PENGUIN BOOKS
DON'T LOOK DOWN

Karishma Attari is curious to know everything about everything, and writing is a way for her to find out. She reviews books and has a background in theatre, journalism and literature. She runs Shakespeare for Dummies, a workshop series for everyday adults, and travels every chance she gets. *Don't Look Down* is the sequel to her debut novel, *I See You.*

PRAISE FOR *I SEE YOU*

'It's a joy to open a book and find doorways in place of pages, crackling embers in place of words. When you can feel a tale's heat for yourself, see its colours and hear its bark, you're no longer reading but living twice, it's no longer writing but alchemy. Karishma Attari has it to spare'—DBC Pierre, Booker Prize winner, author of *Vernon God Little*

'Rarely does the film-maker in me find a horror plot so inviting that the nightmare actually feels like it would be a dream to picturize'— Vikram Bhatt

'A very self-assured work of writing, the novel starts by going straight for the jugular without any kind of lengthy introduction, prologue or preamble . . . Attari constructs her novel with care, satiating the reader's curiosity only in bite-sized pieces and keeping a tight leash on the suspense quotient . . . it is to the author's credit that she gathers all the diverse ingredients of horror, gives them a mighty shake and stir, and serves them as a chilling, cohesive whole. A riveting and deliciously scary novel, *I See You* is perfect reading material for the long winter nights'—*Asian Age*

I See You keeps you hooked right till the end, teasing you along the way with fresh pieces of the puzzle that you'll be struggling to put together and that will keep you hungrily reading on, waiting for the big reveal'—*JetWings*

Don't Look Down

KARISHMA ATTARI

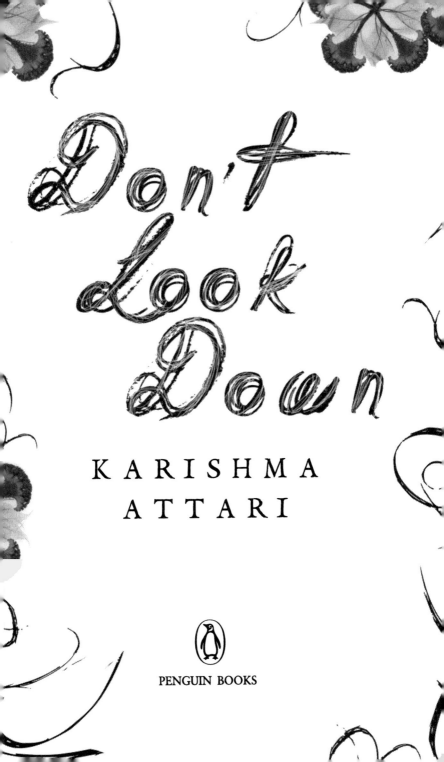

PENGUIN BOOKS

PENGUIN BOOKS

USA | Canada | UK | Ireland | Australia
New Zealand | India | South Africa | China

Penguin Books is part of the Penguin Random House group of companies
whose addresses can be found at global.penguinrandomhouse.com

Published by Penguin Random House India Pvt. Ltd
7th Floor, Infinity Tower C, DLF Cyber City,
Gurgaon 122 002, Haryana, India

First published in Penguin Books by Penguin Random House India 2016

ISBN 9780143434443

Typeset in Linux Libertine by Manipal Digital Systems, Manipal

Printed at Repro Knowledgecast Limited, India

www.penguin.co.in

For Zahra and Adam,
who help me find things I didn't know were lost

'One need not be a chamber to be haunted,
One need not be a house;
The brain has corridors surpassing
Material place.

Far safer, of a midnight meeting
External ghost,
Than an interior confronting
That whiter host.

Far safer through an Abbey gallop,
The stones achase,
Than, moonless, one's own self encounter
In lonesome place.
. . .'

Emily Dickinson

Prologue

You've heard the stories as a child; you know they roam the night—murderers, monsters, and those things too terrible to give a name to. What if they gather one night outside your window, drawn to your human breath whilst you lie helpless on your back, breathing in and out, as though that slack enchantment the world calls sleep is somehow blessed. How can you sleep at all when the only thing that separates you from the darkness outside is a glass window? This question does not bother me; I ask out of curiosity. I haven't closed my eyes in almost a year and there is nothing outside my window that can harm me.

My name is Alia and I am murderer, monster, and that thing too terrible to give a name to. I can have anything I desire, and the moment when I no longer Want anything is when I shall close my eyes and meet the End. Until then, I am a juggler with a flaming torch. I have to keep the hunger for things burning and—here's the hard part—I have to keep it from burning me up.

ONE

My eighteenth birthday was in four days and Sid had a plan.
Sid always had a plan. You could love that or hate that about
him but you sure as hell could not take that out of him.

'Keep an open mind is all I'm saying,' he said. 'It might
do you good; take your mind off everything.' We started
walking up the flight of stairs at St. Xavier's together just as
the bell went.

'Everything is a tall order,' I muttered. 'What kind of
party are we talking about anyway?'

'So you *do* like the idea then?' He paused to look down
at me.

'I . . . no! I stopped listening to you sometime after you
said DJ Razz-T.' I shook my head, trying to wipe the smile
off my face that appeared whenever I remembered the first
time we met on these stairs. 'Why on earth would we hire
a DJ?'

'What do you expect everyone to do, Alia? It's a party.'

'Maybe I could show them some of my magic tricks?
Make a few people disappear? Hey, okay, don't get mad. I'm

just kidding.' I lowered my voice. 'I still don't get why we are celebrating my birthday like it means anything.'

'Oh, you don't get to go back to that argument,' he said. 'You act normal and you stay normal, that's what we agreed on. And that means,' he darted a look at his watch, 'not being late for Ursula.'

I took a deep breath and followed him up another flight of stairs to English class. For someone who could probably attain world domination, I was pretty damn pliable.

Ursula fanned herself with a copy of Milton's *Paradise Lost* and fixed us with the glare reserved for stragglers. I looked around the classroom. Sunlight streamed in through the arched windows and on to familiar faces, but Chris was nowhere to be seen. I met Natasha's eyes and she shrugged. I sat down and opened my copy only the tiniest crack, making sure to keep it on my knees, and thus hidden by the table.

The antique pages were as delicate as butterfly wings, and it was probably not my imagination that they faded a little with every exposure to the Mumbai humidity and sunlight. One of the early editions of the classic published in 1667, this copy belonged in a museum, if not a temperature-controlled vault. Yet, here it was, an object of pleasure for an undergraduate student who had to pick her pleasures with great care.

It had been one of the things I had asked for in the early days when I had been Changed. Those days were a blur to me beyond the first hours of transitioning into my new body. I remember waking up in the maze and finding no sign of the ritual that I had undergone to inherit my father's supernatural legacy. My blood no longer stained the earth in the shape of the Running Man, outlining me as it had when I bled out to undergo the Change. The knife was gone, my body healed of all injury.

My eyelids had batted heavy against my pupils, until focus returned, the stars switching on one by one, suspended like nails in space. Everything was heightened as I came to—the puncturing of fresh grass on my limbs, the heat that arose from the cradle of the earth, the tug of the sea that rimmed one end of the villa, and the breeze rustling through the bushes to caress my skin.

Songs of the sea, songs of the earth, songs of the fire, songs of the wind and songs of the ether crammed into my expanding brain as I was transformed. The lines in my palms solidified—the Fate line that had led me this far—and in response to the transformation, my heart began to beat to a new and terrible rhythm. I knew, even as I walked to the villa to resuscitate my parents who lay in their coffins, that the world was a darker place for my gaining new and profane powers.

I closed my eyes and put the classroom around me on pause as I repeated the three words that helped me stay grounded in all the days to follow that terrible day. *I chose this.* I chose to inherit my father's curse to save him from eternal torment. I chose to bring my fickle, fragile mother back from the dead.

I had done what I could for the father I had never truly known, and in return he did what he could for me. For he had sat me down every day for the drill in the early days of the Change, and we had run through the dos and don'ts of my situation. I had come to terms with it—that it was a long life I would spend without eating or drinking or sleeping; that the only hunger, the only thirst, the only rest and the only desire I would have would be to Want things.

You need to Want things, he had explained, and if necessary, you Want bad things to keep from doing worse things because you have to keep going, you have to keep caring, and whatever you do, you don't look down. He would know; he had spent seventeen years fighting Despair and stretching out his bargain with the Baba of *Saat Rasta*. He had bartered his soul in exchange for unlimited Wants, only to discover the sick trick worked into his deal. I mean, think about it philosophically for a moment; what would fuel desire if everything was there for the taking? He had learnt his lessons the hard way. So he urged me to go slow. Only one Want at a time, never more, or you are lost. And you never, ever, meddle with people. My father had only to look at me and the regret on his face was warning enough of the consequences of interfering with people. Actually, what had happened to my mother was more than warning enough.

As though sensing that I had drifted away, Sid put his hand on mine, bringing me back to the present. I glanced down at the book; the illustration of the author's face was grave. Milton had gone blind composing this poem. Is this what happened when you took on demons and angels? Were you cursed beyond cure? Or did you need to be blind to this world in order to see the one that lay just beyond its surface? Homer had turned blind too, hadn't he?

'Alia? Hello?' Natasha stood in front of me, doing that rapid-fire blinking thing she did.

Class had ended without me noticing. I shut the book as gently as possible and slid it into my bag. Sid gave me a beady look.

'Sorry,' I said, 'I was daydreaming a little.'

'You looked a little lost,' Natasha said.

'Lost in *Paradise Lost*,' I said with a grin.

'Yeah.' She grinned back. 'Now that's a heavy text to get lost in. So . . . I was wondering, have you heard from Chris lately?'

I hesitated for a moment before I lied to her face.

'Nope. He's a reincarnated hippie, remember? He will be back when it suits him. Did you try calling him?' I asked.

'I just get his stupid voicemail.' Natasha grimaced. 'He sounds like such a jerk.'

'You should do what I do,' Sid said.

'What's that?' Natasha asked.

'Not call him ever again,' he said as he hoisted his bag on his shoulder.

'Don't be mean, he's got some adjusting to do. I mean, what that boy has been through! He'll be back to his good old self soon,' Natasha said.

'Sure,' I agreed, the lie congealed on my lips long after she was gone. There was no going back to good old anything for Chris and me, but Natasha didn't need to know that.

I took my phone out of my handbag and dialled Chris.

'Hi, this is Chris the reincarnate. I obviously have better things to do than talk to you. Leave me a message, or don't. Whatever.' It clicked off.

I left a message. 'Chris, it's me. You've disappeared again. Call me.'

'Did you think he would pick up just because it's you?'
Sid's eyes were hard as quartz.

'Well, I kind of did.' I swung my handbag absent-
mindedly in the air. The day at college did not seem all that
inviting any more. 'I need to get home,' I said. 'I'm having
trouble, you know . . .'

'Yeah,' Sid said after a pause, his voice distant. 'You go
do what you need to.'

* * *

What I needed to do was satisfy an itch. I got into the
Maserati and left south Mumbai and the heat of the day
behind, with the air conditioner turned to arctic. The whole
thing about Chris unsettled me too much, and there was
only so much I wanted to make Sid deal with. My cheeks
warmed as I recalled our lingering kiss this morning. I
ran my index finger over my neck, tracing out the trail of
butterfly kisses he'd punctuated his embrace with. My father
had been wrong in one respect; Wanting things was not the
only desire I had left.

The boisterous crowds that used to hem the entrance to
Khanna Villa were a memory now, and I swept right into
what was once the most mysterious and desired piece of real
estate in the country. My father's Bollywood acting career
and superstar status had crashed, like the stock exchange
during recession, the night his powers left him. He considered
it for the best. He had cancelled his remaining contracts
and settled suits by writing out cheques for amounts that
seemed to read like the serial number on a bill. The money

did not matter; money was nothing to us. The new life we had together was everything.

Was he really content just pottering around the villa? He had this 'think positive' thing going on. 'You don't look back, Alia, because that's not the way you're going,' he'd say. All the men in my life seemed to think they were in charge when, really, I had only to wish something and . . . I concealed a smile as I climbed out of the car and tossed the keys to an attendant.

I let myself into the hall and walked past the lifeless furniture, my heels clicking smartly on the marble. I passed under the chandelier that was always aglow in the cavernous room and ran up the sweep of stairs to my room, my hands skimming the handrail.

I unbuckled my sandals and tossed them aside, making straight for the bathroom. The luminaries came on with a hum, running along the ceiling and gleaming off the onyx floor. I bent down and trailed my fingers around the rim of the sunken-in bath.

I realized with a start that I had just taken my first deep breath of the day. I opened the taps all the way and watched the frothy, cold water until it rode up the halfway mark. I slipped out of my clothes and went down the steps, not trying to hold back the way my body shook in anticipation before the deliciously cool water engulfed me. And as I sank to the bottom, the water closing over my face, I knew something not unlike peace for the first time that day.

I towelled myself off roughly later, both feet planted on the white shag rug. It used to disturb me at first, the way time seemed to sink with me, and I would emerge four or even seven hours later from the bath feeling as though I had spent all of ten minutes in it. But I craved this sanctuary too much to question it. I put my ear to the wall and the villa throbbed around me, utterly quiet. Everyone was in bed by now. I grabbed a toothbrush and worked on my teeth for old times' sake.

I had no idea how long this period of calm would last, but all things considered, the past year may have been the best year of my life. I had a family, I had Sid, I sort of had Chris back, and while it was true that I had lost a lot of things, I had also learnt a lot of things about myself. I dabbed at my mouth and went into the bedroom.

Sometimes it felt like I had not made the very worst bargain in the universe.

I leaned out of the French windows and into the dark sky. The night was close and still, the heat setting off a chorus of cicadas buried deep somewhere in the gardens. The tide had sucked out even the smallest breath of freshness as it receded from the shoreline, and a scent of salt and fish and raw bones hung over the suburb.

I picked up *Paradise Lost* and put it away again an hour later. I bit my lower lip. Did I really need to be reading a book about eternal damnation and Satan right now?

I picked up my iPhone and saw that there was an unread message.

3 a.m.? Can do?

I tapped out a reply, hit send and sat back. A half-smile curled around my lips. Sid was wrong . . . Chris was not beyond all reason; Chris was not beyond my influence.

I threw on a T-shirt and a pair of jeans, laced my sneakers, gathered my damp hair into a high ponytail and checked my reflection in the mirror with a tingle of apprehension.

There was no monster staring back at me.

I was going to be a little late, but it was a fair assumption that he would wait for me. What else did creatures of the night have to do?

* * *

The Haji Ali Dargah glowed like a pearl run aground, a blurry haze above the moonlit sea. The sea heaved, thick and dark as tar, flinted with white salt where water broke against rock. Every particle of air between the horizon and us seemed heavy with humidity, waiting to drop its burden with the first rains.

I drew my gaze in and the roads were like a toy racetrack under the jaundiced street lights, signals blinking, cars whizzing by, spitting out music. Chris's attraction for heights had taken me by surprise; he always hung out on TV towers and water tanks and at the top of hoardings. Stained-teeth Su, my counsellor from Woodstock, would have got him talking about what that could mean. It was obvious, really, if you thought about it, why wouldn't a boy who had ended his natural life by jumping off a terrace be obsessed with heights? I chewed on a strand of hair, then slumped down on the wooden rack next to Chris. I had my back to the hoarding we had climbed up.

With his pale colouring and spiky dark hair, he looked like a poster Goth boy, but that was mostly the effect of the backwash of light that rained down the billboard. He had a Grateful Dead T-shirt on, and I resisted the urge to roll my eyes. Some days, that boy crunched through ironies like a bowl of peanut shells. But then, I had help at home, while Chris lived with his awful mother. There was another reason, of course—that I was at peace with what I had done in a way that Chris could never be. I parked the thought where I couldn't see it.

He had been watching my face intently.

'Where do they all go?' I said instead, gesturing at the cars on the streets.

He shrugged. 'From one party to another?'

It made sense; I would be scared to sleep if I were human. Come to think of it, I always was, back then, except your batteries kind of wound down at the end of the day. It was hard to remember what lack of alertness felt like now. It was harder still to remember what it had meant to dream.

'Speaking of parties,' he began.

'Oh no,' I groaned. *How had he found out?* 'Don't say it.'

'You can't be serious,' he said. 'You're turning eighteen? Really?'

'It's Sid's big idea.' I shook my head. 'He won't take no for an answer.'

'And you're letting him run with it, of course.'

'You have to admit he's usually right.' I shifted uncomfortably. 'I really don't know, it seems almost like tempting bad stuff to happen, but he says there's no reason to stop living an ordinary life.'

'Yeah. Like he'd know?'

'He knows plenty,' I said. 'He's stuck with me for one thing; that's education enough, I should think.'

Chris was silent for a few minutes. 'Sid is such a hero,' he said. 'He gets to be with you and then go home and eat the dinner his mother cooked, and go to sleep.'

'You're judging him for being human?' I could not keep the edge out of my voice. It bothered me how these two were so cutting to each other all the time.

Chris shrugged.

'How are you doing?' I asked in a softer tone. 'Chris. Is it bad?'

He uncrossed his knees and turned to me. His black eyes gave nothing away. The pinpoints might have screamed of oxy or heroin abuse to a doctor, but I knew the only narcotic he was on was his pain. He lifted his arm up and I snuggled into his shoulder. We could stay like this for a million years, and never in those million years would I forgive myself for having been the cause of his suffering. We sat there like that, staring into the stars. They stared back at us, riveted.

'Do you think our stories are written up there?' I said at last, nodding at the sky.

'Are you still reading horoscopes online?' I could hear the smile in his voice. 'Because you probably do not have anything in common with the average Gemini at this point. Assuming, of course, you ever did.'

I shifted in my seat. 'I just wonder how all of this works . . . how we ended up here, you know, like this.'

'I'll tell you how it all happened. I sent you a text asking you to meet me, then you checked it four hours later and—'

I poked him in the ribs. 'You know what I'm talking about.'

'Yeah.' His tone changed. 'I always know what you're talking about, Alia. So to answer you as categorically as you would like, no, I don't think our stories are told in the stars. It's the scars we have that tell our tales.'

'Do you still have any?' I leaned forward and looked up at his face. 'Where?'

'Not like that,' he said. 'Everything heals exquisitely, doesn't it? Except, it doesn't. Not really.'

'What do you mean?' I said.

'I remember all of it.'

'Chris.' I shook my head.

'It comes to me in flashes, the way the air tasted in my mouth as I fell from the terrace; it was like water was streaming through me.' He rested his chin on my head. 'I can smell the blood, my blood, all over the tiles. When I see my reflection in a passing car, I don't recognize it. I think I'm still there, on the ledge, about to jump, on the ground, in the hospital, waking up to find—'

'Shhh,' I said, putting my hand to my mouth. 'It's over. We are here now, we are—'

'Where are we, Alia? I mean, really.'

'We are right here.' I kept my voice steady. 'We are in Worli and we climbed up the Diesel hoarding because you're a little bit nuts like that, and I indulge you because I'm a saint. And . . . we are looking at the Haji Ali Dargah and admiring how it shines. There's traffic down there, there's people all around us, sleeping in their houses and on the pavements and—'

'But we aren't one of them, are we? We don't belong here at all.'

'We belong where we choose to belong.' It did not bear thinking of any other way.

'Ah, but there's the thing, isn't it?' His voice was leaden. 'Not all of us chose to end up as we did.' His arm tightened around me, and his hand reached up to cup my chin and turn it towards him.

I felt a shimmer on my eyeballs and closed my eyelids, trying to trap the sensation of unshed tears.

The night settled more fully around us.

I stood up a little later and turned my face to the sea. The rim of water on the horizon flared with the promise of a new day.

'Good morning, Chris,' I whispered.

'Good morning, Alia,' he said. 'Ever the optimist, aren't you?'

'We should go.' I tugged on his arm.

'You go on ahead,' he said.

'Will I see you at college?'

His jawline relaxed as he looked at me. The dawn had filled in the contours of his face so that the high cheekbones no longer held shadows. He ran a hand through his dark hair and looked so heartbreakingly like my Chris for a moment that I almost believed this fantasy I was concocting, that he would come to college and slip into the bench alongside me and everything would be okay. He looked away again, his lips pursed in an expression that suggested he was better left alone.

I began the twenty-foot climb down.

* * *

'What happens to dead people?' I had tracked my father down in the villa's garden. The light was tender and flat, the day overcast; he cast no shadow. He was on his knees, tending the roses. Her roses.

He flinched and then looked around warily before turning to me. 'Alia, I wish you wouldn't spring these kinds of questions on me when we are outside.'

'Come on, who's going to be listening to us here? Don't beat around the bush,' I added with a wink, settling down in the dirt beside him.

He smiled at that and it filled me with warmth. It never got old, having a father around to talk to. His eyes were back on her beloved roses. I leaned closer and inhaled deeply. They were in heavy bloom but I could detect a bit of sag coming. The one closest to me drooped, its redness mottled with veins of rot. He selected a leaf joint under the wilted flower head and clipped the stem.

'You do have to, at some point, give me an answer,' I said.

He sat back on his haunches. 'Why did you bring this up now?'

'I met Chris last night and it just got me thinking.'

'How is he doing? Why didn't you bring him home with you?'

He straightened up just as the sun ate through the cotton-wool clouds, like fire on gauze, and I was dazzled by the halo of light that appeared around him.

'Dad.' I squinted up at his burning head and shaded my eyes. 'What happens to dead people? Why can't Chris forget the way he died? He replays it over and over and it never brings him any peace.'

'Then perhaps he would be better advised to stop.' My father sighed, already regretting the sharpness in his voice. 'Look, I wish I had answers to all your questions, Alia. Particularly this one.' His eyes strayed to the villa and I turned around to catch a curtain flutter.

I went upstairs and knocked on her door and then entered anyway, the floral perfume she covered herself in hitting me before I had taken two steps inside. I was right; she had been standing by the window the whole time in her silk slip. The bed was still made, the magazines for the day untouched, the humongous flat screen locked away behind its wooden doors.

'Mom,' I said, 'it's a beautiful day. Will you come down to the garden? Dad has the roses all cleaned up but I'm pretty sure he's overfeeding them. Someone should stop him before it's too late.'

She turned to me and I watched the light go out of her face like it did every time she looked at me. Her gooseberry eyes had lost their sparkle long ago, but the way she used them when she looked at me—the lids dropping down like a shield—made me feel like scum. It was not personal, my father said. I just reminded her of something that she had lived with longer than anyone should have had to. Knowing that ought to have made it hurt lesser than it did.

Her cheeks had an unnatural blush; she had covered her paleness with rouge and bronzer. It was a close imitation of how she used to look, back when she was alive.

'Are you going somewhere?' The words were out before I realized. 'I mean, I just wondered if you'd join us—'

'I can see from all the way up here how much I was missed,' she said, her gaze back on the garden, the arched eyebrows, exquisite cheekbones, straight nose, and bow-shaped lips that had launched a hundred beauty magazines catching the sunlight just so.

'So come with me,' I said, the cheerfulness in my voice sounding false in the quiet room. 'Let's go save those roses.'

'Give me two minutes.' She walked into her dressing room and emerged quicker than I would have expected. I barely had time to mess up the sheets and pound the pillows so that the bed would look slept in. She had a tan dress on now, her slender legs a mile high in strappy sandals, and her freshly brushed hair fell thick like winter honey. It was her eyes that gave it all away—dead eyes. I held her hand. 'Let's go,' I whispered.

She walked into the garden with me and her footsteps quickened once my father was in sight.

'Overcompensation,' she pronounced with mock seriousness. 'The inadequate gardener's biggest challenge.'

He looked up with a grin, his wide nose streaked with dirt. 'Not all of us were born with green fingers.' He held her hands, getting mud on the heart-shaped diamond she wore on her ring finger. I wrinkled my nose. Fertilizer! She did not seem to notice or care. I took a step back to watch them work together. They looked startlingly young even to my eyes, but then, they had had me so early; they'd been kids themselves. My age, I realized with a start. They had been my age when it all began.

'Well?' My father was watching me. 'What's it going to be? Are you celebrating your birthday with us or do you have something special planned with Sid?'

'We are going to have a party!' I knew this was what I wanted the minute I said it and watched his face light up.

'Now that's a great idea!' My father was still grinning and his eyes were crinkled up all the way. 'You should absolutely have a party. You should have it here.' He spread his arms out. 'It's about time someone saw the beautiful garden in Khanna Villa.'

I blanched and then recovered. This villa had been a dark place, a place with skeletons and shadows and memories of spilled blood. But he was right, of course; all of that was in the past. We were a family now, together, and we kept our darkness in a box, locked, sealed and bolted, just like all the other families who have secrets they must contain. Perhaps doing this would set the place free of old memories, would set us all free. I nodded.

He hugged me tight, and I was so steadied that the world stopped spinning the whole time he had his arms around me. I did not mind the muddy hands either. He was just that kind of guy.

'I can't think of anyone who deserves a good time more than you,' he whispered in my ear. He let go of me. 'What do you think, Reshma? Our daughter's first birthday party at home.'

My cheeks reddened with pleasure, and then my eyes caught the shadows we cast on the dirt as we stood side by side—her elegant length, my own form, and my father's figure, the shape of the Running Man that would pursue us always, through fire and darkness and blood.

The smile died on my lips as I recalled what my birthday truly meant to my parents. His actions seventeen years ago on the day that I was born were what had set this whole tragedy in motion. For what was I, if not the collateral to the supernatural pact he had made. The girl who was trapped between two worlds and would pay for his sins in both? I felt light-headed, and it took all my willpower to keep the terror off my face.

My mother knelt down and snipped a rose off its stem. She turned the fallen bloom over and over in her hands and said nothing. I could feel her distaste for the idea of a party in my honour in her beloved villa emanating like a vapour even as the roses surrendered their essence into the heat of the morning—and I shivered, the humidity gathering close around me like a shroud.

TWO

Restlessness seized me that day, making it difficult to concentrate on anything, my feet tapping out a beat on the wooden floor as I waited for the last class of the day to end. I bolted out of college at the bell, conscious of a need to be alone; I returned home only to find I had carried my unease in with me. I spent the evening pacing in my room, and by the time darkness fell, I was ready to scream. The electricity flickered on and off without cutting off entirely and letting the generator kick in, and with every dip and surge those eggshell-white walls seemed to tilt, closing in on me as I burnt a hole into the carpet.

So I threw open the windows then and looked outside. The moon had climbed up the sky to the size of a postage stamp between my fingers, and the villa breathed quiet, before I slipped downstairs and let myself out through the dining room to the back of the gardens.

The treetops murmured above my head, calling out my location, even though my feet were stealthy in the lawn. The garden pulsed through the bark of a rain tree I placed my palm on; however, it revealed none of its secrets. I had grown accustomed to picking my way through the garden by moonlight, and also to the sounds of the night, the occasional owl hoot, the thundering of the sea beyond the boundary walls, and the staccato burst of crickets and other insects crazed by the late-summer heat. Sometimes it felt as though I was the only truly silent night creature there was. Everything in nature seemed prepared to announce its presence but me. But then, everything in nature belonged there.

A shadow swept over the grass and I staggered back. It circled around and approached me, coming closer, and I looked up in time to shield my eyes from the rapid velvet beat of black wings. There was a sizzle of pain as my cheek was sliced open and I stood there frozen in disbelief, touching it with my hand; it came away wet with streaks of blood. Then the telltale flapping of wings made me spin around and I barely had time to register the red-eyed gaze of the creature, before it was upon me again, shrieking, crashing through my hair, its claws and teeth ribboning my skin in a frenzied ambush. I managed to beat it off, although my arms were wrecked and I stumbled, blinded, my ears ringing when it returned for a third attack. It was too much. My knees caved and I fell to the ground, taking it with me.

Finally, my slippery, shredded hands managed to tear the creature off and fling it away. I wiped the blood off my eyes and followed it as it flew low, circling me, until it winged its way to the cluster of trees at the boundary wall. It perched there and watched me, its eyes glinting in the moonlight, the sable coat of its fur slick and wet.

I blinked in disbelief at the menacing smallness of it, my breath wheezing through my chest. It was a foxy little bat. A startled laugh broke out of me. Vampire bats did not really attack people, did they? That was the stuff of legends.

My body shook like it had been thrown into ice water. What manner of occult darkness had possessed this creature and why? The bat seemed to be weighing me up for another strike; its eyes had never left my face and its body was beginning to tense. Is that how it would be when the bargain between the Baba and me ran out and the End came for me?

Would I be as unsuspecting as this?

This flying rat had made me feel vulnerable.

And I did not like it.

I told myself it was a lucky thing. The urge had been building up again; the restlessness that meant I needed to summon Bobby. I was a patient with a chronic disease and he was the otherworldly stunted doctor, measuring out my lifespan with his evil whispers.

I slid my iPhone out of my pocket and swiped to calendar. I was several days away from being due for another Want. I forced myself to take a deep breath in and let a slow breath out, a reflexive tribute to my boarding-school days with the old stained-teeth counsellor, Su. Yes, it was a risk to jump with instinct; my father had given me enough reasons to adopt his newly patented method of gradual, timely release. 'You never let the desire in the driver's seat.'

Except, every breath I dragged in now was tinged with a corrosive fume. It scorched through my vitals and had eaten into my resolve, until the bitterness exploded like a light bulb, splinters of dark light piercing me, blotting over my pupils, wiping out all thought. The Wants would enslave me one day, but for now I was master.

I picked myself up off the ground, letting the searing currents of pain from my nerve ends hit my mind just so. I was ready but I was exposed here. I glanced back at the building, and walked towards the mouth of the maze. My hand slapped against the hard twigs and the coarse leaves, and I hummed as I wound deeper in. I was committed to it now. I could feel something lighten and tingle in my veins and then tighten as I summoned him. It was a feeling not dissimilar to pain but tightly looped with pleasure. This is what it felt like to be truly alive.

The pointy shrub sparkled around me, jewel-like, the pebbles glinted like black diamonds against my feet. Every electric breath I took filled my lungs, and the blood responded; it thudded through my heart, blooming out of the ventricles, shedding its bitterness and flowing through my body until everything was clear, everything was beautiful. My heart stuttered, slowed, and then suspended its beat. The act of Wanting bore another hook into my skin for the anxiety to catch, for the robe of darkness to drag my shoulders down, but I did not care. In that moment, I was unmatched. I was ready to Want.

* * *

It lay at the exit when I emerged from the maze, like a prize—the poor, once-beautiful foxy bat. Its body was still and crumpled and its skin had been turned inside out like a pelt, so that the sharp teeth protruded whitely in the spreading pool of crimson. Its velvet blackness had smudged against the dirt in a long, curving slash, traces of skid-burnt skin lifted in the breeze, drifting like ash.

It was as I had willed it with triumph in my veins, but to see it was altogether too much for me. Emotion spouted out of me in hot spurts and I fell to my knees and sobbed dry, heaving sobs. I was not crying for the wee bat that lay at my feet.

I was crying because crushing it was what it took to finally make me feel good.

* * *

Would he now see me for what I was? Ever since the bat incident, it was as though a hand mirror had slipped from my grasp and was headed for a slow-motion collision with the ground. Except, what would shatter was the reflection I held of myself—of someone who was in control, of someone who was good and strong. Sid was troubled and he made no attempt to disguise it.

'So you wanted the bat dead,' he said flatly. 'And it made you happy to see it dead.' The bell went, summoning us to class. I had psychology, he had statistics, and neither of us moved. All the psychoanalysis and all the data in the world couldn't help us with this.

His eyes darkened a few shades. 'Alia,' he said, a warning in the word. 'Don't torture yourself over this. You've been doing okay all this time. What do you think changed?'

'Maybe I have. Maybe I'm sliding. Maybe the effort of holding it all in is taking a toll now.' I took another gulp of air in. In the cold light of day, it was that much harder to admit my suspicion that the bat hadn't been there on bat business. I ran my fingers over my cheeks; only some residual redness remained.

He put his hand on mine and squeezed. 'Hey. So you screwed up,' he said, trying to make me smile. 'You're not that perfect, are you?'

'Are you?' I turned on him, even though I knew he had been teasing.

My eyes roved over his familiar face, the sharp jawline, and the cleft in his left cheek showing as he bit it, his go-to cheek in distress. We had played this out before. I could close my eyes and know the way his hair fell over his broad forehead, the brows knit together because of what I was telling him. I might as well say it and be done with it. 'Or are you pretending to be okay with all of this because you don't want to let me down.'

'Hey,' he put an arm around my shoulder and pulled me in close, 'the only person you are capable of letting down is yourself. You know what you can and cannot take or do, Alia, I'm just—'

'Just what? Along for the ride? There are no safe passengers on my trip.'

'Do you think I don't know that?' The fierceness in his voice cowed me. 'I just know that if I had to pick one person in the whole world to give this curse to, one person whom I could trust to handle unlimited power and not turn into a psychotic power-hungry Nazi, it would be you.'

'Tell that to the foxy bat. Even his mother wouldn't recognize him now.' I shivered.

'I don't care about the flying rodent, Alia. The first thing your father did when he was Changed was kill a whole bunch of people and turn himself into a Bollywood superstar, because he could have whatever he Wanted. He was drunk on the power of unlimited Wants. You've kept your head down, attended your classes and killed a total of one bat in half a year of controlling your Wants. I don't think we need to hit the panic button just yet.'

He let go of me as a priest walked through the canteen, parting the students in waves. 'Let's get out of here, shall we?'

'Don't we have class?' I asked with a frown.

'We've got bigger things to worry about, trust me.'

We went to Le Pain Quotidien. I looked with interest at the chocolate pastries, the chubby breads and glazed pies. I could not even remember what food tasted like. I grabbed a passing server.

'I will have a spinach linguine, the salad of the day, three pain au chocolat, a chocolate eclair and a cup of mint tea,' I said. 'Heck, cancel the tea and make it an espresso—I don't sleep much anyway these days. With that fancy biscuit on the side, please.'

'Don't mind her,' Sid told the startled server. 'She's on a really tight diet. It makes her a little crazy.' He leaned forward conspiratorially. 'The thing is, if she eats carbs, she bloats up like a pufferfish and I don't like my women fat.'

'And then he won't have anything to do with me unless I cleanse with the Whole30 diet,' I added. 'It's rough, you can't even eat dairy.'

'Or cereal,' Sid added.

'You should eat what you like. Do you know how thin you are?' she said to me, darting a furious look at Sid. 'Your boyfriend is a pig! Lose him!'

'So,' I said when we were seated at a table by the corner. 'Everything you order here henceforth is going to have twenty grams of spit in it. But that aside, what do we need to worry about?'

'Saturday night,' he said with perfect seriousness, pushing his uneaten ravioli aside. 'I'm thinking we should go with a fancy-dress party.'

'What will I come dressed as, Sid? A regular person?'

He leaned in and whispered into my ear.

I burst into laughter. Turning eighteen had never been this ironic before.

* * *

One week to go for the party and the guest list was officially out of my hands. Which was just as well, considering that if I invited every single person I had ever spoken to in the last year at St. Xavier's, I would still be hard-pressed to bump the number over twenty. Sid had turned the whole thing over to the one person who knew how to throw a good party—Maya.

I found her in the canteen punching numbers into her phone. She had managed to spot me and hail me over without even looking up from the screen.

'These invites won't send themselves, you know?' she said. 'What are you wearing? I hope it's, like, really unique, because you don't want to clash with someone at your own party.'

'What are you coming as?'

Her eyes widened. 'Supergirl, of course. No one else ever comes as Supergirl because it's *my* thing.'

'You don't mind being predictable?'

'People should know what to expect at a fancy dress,' she said in all seriousness. 'Nobody really wants surprises.'

'That's quite a smart—'

'I like to think I set a standard of sorts. You don't put on a scarf and an eyepatch and say you're a pirate, you know, you get the whole outfit going. Which is why I stick to Supergirl.' She tossed her ponytail in the air, put her hands on her hips and stamped her foot on the bench. 'I've got that nailed.'

'You sure have.' I turned just in time to see Ronjita and Raoul saunter up arm in arm.

'So I'll see you guys Saturday night?' I asked them.

'Yeah.' Ronjita wore one of her slow, warming smiles. 'I still can't believe we are finally visiting Khanna Villa. I bet your outfit is really stunning. Did you get a stylist to do it?'

'Yeah! What did you say you were coming as?' Maya asked.

'She didn't.' Sid appeared and slid his arm around my waist. I leaned into his musky scent.

How was it possible to miss someone so much in the one hour you spent apart?

'What about you?' Maya turned to Ronjita.

'It's a secret, too,' Ronjita said, smiling, 'but you will think it's perfect.'

'What will you come as, Raoul? A gold-digger?' Binni said coyly. When had Binni joined the group?

Raoul gave her a dirty look and Ronjita coloured and fiddled in her Guess handbag.

Sid cleared his throat loudly. 'So are you getting RSVPs yet?'

Maya turned to him. 'You should worry about your end of the party,' she said with excessive sweetness. 'And leave me to mine.'

'Come on,' I tugged on his arm, 'we can't miss class again.'

We slipped in with seconds to spare. I opened my copy of *Paradise Lost* under the table again and turned to the passage Ursula was reading aloud.

> 'So hand in hand they passed, the loveliest pair
> That ever since in love's embraces met—
> Adam the goodliest man of men since born
> His sons; the fairest of her daughters Eve.'

I looked up to see Sid bent over his copy, his pencil to-the-ready for markings that Ursula might suggest, and my throat constricted at the nearness and dearness of him. I did the unthinkable. I marked my copy. Turned out the lightest of pencil marks was enough to tear through the centuries-old paper. I narrowed my eyes and squinted at it; the passage was still readable.

> *Should God create another Eve, and I*
> *Another Rib afford, yet loss of thee*
> *Would never from my heart; no, no, I feel*
> *The link of nature draw me: flesh of flesh,*

Bone of my bone thou art, and from thy state
Mine never shall be parted, bliss or woe.

Did Sid feel the same way about me as I did about him? I peeked at him sideways from under my eyelashes.

I had no illusions of being a dream girlfriend and yet he was mine and I was his, 'bliss or woe'. Except, didn't he deserve more bliss and less woe?

I held the copy in my palms when the paper parted into neat slices right where I had tried to mark the words out.

The burst of panic died down when I realized that this was the perfect scheduled Want. The wish born cold and to be asked in heat—the wish that these lines I had drawn should be erased, and the rents in the antique paper vanish. My mind skittered to the memory of the dead bat and I shook the thought off. Not all mistakes could be easily undone.

I shut the book and leaned back against the wall, feeling an exhaustion that was not even remotely physical.

'Alia? Anything you would like to add to our discussion?' Ursula's eyes narrowed on me like a steel trap.

'I'd say the Fall was necessary.' I reached under the table to squeeze Sid's hand.

Ursula's expression changed. 'Tell us why,' she said, encouragingly.

'Because without the Fall, they wouldn't be who they are—Adam and Eve, I mean,' I said.

She frowned. 'The Fall had to do with humanity at large. Are you treating it like a character-building exercise for two individuals?'

Someone in the front snickered.

The trilling of the bell saved me from any further questioning.

* * *

I drove with the windows down after having dropped Sid off to a group-study session.

As I passed by Juhu beach, something made me pull over and look out at the setting sun.

Chris had once said that nostalgia was just extended self-pity. But as dusk fell like a lilac net tightening its drawstrings around the city, I wished I'd spent more time watching sunsets back when sunsets actually meant something.

THREE

The days flew by and only bumped to a stop when they hit the weekend curb, and before I knew it, it was the night of the party. The massive electronically guarded gates of Khanna Villa were thrown open for the first time, and cars and bikes wound their way like fireflies, past the topiary bushes and lawn, to park in the driveway. Reflected headlights danced off my ceiling, shouts and laughter made their way to me in an updraft, and I could hear the speakers spit out soundchecks from the back of the grounds.

This party was going to start with or without me. I went back to the vanity mirror. The dress that Ayesha the stylist had sent me this morning was exquisite and in so many pieces that I had to have her explain to me how to wear it twice over. I slid on the dark green slip and then began to connect the emerald-green sequinned elements. I scrunched my hair and let it fall on to my bare shoulders in ripples and then fixed the crown of leaves on my head. The last thing to add was the sparkling apple pendant that slid down to the hollow in my collarbone.

I tried on the blood-red sandals but they were too high and I did not trust myself to totter down the pebbled driveway and walk through the garden on stilettos. And then it struck me that being barefoot would complement the look perfectly. I laid the lipstick on thick and smacked my lips to make it blend, and then applied a layer of mascara. After all, this was a fancy-dress party.

I padded around the banister at the bottom of the stairs; I would sneak into the party through the dining room that opened to the back gardens. I swung in through the doorway and came to a sudden stop—there was a figure standing by the French windows. It was my mother in a white shift, her hair tied into a knot. She was humming a tune to herself.

'Mom,' I cleared my throat. 'It's me, Alia.'

'My, what a marvellous look you have for tonight. Ayesha really came through! Of course, your figure is not half bad; you take after me.' She narrowed her eyes, studying my reflection in the glass just as I studied hers. I patted my skirt down self-consciously.

'Are you coming out to join us?' I was uncomfortable at the thought of her actually doing that but her standing half concealed in the room, watching the party in her nightdress, was even creepier.

'All your friends are here, aren't they?' she said. 'It must be nice.'

'Yeah,' I said cautiously.

'Except for the one you brought into the villa that night, of course,' she said softly. 'You know whom I am referring to . . . the young man we never saw again.'

I felt the rush of blood to my cheeks, and touched them with my fingertips, another phantom sensation from the old days.

Why was she bringing Deesh up? Why tonight, of all nights? I leaned against the door, tapping the wood with my fingertips, trying to draw from it some solidity, some support. 'Where's Dad?'

'Happy birthday, Alia.' She flashed me a smile so bright it made the lights of the party behind her appear dim. 'Except it isn't really your birthday at all.'

'What?' I swallowed with difficulty.

'What I just said, baby.' Her smile was different now; something feral reached out to me and I had a vision of a cat that ate her young.

'I thought 11 June . . .'

'Sure, you would think that, as does your father. I had to pick a different date, silly.'

'Why?'

She frowned at my confusion. 'He was never meant to know that he had used his own child as collateral. You know how dangerous Despair is to one who has suffered the Change. You had to both be kept in the dark.'

I pulled a chair and sat down; the skirt rustled around me like a whisper. Where had her protective instinct been when it came to me? Her own daughter! She had used this secret to twist my arm when I faced my moment of choice. And I had done exactly what she intended for me to do all along. I had chosen to save my father's life even if it meant tying my own into a fatal bargain with the dark side.

'What is my real birth date?' I asked with difficulty.

'1 January—you made it out a few strokes after midnight. Two-faced Janus, that's what I've always thought of you as.'

She smiled again, the viciousness in full display.

'I am not two-faced,' I said.

'Dates don't lie. Have a rocking party, sweetheart.'

'Mom!' I cried out.

She walked past me and turned back at the door. A spasm crossed her face. 'I have something for you,' she said in a whisper. 'Your Sid was persuasive . . . and I . . . you'll get it later tonight.'

'Okay,' I said, light-headed with the suddenness of her turnaround. If I hadn't known better, I'd have labelled the expression as guilt.

I shook myself out of the stupor I was in once she left and stepped out into the garden and followed the stream of supernaturals, music legends and movie characters to the brightly lit canopy. I entered the clearing where they'd set up a small platform for the DJ console and arranged the food and drinks tables. The canopy of fairy lights reflected off the highly polished plates and crystal glasses, and the bushes were studded with so many glittering pinpoints that it felt as though the night sky had upended itself into the garden.

'Are you a nymph?' I felt a hand on my shoulder and looked up to find a stocky Batman with bad breath.

'No.' I shook his hand off.

'Are you a leaf goddess?' The hand was back on.

'Are you high?' I shook him off. 'Stop touching me.'

'It's a party.' He held his arms out. 'Of course I'm high, and you're hot, so what do you expect. Are you a nymph?'

'I'm none of your business, okay? Now get lost.'

He lurched away. I frowned and scanned the crowd for a familiar face. Sure enough, whispering into the DJ's ear was Sid. The music amped up. Before I could make my way to him, Supergirl and an irritable-looking Iron Man accosted me.

'Hey, hey, hey, great party, Alia!' Maya was tipsy and swayed on her fiancé's arm. Not the most wholesome Supergirl on the planet, but definitely the cutest. 'Krish couldn't believe it when I told him we were going to Khanna Villa and that you're, like, Khanna's daughter.' She giggled throatily. 'No one really knows you, and so they're, like, all here to satisfy their curiosity.'

'Is your dad around?' Krish cleared his throat and made an effort to look sociable. The lights glinted off his breastplates. 'He's been laid-low ever since he got cancer, hasn't he?'

'Um, sure,' I said. So here was another Page 3 rumour about my father that had obviously caught on. Well, people did need an explanation as to why an actor would step down in his prime.

My eyes strayed up to the villa.

'So he's like, upstairs, watching us, and wishing he had his strength, and good hair?' Maya had followed my eyes. Her bright pink lips formed a perfect O.

'No, no, of course, he is not watching us.' Startled, I turned away from the villa and tried to shake off the apprehension her words had filled me with. 'No one is watching us.'

By the time I made it to the DJ, Binni had replaced Sid. It was no use asking her where Sid was.

'Madam, I'm Adam and you're—' It was Batman again.

'I'm not a nymph, okay?' I snapped. 'And if you touch me again, I'm going to break your wrist.'

'Okay, okay,' he backed off, 'I never said you were a nymph, babe. I mean, it's pretty obvious what you're dressed as.'

The posh accent was a giveaway, as was the straight-backed posture. 'Damn! You have that mask on. I thought you were somebody else.'

Khan stuck his chest out. 'There are other Batboys around. But there's only one Batman. Nice place, by the way, what were you hiding it for all this time? Too cool for school?'

I remained staring into space after Khan was gone. *What was I hiding this place for all this time?* He had no idea what it was like to grow up with secrets. Even now, he had no idea what I was, and what I was capable of. I glanced back at the shadowy building, thrown even further into shade by contrast with the garden, and I shivered.

The lights were burning down on us and not a leaf stirred. I stepped off the platform, dizzy with confusion. Who were all these shiny, perspiring people? What was I doing here with them when all I wanted was to find Sid? A Jack Sparrow pirate began to walk towards me. His wig of stringy hair unnerved me so I backed up as far as I could, stepping on a fairy's foot. She shot me a dirty look.

'Sorry,' I muttered, trying to move past her, and only succeeded in having the contents of someone's glass poured down my side as I rattled the arm of a stoned Snow White.

'That's stooooopid,' she slurred. 'She's stooopid.'

A Cat Girl glared at me through heavy mascara. I pushed myself through the crowd to a table and grabbed some tissue paper. I lifted the side of my skirt and mopped at it as best as I could. The sequinned leaves on my dress trembled but stayed on.

Where the hell was Sid? I needed a timeout. I could hear someone call my name but I passed the refreshment tables and went into the thicket, heading to the back of the garden, far away from the pulsating music. I leaned against a tree trunk, my eyes adjusting to the gloom, and fought the urge to get into the Maserati and drive as far away from my own party as I could get.

A twig snapped behind me and I spun around, instantly alert. The woods were shrouded in darkness, the clipped nail of a moon floated in ether, too far above to illuminate much. Then two red eyes glowed in the dirt and my heart jumped up in my ribcage; the scream for help choked to a gasp in my throat as a sense of inevitability numbed my senses. No mortal could help me.

I was frozen in position as a whisper of breeze displaced the dirt, and the red eyes scattered, dimmed, flickered, and revealed themselves to be nothing but cigarette butts. I hugged myself and looked around. The smokers must be close; however, the throb of electronic music made it unlikely I would hear their footsteps.

Two cigarette butts . . . I mused, examining them on my knees. Then I remembered Deesh, the mysterious stranger who had befriended me, bunching up two cigarettes between his fingers, and lighting two cigarettes at a time on New Year's Eve, and I dropped them at once, my hand shaking with fright.

Deesh, the young man who did things in twos, in tribute to his lost twin. Not lost, I gritted my teeth; murdered, murdered by my ambitious father who sacrificed the boy in a dark ritual to save my mother, and buried his ashes in the villa, around which rose the maze. So much of what followed spun back to that one terrible event . . . was Chris wrong to think my father a monster?

I may have taken on the curse from him in an attempt to save my parents, but was I any better? My thoughts strayed back to a night not unlike this one, when I had sneaked the young journalist named Deesh into the villa on a mission to redeem us all. Had I really believed that salvation from my father's crimes would be so easy? That allowing Deesh to liberate the spirit interred in the villa would set us all free? I knew now that this restless soul spiel was the stuff of urban legends and horror movies, a fake feel-good cushioning, for there were no happy endings when you messed with the dark side.

It was true that I had tried to stop him. I had had my doubts, and yet my warnings had only enraged him. Deesh had waited seventeen long years to be reunited with his twin brother and there was no stopping him. He had knocked me down without hesitation to dig up the urn buried deep in the maze; what was meant to be the redemption of one brother turned into a deathtrap for the other. For Bobby was no longer an innocent victim of child sacrifice; his spirit had become a manifestation of the Baba's evil powers. Just like I would one day.

Things would unravel soon enough for me; for now there was only waiting.

I shook myself out of this bleak knowledge and dismissed the premonition contained in the glowing cigarette stubs. I extinguished them with my heel, the heat flaming against bare skin, and crushed them into the mud.

I walked back as quickly as I could to rejoin the party.

Chris was milling around in the crowd, talking to no one in particular.

'Oh, is this a costume party?' he said, when Natasha came up to him and complimented him on his look. 'I just came as I is, you know, kept it casual like.'

'I think you went through a little more trouble than that,' I said. He had worked his whole body over with white paint.

'You look great!' Natasha gushed. 'You're the best zombie here.'

'I was going more for a generic Undead. So, birthday girl.' He turned to me. 'Didn't they have a costume for what you are?'

'Yes, they did,' I said as lightly as I could manage. I dangled the felt snake I had been carrying around my shoulders. 'I am Eve.'

'I'm Xena, the warrior princess,' Natasha added. 'In case you were wondering, a lot of people did not get it. I should've worn lenses.'

'No, I mean, do they have a kind of creature for what you really are?' Chris said. 'You could've asked for horns and a tail, what stopped you?'

'Don't be a jerk,' I said, my face burning.

'Chris, will you stop talking nonsense?' Natasha turned to me. 'I think you make a great Eve. You have such delicate and sharp features and you never ever eat fruit. Hey! I know!

Let's go to where the music is and dance!' She turned tail and raced away.

I looked up and saw Sid at last; except he was dancing with Princess Leia. I groaned aloud. How had Darth Vader found a Leia? I mean, seriously, what were the chances? This party sucked. I felt a hand on my arm and it was Chris.

'Care to dance with a mean dead guy?' he asked, taking my other hand in his and bowing.

'Go away,' I muttered.

'Did I hurt your feelings?' he said, ruefully. 'I don't know what got into me.'

I glanced beyond his shoulders to where Sid was still slow-dancing. Wasn't this their second song together?

'Be careful,' Chris said.

'What do you mean?' I looked back up at him.

'You're emotional, really strung up,' he said. 'And that's dangerous for you.'

'No, I am not!'

'Your boyfriend found a beautiful princess to dance with on your eighteenth birthday. Of course you're angry, and confused. I'm a little mad too, for you.'

'Okay, maybe a little,' I gritted my teeth. 'What the hell, Chris!'

'My sentiments exactly.' He drew me closer. 'I'm sorry about before, okay?'

The music changed and he folded his arms around me and I slipped my arms around his neck. His white face was very close to mine, the blood-coloured teardrops distorted from up close.

'What would I do without you?' I said.

'Only reason I stick around,' he murmured.

A humourless chuckle bubbled up inside me.

A heartbeat passed.

'What do you feel when you look at me, Alia?'

Another heartbeat and I cleared my head.

'You're a zombie, what do you think I feel? The urge to run really fast and scream really loud for the camera, is what I feel.'

He chuckled and kissed my nose. 'As a zombie, I feel obliged to make you mine.' He rubbed his forehead against mine, transferring the white paint, and I squealed.

'What are you doing?' The voice was harsh.

We fell apart, startled.

Hey,' I said, trying to gather my scattered thoughts. 'What's up, Darth Vader?'

'I've been looking everywhere for you.' Sid sounded annoyed.

'Didn't look like that at all,' I said.

He pulled his mask off and ran a hand through his crumpled hair. He gestured towards my forehead. 'You've got zombie all over yourself. It stinks.' He gave Chris a hard look. 'There's the small matter of a very big cake that you need to cut in front of about two hundred people.'

'Oh no,' I groaned.

'Believe me, I'm not the one that ordered a cake shaped like a—'

'Like what?' I gasped. I pushed past him to go see, just as someone let loose a whole bunch of fireworks into the sky. They exploded simultaneously, shaking the still night and showering us with heat and polychromatic streaks of light.

'You're not going to like it,' Sid called out over the eruptions. 'Just don't freak out, it's a costume party, remember?'

'Who ordered the cake?' asked Chris.

It was a grave. It was brown chocolate with a border of fresh green-grass icing. It had a plastic doll's hand sticking out of the chocolate, and candy worms writhed on the surface. A plaque said, '18 till you die . . . Happy Birthday, Alia.'

'I am not cutting that,' I said, feeling ill. As though I had anything in my stomach to sick up. The last time I had thrown up was a year ago, to coincide with the last time I had eaten. Flashes went off in my face and the ring of people that had formed around the giant cake pushed me forward.

Sid had his hand under my elbow. 'I know,' he murmured. 'What do you want to do?'

I looked around helplessly. Maya was leaning into the cake and counting the candles. They were shaped like shovels.

'We need one for good luck,' she called out. 'Where's the one for good luck?' Krish handed her the nineteenth candle and she stuck it in clumsily; her hand came out covered with chocolate.

'Oh, oh!' she giggled. 'I dug up Alia's grave.'

The table bumped again as the crowd began to press further in and the grave lurched, the depression Maya's hand had made yawning open-mouthed.

'I can't do it, Sid,' I whispered. I'd never believed in omens before but this cake felt like a prophecy of the End I was doing everything to try and forget about.

'Okay,' he said. 'Let me think of something.' He turned around.

'No, don't leave me!' I shouted. There was silence as everyone turned to stare. Someone had lowered the music all the way down.

Natasha's face swayed in front of me. She was bending over and lighting the candles. They were shovels, yet they hissed like snakes.

'No,' I whispered, feeling all the strength leave my knees. 'No.'

Khan put a silver knife in my hands. 'Blow your candles!' he shouted. 'What are you waiting for? Eighteen years old and you still don't know how to blow?'

Dark spots danced before my eyes. The last time I'd held a knife it had been to plunge it into my stomach. I dropped the knife and it fell to the ground with a subdued clink.

'What are you doing?' Natasha said. 'Are you okay, Alia? Do you need some air? You look like you're going to faint!'

'I'll get you out of here,' Sid said, and put a hand on the small of my back, turning me around.

And then the cake exploded and pieces of it flew everywhere. Everyone ducked and I screamed, and kept screaming until Sid put his arms around me and squeezed real tight.

'It's okay,' he said. 'Relax. You don't need to cut the damn cake any more.'

Someone had tossed a red mask right into the centre of the cake. I picked it up; it was a joker with big shiny bells atop it.

'Real mature,' Sid said, and gestured to the staff to start slicing up the cake. People muttered as they dispersed. The music came back on.

Ronjita and Raoul broke through. 'I'm sorry, Alia,' Ronjy said softly. 'Who could have done that?'

'I'm going to kill whoever it is!' Maya turned around and stamped her foot down hard. 'Who the hell was the joker at this party?'

'That was intense,' Raoul said. 'Come on, Cinderella, I know a bear who wants to have a word with you.'

'Wearing brown clothes and painting your face does not make you a bear!' Maya shouted after them. 'Honestly, what does she see in that guy?' she muttered to Krish. 'He has nothing going for him.'

He smirked and walked off with her trailing behind him.

I took a deep breath and told myself to calm down.

Sid's eyes sparkled with uncomplicated joy as he put his arms around me and held me close. 'So what's left?'

I shook my head, still too overwhelmed to speak.

'The birthday gift.' And then, in a teasing voice, he said, 'Really, one would think this is your first party ever.'

It *was* my first party ever, but I had no intention of throwing myself a pity party on top of it.

'So what do you get the girl who has everything?' he asked.

He turned me around and lowered a chain around my neck. An old-fashioned oxidized silver pendant dangled against my ribs.

'It's beautiful, thank you!' I picked it up and examined it. I popped the tiny clasp and it swung open. My breath caught in my throat. It was a picture of my mother and a baby.

It was the first photograph I had ever seen of the two of us. I closed my eyes and focused on the image I'd seen; perhaps it would jog loose a memory, some hidden memory of her holding me this way with what looked like love.

I turned around and buried my face in Sid's neck. I guess we were dancing soon, because I was swaying in his arms and the night melted away by inches. So that's what she'd been referring to when she'd said she had a gift for me.

'Thank you for doing this,' I whispered into his ear.

His only reply was to hold me tighter.

The party ebbed and flowed around us, and at some point the music stopped. People were leaving but Maya took care of the goodbyes, saying the 'cake incident' had been too much for me. Hardly anyone cared or knew me anyway. I hummed to myself, cocooned in the warmth of Sid's arms, sensing the drip of dew on the blades of grass under my feet, and the slow slide of sunlight over the horizon somewhere beyond the walls of the villa. Today was a new day.

Sid murmured against my ear, his hand stroking the back of my head, and I mumbled back, lulled by his touch.

He gave me a peck on the cheek just as a shout reached us across the lawn. I looked up to where Chris and Natasha were seated on the empty drinks table, playing rock, paper, scissors.

'Come on.' I pulled Sid to join them.

'So there's a zombie who walks into a bar,' Chris said. 'And he finds Darth Vader, Xena, Eve, and there's a jazz song playing, you know, Queen's "Dead on Time".'

'Chris!' I was laughing despite myself. 'Behave yourself.'

A sharp pain drew my attention just as I hefted myself up the table. A shard of glass had pierced the arch of my left foot.

'Oh my God!' Natasha leapt up and grabbed a napkin. 'You're bleeding all over.'

Sid and Chris exchanged glances. Sid turned Natasha towards him and spoke to her earnestly in a low voice. Chris jumped down and pulled the offending piece of glass out before I could react. He wrapped a handkerchief around my foot.

By the time Natasha managed to turn around, I was sitting pretty, as though nothing had happened, which, in effect, was the truth. I felt a sting, and yet within an hour this would be completely healed, the skin unbroken.

'I don't get it?' Natasha said, yawning. 'How does the glass in the foot add to the Eve costume? You're full of shit, Sid.' She blinked at him in her customary confused way. 'Doesn't she need stitches?'

'Have another Bacardi,' Sid said in a kindly voice and ruffled her hair.

I would have worried about this kind of thing ordinarily. Too many slip-ups, too many deviations from the norm, and someone sometime could start observing me carefully. But I let it go because I had to admit it was kind of funny how gullible drunk Natasha could be, or perhaps it was I who was kind of light-headed after all the drama from before. I felt a shiver run through me that had nothing to do with the temperature.

Sid draped his black cape around my shoulders. The cleaning crew were already at work; perhaps it was my father's not-so-subtle way of getting this party to wind down. I leaned my head on Sid's shoulder and closed my eyes, breathing in the stale perfume I'd gifted him a month ago. Everything was bent the wrong way, like a spoon in a magic trick, but at least today was going to be okay.

FOUR

The Wants were like an inhaler to my asthmatic soul; they released the unbearable tightness that built up in my heart and they filled my empty veins with life. But they, like all good medicine, could not be taken off schedule. I tapped open the calendar on my iPhone and switched to annual view; I slid my forefinger over the red dots.

I groaned and fell back in bed.

It was 2 a.m. I had reread *What Maisie Knew*, watched a cat walk in heels on a Facebook post and divided my hair into elaborate, tiny plaits by following a YouTube video.

I could not take the restlessness any more. I dialled Chris and he took the call on the first ring.

'Are you okay?' he asked.

'I . . . why do you ask?' I said.

'You never call me after midnight.' I could hear the smile in his voice.

'And why don't I do that?' I said, smiling back. 'Mr Know-it-all.'

'Because you like to pretend we sleep, I guess. Normal not working out for you any more?'

I shook my head. 'So what are you doing right now?'

'The usual.'

'Can I come?' I said.

'Yes.'

I had not changed out of my clothes this evening when I returned from college. There just did not seem to be any point to keeping up the charade of nightwear. I let myself out quietly without disturbing the skin that had formed like cream around the sleeping villa.

The drive to Kala Ghoda filled me with impatience and I sped down the Worli Sea Link, pushing the Maserati into an extended purr as I shifted into a lower gear, the steel suspension cables blurring into each other. I wanted to be there already. And once there, then what? Was there a cure for the hours and the days that I felt pile on me so acutely, now that I lacked the ability to switch off?

I had taken that last rotary turn way too fast. I forced my foot off the accelerator and pulled over to the side of the road with a sigh, sliding the gear into Park. It would take very little for this sports car to create a pile-up of epic proportions. When I took my hands off the wheel, they shook. This edginess was not a good sign. I knew that the one thing that would ease it was the one thing I had to stay away from until the time was right. Until then, I just had to fill the hours.

My phone buzzed.

'Stay where you are.'

I got out of the Maserati and there he was, standing under a street light. I crossed over to the promenade.

'How did you know where I was?' I asked.

Chris grinned as he turned away. He went to the parapet and looked out at the sea, where a retreating tide sucked at the rocks like they were hard candy.

'I could tell you but you have to promise not to get upset about it.'

'Nothing calms me down like being told to calm down,' I muttered.

'Okay, but you're going to hate this. Sit down.'

I slid down next to him, holding my skirt down as a burst of wind buffeted upwards from the shore.

'I always know where you are, Alia.' His eyes trawled the restless sea.

'I don't get it.'

'Ever since I came back, I've had some sort of connection with you. I can sense you; I feel this pull to where you are. And if I go with it . . .' He shrugged. 'Then I find you. Like I just did.'

'What? That's terrible!'

He smiled. 'You would think that.'

'You know where I am every moment. You are stuck with being tied to me. We are like . . . weird psychic twins.'

'That's one way to put it,' he said. 'It took some getting used to. Not just turning up where you were all the time.'

'But what does it mean?'

'Everything. Nothing. Who knows.' He shrugged. 'It just is.'

'How come I don't feel it? I feel nothing,' I said.

'Maybe you will one day.' He swallowed and broke his gaze.

'Good God!'

'I don't think God has anything to do with this. Do you?' he said.

I shrugged. 'Does He even exist?'

'I'll toss you for it.'

I stared at him in surprise.

'Heads He exists, tails He's the tooth fairy.' He pulled a coin out of his pocket.

'I know you're really into coin tosses these days, but isn't this like really sacrilegious or something?' I said.

'Depends on which one you pick,' he said with a wink.

'Fine. Tails,' I said. 'He doesn't exist.' I glanced around to check for lightning bolts.

He tossed the coin.

'Oh,' I said at last. The verdict was in and I was surprised at how disappointed I felt. 'It makes sense that it was tails I guess. It feels like God has been missing my whole life. You have it, don't you? Faith, I mean.'

'Faith? We are outside God's plan, Alia. Surely you see that. We are aberrations, mistakes at best,' he said.

'Maybe, but . . .' I shook my head. 'Learning that Khanna was my dad changed things for me. He bargained away his soul to save my mom.' I shrugged.

'You think love is godly? Even if you make a pact with the devil for it?' His voice was harsh with contempt.

'No! I'm just saying he did it to save her life, not his.'

'You don't think it was a sin of pride or selfishness?'

'So would it have been more godly for me to let them suffer when *I* had to make the choice?' I didn't say what was on the tip of my tongue. *Would it have been more godly for me to have let Chris go instead of bringing him back out of his coma like I had?*

I hugged my knees to my chest. 'This God guy is cryptic, huh. I could have used a sign, some direction.'

'God doesn't need to come down to your level, Alia. You need to go up to His. He's already told you what to do. He's sent His prophets and He's sent His books.'

'Then why aren't you reading your Bible every night when you can't sleep? If you think it has all the answers—'

'Don't you get it?' The fury in his voice made me jump. 'I cannot touch the Bible. I am an abomination and I belong in this hell.'

'Hey, hey, slow down.' I put an arm around his shoulder. 'What have you done to anyone, Chris, to earn that title? Look around you; we are still here. And this moment when I'm sitting next to you, this is no type of hell.'

'This is a memory of what it feels like to be human, an echo. Don't kid yourself; we are living an imitation. We don't belong here any more. The darkness is coming for us.'

'Gee, Chris, you sure know how to get a party going. I feel human enough, thank you.'

'Why are you here, Alia? You're restless, aren't you? It's starting to pull you in, the darkness, the Wanting. Why aren't you at home with your precious books or watching cable if you're so human.'

'Lower your voice.' I looked around. Cars whizzed behind us on the street but there were no walkers out this late. The deserted promenade stretched out on either side of us under the yellow street lights.

'Chris?'

'Yeah?'

'Do you ever wonder if we aren't alone?'

'What do you mean?'

'What if there are more of us? I mean, if we exist, then there must be others, right? What if we found them? Other people who made pacts with the Baba or were collateral somehow and are—'

A loud crack rang out as a lathi hit the cement wall by Chris's knee, the shock of the vibration tingling through my thighs.

The policeman gestured with his lathi, his thickset body swaying as though under the influence of some kind of intoxication. 'There you are,' he said, displaying gold-capped teeth. 'Are you deaf or stupid? Get out of here. Does this look like your bedroom?' His belt buckle flashed in the street light.

'Does it look like yours?' Chris turned around at last and his expression was not pleasant. His brows drew closer, dark eyes hardening like steel underneath.

I jumped off and dragged Chris with me, unnerved by the man's slurring. 'It's okay, I have my car right there.' I pulled my keys out of my pocket.

'No, wait a bit,' the man trailed us, 'let me get to know this hero a little better. It's time someone taught him some manners.'

'Who's going to teach me? You?' Chris's tone was a taunt.

'Here.' I pulled my wallet out of my pocket and flipped it open. How had this policeman materialized out of thin air? I pulled a bunch of notes out and shoved them in his direction.

'Don't worry, sister, I will get to you later.' He brushed them aside.

The notes were caught by the wind and snatched away, scraping over the ground and whistling down the empty promenade.

'What have we done? Is there a curfew on?' I asked. A policeman ignoring that kind of money? There had to be a good reason.

'Lingering. Loitering. Bribery. Indecent behaviour. Misbehaving with a cop in the line of duty.' He licked his thick lower lip and the leer he gave me was enough to get Chris's attention.

'What about punching a cop?' Chris said. 'Or did I not do that yet?'

'Shut up, Chris,' I pleaded, but it was too late.

He swung into the man and landed a good one, except the policeman was unfazed by the punch, and then, without a change of expression, he turned from me and took a heavy step towards Chris. His eyes were onyx under the street light, and I felt my throat dry out as I looked into them, for where there should have been malice and anger, there was no emotion at all.

My fear must have communicated itself to Chris or perhaps his own radar had gone up now. He dropped the act and gave the policeman the full effect of his gaze. *'Leave us, and go,'* he commanded.

The man visibly resisted the Haze; his pupils dilated, and he grew rigid. The air was thick with the struggle. I had never seen anyone put up a fight to Chris's compulsion before and my skin began to tingle with tiny pinpricks.

'*Leave us, and go,*' Chris repeated, his voice low and dangerous, the skin on his face taut as he strained to overcome the man's will.

I uttered a small cry as menace surged through the atmosphere. Surely, the man should've snapped by now. Instead, his face hardened and his fist flew out to punch Chris in the jaw. Chris's scrawny body crumpled back with the force of it and I heard rather than saw him land hard on the pavement. I glanced at my car in desperation and it struck me that I had the keys in my hand. I hit the panic button, aiming it at the car across the street. The alarm blared out loud and clear, alerting the neighbourhood but there wasn't a flicker of expression on the man's face. I pressed the alarm a second time and it sped up, impossible to ignore.

I retreated and grabbed hold of Chris who was sitting up now and groaning. 'Come on!' I grabbed his arm. 'We have to get out of here!'

A dark blue van pulled up beside us, and uniformed policemen scrambled out. We looked at them in relief, and by the time they had surrounded us, we were all alone on the promenade. The phantom policeman had vanished as suddenly as he'd appeared.

* * *

'I have to thank you, by the way, for the stunt you pulled at the party,' I said as we walked away at last, Chris having Hazed the policemen into letting us go without filing a FIR.

'Why did you get that upset, by the way?' He grabbed my arm and gave me a squeeze. 'Maya was just being funny with the cake. You know nobody knows anything.'

'I guess some things cut too close,' I said.

'Hmmm . . .' He rubbed at his jaw.

'Hurts, huh?' I looked at him sympathetically, but the bruise was already fading and gone by the time we'd crossed the street. 'So where are we going?'

'To your birthday gift. Or did you think I'd forgotten to give you one?'

'Look, about my birthday . . .'

'Uh-huh?' He guided me towards the car and was clearly uninterested in anything but showing me what he had to. What did it matter what my real birthday was, when my birth was ancient news anyway.

'Never mind.' I pitched him the keys. We'd had enough drama for one night. 'Let's go.'

He parked across the trundling, prehistoric JJ flyover and we crossed over to the middle of the street to walk along its foundations. He unlocked a chained-up recess in the span between two piers and went inside. Then he dragged what sounded like a metal trunk out from which he produced battery-operated tubes that he set around the floor.

'This is your Batcave?' I couldn't keep the astonishment out of my voice.

'Close your eyes,' he said, and then I could hear him switch the lights on. He turned me around and I opened my eyes to find a larger-than-life picture of my face sketched on the wall. My hair fell in tumbling waves around it. I gasped and walked towards it, getting on my toes, running my hand over the wide-set brown eyes, the pointy chin, and the high cheekbones that he had smudged, as though the girl on the wall had turned around to talk to someone and had grown flushed in that instant. My hands went back to the eyes; the expression in them was sharp and vulnerable at the same time. I took a step back.

'Chris.' I swallowed.

'You don't have to say anything,' he said. 'You don't even have to like it. I wanted to put it up somewhere, sort of have our story out there.'

'What were you doing in St. Xavier's?' I said. 'Why didn't you enrol in JJ School of Arts or NID or something?'

His skin was anaemic under the tube light.

'Your mother. Of course! Let me guess, she told you that you were a shit artist and to get to the IIMs like your brothers?' I traced my hands over the drawing of parted lips, the tiniest gap between them, with the hint of teeth. 'You were such a sap, Chris,' I said in wonderment. 'If I could sketch like that, I wouldn't let anybody tell me I was less than a genius.'

'Helps to jump off a building.' He stretched. 'I have loads of confidence now.'

I cringed at how lightly he mentioned his suicide. Seeing him in a coma at Lilavati hospital was one of the most painful episodes of my old life. 'So where are you in this picture? You said this was our story.'

'Who do you think you're looking at?' he said. 'This is the time we met; this is how you looked to me.'

We were both quiet for a few minutes. A heavy vehicle rumbled over the flyover, creating ripples of sound that eddied out into silence.

'If I ask you something, will you tell me the truth?' I whispered.

'Always,' he said.

'How do I look to you? No!' I said, when his eyes strayed to the picture. 'Not from memory; I mean, now, now that I'm Changed. I see why you did this—you wanted to remember me as I was. How am I now, Chris? I know I look like this,' I waved at the drawing, 'to everyone else, and I always will. But I could see the worsening in my father when he carried the curse because he was my blood. And you might not be my blood but you are my kin in some way, aren't you? It's obvious that I've joined us together. So I'm asking you to be honest. How do I look?'

'In my eyes, you will always be this girl,' he said.

'I see.' I turned on my heel and walked away. He had said enough.

I drove back, taking care not to attract any attention to my driving. Two run-ins with the police in one evening? It was enough to make me want to keep a low profile.

I waited for the electronic card reader to admit my car into the villa. 'There you are,' I said as the gates swung open, and it was when I hit the gas that it came to me at last, what had so unnerved me about the way the policeman had accosted us on the promenade. I had just echoed his words— 'there you are'; that's what he had said on finding us. Why had he been searching for us in the first place? I ran up the stairs to the villa and hesitated for a moment, the key inches away from the door lock. I would have to ask Chris if he had ever come across someone who had resisted his Haze before because if he hadn't, then there was only one likely explanation for what had happened tonight. The Baba was sending out his vassals.

A hiss filled the air as I stood there, stumped in disbelief, drenched, as the first rain of the monsoons came down in sheets, releasing the odours of hard dirt and feeding the dry roots that clamoured for water beneath the soil.

FIVE

I could not stop thinking about the girl in the picture. Sid touched my cheek as we sat in the canteen.

'What is it? You're lost.'

'Chris thinks we are all lost. My mom, my dad, me.' I bit my lip.

'Alia, geez. You have to set less store by what Chris thinks. He isn't you.'

'What do you mean by that?'

'Look, far be it from me to speak ill of the dead—'

'Not funny,' I snapped.

'Jokes aside, Chris has never been a strong person. You are different; you are resilient, and things don't break you. I can't say the same for him but I know you will get through this, and that somehow things will be okay with you.'

'Because?'

'Because you're you.'

I held his hand, turned it over to look at the palm. Something in my expression must have given away the sadness in my thoughts because he pulled his hand away, a frown crinkling his forehead. 'What are you doing?'

'I'm reading your future,' I said. 'Because you have one. And I don't. I have only this restlessness; killing time before I can feel good again and then it's back to killing time before I feel good again. I don't have a future, Sid, I have a schedule. I don't have milestones; I have red dots on an iPhone.'

He exhaled sharply through his teeth. 'Are you done? Maybe if you spent less time with someone who saps you of all positivity, you might see things differently.'

'You mean I might see things your way,' I said.

'Why the hell not? You have to admit my way is better. And so is yours, Alia, when you stay away from toxic zombies.'

'Don't call him that.'

'Agreed.' He held his hands in the air in a conciliatory gesture. 'I went too far. He's just toxic and a zombie, putting them together is creating a dubious new category.'

He made a goofy face and I had to laugh even if I did not agree with his name-calling. Sid was impossible to resist in the sunlight. It was like he was made for sunlight, with his rumpled hair and tiger's-eye irises, brown enough to melt glaciers.

'So listen,' I said, 'I was wondering if you'd like to come over for dinner tonight?'

'To the villa?'

'Yeah. My dad wanted to thank you for the party and everything.'

'I didn't do it for him. Heck, I didn't even do it for you. Sid likes to party.'

'So I'll take that as a yes.' I gave him a peck on his jaw, and held it just to feel the way his cleft dimpled under my lips when he smiled. My phone buzzed in my pocket. I pulled it out and was about to cancel the call when I saw the digits and snatched it up.

'Hello, Aleifya?' I asked.

Sid widened his eyes when he heard her name. 'Seriously?' he mouthed.

'You got that right.' Her throaty cackle was joined by the sound of loud honking. 'I'm driving, can you believe it? I've figured out how to drive and talk and not kill anyone, all at the same time.'

'Are you back?' I sat up. 'It is so good to hear your voice, you have no idea.'

'Sounds like you have a shitstorm waiting for me. It's not very attractive, Alia! It's not terribly appealing! The last thing I want is a world with emotional complications of any kind! It's—damn—' There was the sound of tyres shrieking, and the line disconnected.

'What happened?' Sid asked. 'Is she okay?'

I shook my head. 'Jesus Christ, it's really her, after all this time. It sounded like she hit something,' I winced, 'or possibly someone.'

'She's not one to hold back punches,' Sid grinned.

'No, no, I mean she's driving and—'

The phone vibrated on the table and I grabbed it.

'Are you okay?' I asked. 'Have you pulled over?'

'Nah. I ran over a tiny bicycle. Wait! If it has three wheels, is it a tricycle? Good thing there wasn't a kid on it, huh.'

'Aleifya!'

'No, no, there really was nobody on it. I got out and checked. I mean, how can you see what's going on all around you when you're driving a van, right?'

'You're driving a van? You're less than five feet tall. How can you even see over the dashboard?'

'Driving is 80 per cent instinct. Brain fact! So, what's happening? Tell me everything.'

'Hang up the phone, you idiot!' I said.

'No need to yell, I'm just parking. I'll see you in two minutes.'

The line disconnected.

I grinned. 'I know this sounds crazy, but I have a feeling she's really here outside the gates.'

We found her arguing with the security guard at the gate. 'What do I look like? Some old perv?' she was saying. 'Come on, man, it's obvious I'm a student, I've just been in the sun a lot.'

'She's an ex-student,' I said. 'And she's here to meet Father Clarence at the Counselling Centre. You can call him to check.' I gave the guard what I hoped was a reassuring smile.

Aleifya grumbled more than he did as he let us go.

'My skin is a bit leathery, you know,' she complained. 'That's no reason to go all Gestapo on me.'

'Must you always take the path of most resistance?' I gave her a hug.

'Where's the fun when you do it the easy way.' She winked slyly. 'After all, I can see you two are still together.'

Sid chuckled, 'Touché. It's good to have you back, Ally; now why do you keep disappearing on us?'

'You know why,' she said crossly.

'Kashmir,' the three of us said solemnly.

'You guys have no idea.' She shook her head, the look in her eyes making her seem far older than her eighteen years.

'But there's nothing in the news these days,' I said.

'That's because no one cares about what's happening there or anywhere that isn't here.'

'That's true,' I said, struck by the intensity of her feeling. When had I bothered to think about what the wider world looked like? 'So what is going on there?'

'The army controls—' she began, and then the bell on the wall next to us went off shrilly. 'What the hell is this?' She rubbed her ear and moved from under the device. 'Did we turn into a fire station?'

'You've just forgotten what college is like,' I said, rubbing her back.

'So what do you want to do now?' Sid asked. 'I'm guessing you're not here for class?'

'I need to go check on Father Clarence. Tell me you've kept him alive, Alia? I left specific instructions, so you'd better not have screwed it up!'

I winced. I hadn't paid the old counsellor at college many visits ever since I was Changed. It was hard to face someone who expected honesty when you were living a charade.

'Really?' She shook her head. 'Alia, Alia, Alia, I expected better of you.'

'I'm sorry, okay?'

'Sorry won't alive a dead man, Alia. You had responsibilities to keep a check on his pills and not to let him overwork himself. What is your excuse?'

'He's okay! I mean, he's old enough to manage his own—'

'This is not making you look good, Alia! I won't lie to you—it's terribly unattractive!'

'Geez, Ally! Stop interrogating me!'

'Okay,' she said in a conciliatory voice, 'who am I to assign people missions anyway. So he's still alive?'

'I swear it,' I said.

She turned to Sid. 'You confirm this?'

He made the sign of the cross.

'Okay,' she said, turning cheerful as quickly as she had been fractious. 'How about I go visit him, see a few assorted souls I've missed, and meet you back here in an hour? We can go to the Kala Ghoda Cafe?'

Sid grinned. 'I have to look up some references in the library for Professor Evans, but why don't I join you guys there at two?' He pecked me on the cheek and whispered, 'We can head over to yours after?'

I gave him a grateful grin. After that odd conversation I'd had with my mother on my birthday, I was in no hurry to confront her on my own.

* * *

The tiny cafe was predictably full during lunch hour. We crawled into the upstairs seating area and I scrunched my jeans up around the knees to get comfortable as we sat cross-legged.

'So Kashmir, huh?' I asked. 'Didn't you promise me postcards and phone calls?'

'My fingers were frozen stiff all through winter. And spring in Kashmir is not meant for postcard writing and telephoning,' she sniffed. 'It's meant for love. And curfews.'

'No way!' I sat up straighter. 'Who?'

'It's no use. He's a foreign student and wants to become . . . guess what?'

'Aleifya!'

'A monk. He wants to get tonsured, instructed, draped, flagellated, spirited—whatever it is monks do, he wants to do it. Alone. Monk style. So that's it then; there's no future with a guy like that and I'm officially heartbroken.'

I could not help but laugh. 'Are you really heartbroken?'

'Not sure,' she said, smiling. 'It is kind of both funny and sad.'

She ordered a fennel infusion and a slice of cake. 'What are you having?'

'I . . . umm . . . nothing.'

'Geez. I don't think an infusion will do much. It may help.'

'I'd rather not.' I could barely tolerate the scent of the freshly baked bread that wafted up.

'You're not actually dying, are you?'

'What do you mean? Why would you ask something like that?' I said.

'Because you kind of disappeared before I left; you got sick with that weird amoeba thing and you couldn't see anyone for months. And now you're better but you're not eating anything and, well, I just feel like it's polite to ask.'

Sid had handled the social side to my disappearance in the early days of the Change when I went undercover. 'I am not dead,' I said, trying to shake off the memory.

'You mean you're not dying. I can tell you're not dead. You're an odd cookie, Alia.'

I kept the smile frozen on my face. She had no idea just how odd I was. Maybe hanging out alone with Aleifya was not the best thing; after all, she had the strongest instincts of anyone I knew.

'Alia!' I glanced downstairs when I heard my name. It was the gang. The cafe had got crowded and they had spotted the empty space around our table.

Maya made it up first and sank in next to me, balancing her large duffel bag on her knees. 'I am starved!' she said. 'What are you having?'

Binni lumbered up and sat by Aleifya, ignoring me completely. 'Welcome back, explorer girl.'

Raoul and Ronjita followed. Khan brought up the rear and sneezed into a large handkerchief, which made everyone uncomfortable. I had to bite back a sigh. Could this get any more crowded? And then it did. Sid walked in with a radiant girl in a balloon dress and with so much bounce in her tennis shoes that she was almost on her tiptoes as she scanned the crowd. Somya was back.

The upstairs was looking more like a dare or a joke—how many kids can you fit into a car or lift? So Sid and Somya had to sit at the top of the stairs, with their backs to us after they'd said hello.

There was no question of having a conversation after that; my mind was in free fall anyway after seeing them

together. Aleifya ended up recounting her adventures
to everyone. They were met with a mixture of derision,
amazement, disbelief and laughter. Which was just as well,
because I could tell that most of them were untrue. She
winked at me after a particularly bizarre story and her
eyes radiated sympathy. She could tell how uncomfortable
I was with Sid and Somya pressed so tightly together,
their heads nearly touching, as they carried on a private
conversation.

I bit my lip. What was I doing here with these people?
Nothing seemed to fit right these days.

'Pass me the chai na, Alia?' Khan wheezed.

I reached out to pick it up and slammed it back down
when I spilt most of it on my skin. My hands were shaking
again. This mood, this restlessness, was not small. I felt my
face flush with anxiety and the desperate need to escape. It
seemed like an impossible task; I would have to step over
people and food and bags, and then how would I frame civil
words to make Sid and Somya let me through?

I staggered, with one hand touching the low ceiling, and
made my way out through the thicket of arms and legs. Sid
turned around just as I made it to them.

'Alia,' he said, alarmed.

'Female emergency,' Aleifya piped up from behind me.
'Let us through.'

He moved out of the way at once.

'Let me know if you need something?' Somya asked.

I shook my head; I just had to get down the steps in one
piece and I would be all right. It amazed me that Aleifya's
words had worked with Sid; did he really think I still had

female emergencies? How clueless could he be about me? Time had stopped for me; and so had everything of a biological nature. Another thought hardened the blood in my veins; perhaps he was just too comfortable squeezed up there with Princess Leia to think straight.

We popped out of the cafe and into a burst of rain. Aleifya seized an umbrella from the stand by the door and examined my face.

'What's wrong with you?'

I shook my head, not trusting myself to speak.

'Do you need a doctor?' Her eyes roved my face. 'You're ill, aren't you? Tell me you'll be okay?'

'She will be okay.' Chris stood before us in the rain. His clothes were drenched and his frown was dark. His black hair fell like needles on his forehead. 'Because I'm here now.'

'How did you know?' I said through chattering teeth. How fine-tuned was his radar when it came to me?

'I texted him to come hang out with us, love,' Aleifya said, sounding confused. 'Are you guys not talking or something?'

'I am the only one she actually does talk to,' Chris said with a smile. 'Isn't that true?' He held his hand out. 'Come on, let's take a walk.'

'You are not getting her wet!' Aleifya snapped. 'Don't be silly.'

'She thinks you are ill,' Chris said with a chuckle. 'What do you have in mind, Aleifya? Cancer? AIDS? You have something tragic chalked out for our pale, skinny friend, don't you?'

'Chris, don't,' I said.

'Don't be an A-hole!' she snapped. 'What is going on with her?'

'Oh, this is her secret to share,' Chris said. 'I wouldn't dream of interfering.'

'Stop it, both of you,' I bit out. 'I'm going home.'

'I'll come with you,' she said.

I shook my head miserably.

'Oh, come on.' She sounded more worried than exasperated.

The door opened and Sid emerged. His jaw hardened as he took in the little group in the rain. Then he saw my face and softened.

He took hold of my elbow and steered me out of there. 'You don't mind a little rain, do you?' he said. 'Sorry, love, we had dinner plans,' he spoke to Ally, snubbing Chris, who glowered silently by her side.

'Hello? It's afternoon?' Ally shouted after us.

Chris turned around and stalked off, but not before giving me the eye.

I waved at Ally, feeling shame wash over me for leaving her standing open-mouthed like that.

SIX

It was early evening by the time we made it to the villa, and Sid hadn't eaten lunch, so we got some sandwiches made and went to the back of the garden. Sid ate them and flipped through a *GQ* magazine while I scratched a pattern into the dirt with a twig.

'You're a rubbish artist, Alia,' he said lazily.

I opened my mouth to tell him about Chris and the place under the bridge, and then shut it. Damn Chris! Why did he have to make everything so complicated?

'It's my new star sign,' I said.

'Ah,' he said. 'The constellation of Alia. Of course.' He lay on his back and smiled. 'You know what this place could use?'

'What?'

'A dog. A lot of dogs.'

My face must have fallen, because he sat up. 'What? What did I say?'

'It's nothing. Just that animals . . . they don't like me too much these days.'

'Hell! I'm sorry. What was I thinking!'

'Yeah, well. They have instincts, right?'

'Does it bother you a lot?'

'That animals treat me like demon spawn? Sure.'

He put his finger to his lips.

I could tell from the tread that it was Mary even before she appeared. She had a jug of nimbu pani, with two glasses and a bowl of peanuts on the side. The little plastic umbrellas in the glasses made me smile. She always had tricks lined up for visitors.

'This is just what we needed,' I said, trying to keep the dryness out of my voice. 'Thanks.'

'Sid baba, how are you?' She had a smile big enough to hug him with. 'So happy everyone is you are coming for dinner. Boss is making special chops.'

'Mr Khanna is cooking again?' Sid grinned.

Mary sighed. 'He not cooking, but he not leaving the kitchen when chops is on.'

Sid laughed. 'Well, I'm honoured anyway.'

'You are such a fanboy.' I shook my head. 'Grow up.'

'Where's Mom?' I asked Mary. 'How is she feeling?'

'So so.' She smiled at Sid again and left.

'My mother has been lying low since the party,' I said. 'I'm not too sure why.' I felt the locket around my neck with my fingers and thought about how, in some faraway forgotten time, she had carried me in her arms.

'Maybe your villa is too damn big,' he joked. 'Try living in an apartment. Keeps us close.'

'Yes. You're all so heavily normal, your mom and you,' I teased, ruffling his hair. 'It really makes my skin crawl!'

'She's been waiting to meet you, you know.'

'I know.'

'Alia, my mother is not going to pick up any weirdness off you. She wants to meet my girlfriend. And you do not give off some kind of bad-girl vibe, or whatever it is you're afraid of.'

'I don't feel ready.'

'It's not an interview.'

I held my hands up to show him the slight tremors that were running through them. 'Maybe one day just after a red-dot day. When I'm less shaky than this.'

'No matter how shaky you feel, or how badly you sketch a really, really simple star sign that most four-year-olds would . . .' He held his gaze steady until I looked into his eyes, and when I did, the smile was gone. The setting sun inflamed the iris, setting off streaks of fire in the amber and I was transfixed by the metamorphosis of his cat eyes. 'No matter what, you're my girlfriend.'

We lay back down, side by side. The sun-warmed ground was good against my back. He lifted himself off and leaned on an elbow, saying, 'You think I don't know you're not ordinary? You were never ordinary. Get over it.'

I stretched and looked at the sky. Threads of clouds pulled the setting sun down into the western horizon. They took Sid's cat eyes with them; they took the daylight away.

* * *

We went up to my room. Sid kicked his shoes off and settled into an armchair with my iPod. I went into the bathroom and shut the door behind me. Who was I kidding? I wasn't really here for a shower. The tub shone in the spotlights, practically sparkling with tiny flashes. I sat down on the side and ran my fingertips over the inner rim, breathing deeply.

I filled the tub with fast-foaming hot water. I emptied out the bath salts and lowered myself in, feeling the sizzle of heat on my skin. I shut my eyes. I knew Sid was waiting outside but I needed five seconds, just five seconds to feel at peace, before I faced my parents downstairs. I knew it wasn't good for me, this slip and slide I took into oblivion. What if I didn't come out of it one day?

But I'd worry about that another day; today I just had to buy some time until I could face this dinner with my mother. So I abandoned my body to the flow of water. I let it float outwards, my feet tilt upwards, and my head slide off the edge and dip into the water. I kept my eyes open, the water covering my chest, slinking around my face, up my chin, lapping around my protruding toes. And then I felt the pull and tug of depths that had nothing to do with the shallow tub; something made my limbs grow heavy, and sucked me inwards, into the water.

I struggled for an instant to keep my eyes open, only to see the chandelier and spotlights above me swirl into the churning water like a galaxy of stars that imploded, and then the most hidden of sounds, the softest of silences settled against my eardrums and my gasps were hushed; the bubbles of air floated upwards and out of reach. Darkness closed over me and I was away.

I was in the womb again. But I was more constrained with every beat of my new heart. As I grew, I filled the recesses in my host's body, I pushed the weight of me against her spine and felt the hostility in her embrace as I became a body to rival her own. Then the waters around me broke and I lay on the terrace tiles shivering in paper-thin skin beside a mother who turned her face away from me.

A figure with a blurred face picked me up and claimed me in a way my mother never would. The heat I felt now was not love; it was the scorch of a sacrificial fire. The Baba of Saat Rasta *had carried me into the other world and initiated me into the unholy ritual.*

He had a mask on now, a bronze downward spiral with wings, like a flaming bird. Twin boys watched, their childish faces in thrall, but only one was marked out for sacrifice with the tattoo of the spiral. The flames lapped at their feet, yet they showed no pain; and my father's face showed no pain either, as he wagered me. To him I was a clay doll, the symbolic fruit of his loins.

The flames ate me, and the divinities of balance were appeased. I was forged into the bargain with the sacrificial child and my father's transgression was accepted. I was lifted out of the embers, still intact when my father held the sacrificial knife, stained with the blood of the boy, Bobby. His face was rigid as a statue's when he smashed its hilt against my frame, little knowing that somewhere in the real world he had spawned me and I had been born into a curse.

I felt my lungs constrict and then cry out for the first time as arms reached down in earnest to drag me out into the waking world. The waters fell back as I was dragged out; the veils lifted, and I opened my

eyes, blinking rapidly to see the constellation of ceiling
lights before I focused on the face before me.

Someone was shaking me by the shoulders. The world
around me heaved and bucketed as I was half dragged, half
lifted out and dumped on the bathroom floor. Sid's face
swam in and out of focus.

'Alia,' he said. 'For God's sake, open your eyes, say
something!'

'I'm okay. I'm okay!'

He pulled me up against the side of the tub. I slapped his
hands away from my face. 'Just leave me alone!'

He was pale as he sat back on his haunches. 'Okay,' he
bit out. He put his hands over his eyes.

'Are you all right?' I knelt before him, dripping, a minute
later; I was getting him all wet. 'Sid? Are you crying?'

'I thought you were . . .'

'Dead?'

'Gone. I thought you were gone, that I'd lost you forever.'
His voice was raw.

'Hey,' I joked, trying to lighten his mood, 'I don't think
you have to worry about me drowning.'

He hauled himself up, walked out and slammed the door
behind him.

I wriggled out of my now skintight jeans and peeled the
blouse off me. I wrapped myself in a towel and blow-dried my
hair. I had revisited my father's initiation ritual somehow, and
the day of my birth, but how and why? It made little sense.

He was staring out of the window when I came back in
to pick up something to wear. He turned around and took

me in, the towel wrapped under my damp arms, the hair
that had doubled in volume and had yet to go into a bun, and
he turned back to the window. I grabbed a dress and went
inside to change and do my hair.

I came back out and put an arm around his waist.

'Hey,' I said.

'What just happened, Alia?'

'I don't know how to explain it.'

'Try,' he said. I could feel him tensing up. 'How often do
you do this?'

'I haven't counted,' I said. 'How long was I in?'

'You were not breathing,' he said at last. 'You were under
the surface of the water and you just lay there like a block of
cement. There were no bubbles, no movement, nothing. You
were not breathing.'

'Yeah,' I said at last, looking at my bare feet, the nail
paint on my big toe chipped from where the sandal had
rubbed against it. I had not wanted him to see that. 'Turns
out I can do without breathing.'

* * *

We went downstairs and the hall was ablaze with light. The
dining-room chandeliers were lit up, and fancy crockery was
laid out on the table. Sid was startled and then rueful. 'Did
they expect me to turn up in a jacket?' he asked.

'Relax,' I said, 'nobody cares how you dress. It's just
been a while since they had a guest over.'

It did not help that my father walked in wearing a
jacket.

'Were we dressing for dinner tonight?' I asked a little sharply. 'Because no one sent us a memo.'

He raised his eyebrows at my tone and gave me a kiss. He shook Sid's hand warmly and grinned. 'Handsome young men always look good, don't they? It's us old guys who need to dress up. Good to have you back, Sid.'

Sid blushed and grinned back.

He maintained his admiration for my father based on his career as an actor. It surprised me when he did not revise his opinion once he knew that it had all been fixed. Sid claimed the stardom had been fixed, but the acting had been real.

'I hear there are chops,' Sid said. 'And that you were somehow involved.'

'I could be a world-class-chef.' My father winked at Sid. 'Only Mary won't let me stay for long in her kitchen.'

The door opened and my mother appeared, resplendent in an evening dress. Her eyes were heavily shadowed and outlined, yet when they met mine, she could not disguise that they had lost all their hazel warmth; they were opaque now, as though the long eyelashes framed smoky gemstones. I felt rather than saw Sid's look of admiration.

'Alia,' she said, 'Sid, good to see you again.'

Mary and the servers set up the plates with steaming chops, grilled vegetables and potato mash.

Sid looked at me, shrugged and began to dig in.

'It's always a pleasure to have someone to share good food with,' my father said to Sid. 'It's the one big indulgence I have now,' he said in a low voice. 'Although I have to start watching my weight, according to Reshma.'

Sid grinned. 'Glad to be of service.'

My father raised his knife and began to carve his meat.

I looked at my mother and she looked back at me with a chilly smile.

'At least with you we needn't pretend,' she said to Sid, even as she spooned potato mash and gravy into her plate and pushed it around, uneaten. She smiled and put a ringed hand on my father's left hand. The princess-cut diamond played peekaboo with the chandelier lights. 'It is a good thing that Alia has such support.'

'Alia has a lot more than my support.' Sid gave me a long, lazy smile.

'Hear, hear,' my mother said, eyes only for Sid. 'Ah, the passion of young love.'

I withheld a groan. Trust my mother to turn any event with Sid into an Addams' Family experience.

My father scooped up grilled vegetables with his fork. 'I hope you didn't mind us not coming for the party, Alia. The thought of running into hundreds of teenagers was too much to take.'

'I understand,' I said. 'You guys are probably all partied out,' I added, remembering how much they used to socialize before.

'I've started going out again,' my mother said to Sid. 'Keeps me from getting bored when this one is asleep.'

'You must be very secure if you're letting Mrs Khanna go out alone like that.' Sid nodded at my dad in mock admiration.

Before I could even react to the shocking caveman statement, I was taken aback by the sound of my mother's laughter. It was a sound I didn't even remember hearing, and it jarred like a false note.

'I would have thought you'd want to take a break from all that socializing, now that you don't actually need it,' I snapped. Why was she still playing the trophy wife? Was it too late to grow a heart?

'Come, come, Alia. Isn't it time your mother started moving around again?' My father's voice was strained.

'We do what we must to get by.' My mother gave Sid a good imitation of a wounded look.

We ate in silence after that; only Sid and my father kept up a light patter of conversation.

Sid and I remained in the dining room after my parents drifted off to coffee in the lounge.

He reached for my hand, knocking his iPhone off the chair where he'd parked it. It vibrated and lit up with a message just as I bent down to pick it up. I handed it back to him but not before I had read the message that flashed across the screen.

```
Since U insist, I'm mkng an apprnce tmrw. C U
ltr Darth Vader! xxx P. Leia.
```

I looked at him questioningly.

'That's Somya,' he said.

Somya. The intensity of my jealousy took me by surprise. It was all I could do to compose my face.

He cleared his throat. 'I've been trying to get her to show up for classes. She thinks it's a waste of time to graduate when she's already doing shows with the troupe.'

'It *is* a waste of time. She's talented,' I said.

'What if she changes her mind when she's, like, twenty-five, and then it's too late to change careers because she didn't get that piece of paper?'

'What do you care about what she does when she's, like, twenty-five?' I said. 'In any case, I give her life expectancy till the end of the week.'

Sid burst out laughing. 'Alia, are you serious?'

'Dead serious,' I said, realizing with some alarm that I meant it, and then I choked back the anger and forced a smile to infuse some humour into the words.

* * *

I walked Sid to the driveway just a little before midnight. The clouds hung thick as show curtains, and the heavy tug of the sea behind us brought no breeze. Sid's face was shiny with sweat as he glanced up at the sky.

'Will be a full moon soon,' he remarked. The dark clouds moved in, eating away at the moon until even its pale phosphorescence had been blotted out. Not a star dotted the sky. 'Or not,' he said, with an uneasy laugh. 'That was spooky timing!'

'Indeed,' I said, opening the door to the Maserati and sliding in. The keys were in the ignition as expected. I fired her up and backed up a little before swinging into the gravel path that led out of the villa. The shadowed menagerie of topiary bushes accompanied us all the way, eerie features caught by the garden lights—great bears and elephants, horses and bulls, big cats and wolves.

I felt a catch release in my throat as I zoomed out through the villa gates and into the deserted road. It confused me; the last time I'd felt this way had been nearly a year ago, but hadn't we taken care of what haunted me once and for all?

SEVEN

I could have asked him to stay. Instead I dropped him home, kissed him lightly on the lips and ignored the question in his eyes. Perhaps I was more committed to this whole normalcy thing than I realized. I reversed out of his building compound, keeping my foot firmly on the gas until I was back on the road.

I ground my teeth and kept my eyes on the street, trying to shake off the uneasiness from the evening. It was claustrophobic in the car even though I'd blasted the air con to what Sid called brain-chill setting. I switched it off and lowered the windows, breathing deeply into the balmy summer night. The lanes were deserted except for the occasional car that whizzed past with its headlights flickering. I took the inner shortcuts and cruised alongside Juhu beach, the wind in my hair—when I felt it. I felt it before I saw it; the seam that stitched everything together was coming apart. Something darker than night spun out from the tarmac and flashed upwards on the street ahead of me, glinting in the street lights for a microsecond before time jumped forward and it was upon me. It slammed into my windshield just as I pounded on the brakes, and I sat there, having rocketed to a stop, the seat belt cutting into my heaving chest, every nerve in my body alert with terror as the black, feathery creature slid slowly down the glass, its bloodied, mangled remains leaving me in no doubt as to what it was.

Except it wasn't possible! The shape shuddered and moved, veined across the windshield, rounded up to my side window, and I hit the window switch just before it could slip over the rubber hemming and enter the car. My breath was jigging and jagging in and out of me now, my mouth sour with panic. It hovered outside, as though confused by the windowpane, before it began to take a bumping, scraping drag around the Maserati again. I sat there, my heart racing as I struggled not to react, to think about what I should do.

My hand grappled for my phone, even as my eyes followed the smear it left behind. I had to call my father! I had to summon a Want and stop this confounded thing! My hands were jittery as I emptied out my purse and the contents slipped between my legs and fell to the floor, the phone clattering into the gap between the gearbox and my seat. I grabbed it and dialled his number, only to be told the phone was switched off or unreachable.

By the time I looked up, the thing had made its way to the windshield once again; it rested there for a few moments until, with no warning, it began to tap against the glass, hard, and then harder, its insides mashed bloody, pulping over the glass. A tiny crack occurred at last, and then a starburst of cracks spread across the centre of the windshield.

My limbs surged with adrenaline. On an impulse, I switched gears and pushed on the accelerator, taking the car forward in a massive leap, flooring the pedal and touching a hundred kilometres an hour within seconds. The speedometer climbed steadily up to 150 before I forced my leg to ease up on the gas. I cut my eyes on the turns of the road ahead, keeping my focus off the object that hung on like a primeval stain, an inkblot from hell. I was breathing in great gulps of air that did nothing to calm me. The world whizzed by faster than I could take it in, the road in front of me bumped and buckled furiously, and yet the creature wouldn't slide off. I kept going for as long as I could, praying that any oncoming traffic would keep out of my way, and I found myself on the turn confronted with a pair of little boys in chappals, flapping down towards the middle of the road. It all happened so quickly that the event was like a snapshot, the chemical flash of a bulb.

I careened furiously to the left to avoid them, and hit the brakes so hard that it felt like my ankle was dislocated, stuck to the pedal, which was the centre of gravity, while the rest of my body lurched around with the car. The tarmac met me head-on and the car bent and twisted around me, the airbag punching me in the gut, the chest and the face. There was an awful bone-crunching sound and I looked down with terror to see my legs bent the wrong way, the telling wash of dark blood gushing through my jeans. Then there was a hum; a sort of awful groan rent the air, and the windshield shattered in a spray of hail. I lay there, or rather hung there, for I was upside down by the time the car settled and unable to move. The only thought in my mind was that there was nothing to keep that thing outside now.

My mouth was filling up with the taste of blood, my eyeballs popping as the pupils dilated, the immortal in me kicking in as a shard of metal cut into my side, slicing my organs and flesh into butcher's meat. Pain sluiced right through me at last, blooming through my veins and arteries, and my eyelids flickered as I transitioned.

* * *

'Give her some water,' the child said, nudging his companion.

'She doesn't need water, she's dead,' the other boy responded, authoritative. 'You're such a dumbfuck.'

'Scram!' The voice was familiar; it dug into my skin like a hook, pulling me out of the place I had gone into, a blank space where I floated between thoughts and pain. 'Get out of here!' he said. 'Take this, and go. Forget this happened or I'll come and get you. And you will look a lot worse than this. Got it?' There was a pause. 'It's okay,' he muttered, in a different tone. 'I got you.'

I opened my eyes. I was still hung like a slaughterer's carcass in the twisted metal of my car. I shifted slightly as I felt him cut me loose. I slipped down, one limb at a time, but he had me, cradling my body against his own in the wreckage.

'What the fuck, Alia,' he whispered through the broken window, his eyes wide. 'What were you trying to do?' He kicked the door open and it gave way like cardboard.

I shook my head mutely, feeling the delicate bones at the back of my neck snap back into place. Who would have thought the healing would hurt as much as the breaking of bones?

'We should get out of here,' he said grimly. 'I've set up some distractions in the area but this place will be crawling in minutes.'

I half scraped, half crawled out, while he pulled with all his might. I grabbed a portion of my dress that had ripped right open, exposing a lot more than my waist and a side boob; a great big flap of skin hung open and it looked like my internal organs had been in a mixer-grinder. My head spun. Chris unbuttoned his shirt and put it around me, before he bent down and scooped me up in his arms.

'It's okay,' he said when I gave him an embarrassed look. 'It's my least favourite shirt.'

'Ass,' I croaked, and spat out a mouthful of blood; it was something of a relief to realize my vocal cords were functioning.

'Do you want to go home?' he asked.

I shook my head. The bat had obviously followed me from home. Pain made my tongue thick. 'Somewhere . . . hide,' I gasped out.

'Okay,' he said, his eyes narrowed as he surveyed the street around us. 'Let's get ourselves a ride first.'

* * *

The day was a flickering strip of light under the shutters. I turned my head sideways and looked at it until my eyes watered. I tried to hoist myself up and winced with pain.

'I'd give it another few hours,' Chris said. 'What's the matter, bored with the view?'

'A little.' I pulled up my shirtsleeves. 'Just splash out with some plastic wrap, and your little den will have all the charm of a *Dexter* kill room. Also, I don't think I've ever spent so long in the company of my own face.' I gestured towards the graffiti.

'You did have the option of going home,' Chris said mildly. 'This is what a hideout looks like. And why exactly are we hiding out?'

I shook my head.

'You okay?' His frown deepened.

'I just saw my own kidney, or at least that's what I think it was. My legs were gone. I knew I'd survive the accident but I can't believe I just saw my body get wrecked like that.' I blanched. 'My insides were practically on the outside by the time I transitioned.'

'Well then, you left it too late. So what was that about anyway?' Chris asked, the impatience in his voice rising. 'Ten ways to test your immortality?'

'How's my car?' I said, with difficulty.

'She's jam,' he pronounced. 'Alia, you were incredibly lucky not to have killed someone the way you were driving.'

'Luck is for people who have no skill,' I said, counting my still-standing teeth with my tongue.

'Knock it off,' he said. 'You weren't drunk, and you weren't drugged, so that leaves just one reason that you'd drive like that alone in the middle of the night.'

I refused to meet his eyes.

'You were running,' he said. 'What is out there that can scare the big bad wolf herself?'

'How long have I been here?' I peeked at myself under Chris's shirt.

'Two days,' he said.

'Two days! You're kidding me!' I rose, slowly. 'No wonder I'm nearly mended.'

'I think you were knocked out for most of it,' he said gently. 'The pain was bad at first; you babbled.'

I gathered the shirt around me and looked for my shoes. They'd been dumped in a corner. I sat up slowly and tried to breathe through the ache gnawing into the root of my stomach and spine. 'Thank you,' I said when Chris threw me my Keds.

'You're still hurting,' Chris said. 'Why are you hurrying out of here?'

I looked around me.

'Alia, you totalled a very solid car. How do you expect I'd find your phone in all that? Are you thinking straight? Wake up!'

'Yeah, yes, sure I am.' I tried to appear calm; I just had to get to my father and ask him what this whole thing meant. Why hadn't he prepared me for this? I had been lying here defenceless the whole time; worse, I had put Chris at risk with whatever that thing was. 'Was there any, um, disturbance while we were here?' I said, holding my side.

'Define disturbance?' Chris said.

I grunted, hoisting myself to my feet. The room spun around me too quickly and I staggered and reached sideways to balance myself against the pillar, except it wasn't where it had been a moment ago and I staggered some more, my hand swiping at air, before my mind shut down and I fell, knocking my head with a sick thud against the wall.

When I opened my eyes, my insides were screaming, my head was on fire, and Chris hadn't moved an inch. His eyes were dark with anger.

'You let me faint and hit the floor? Seriously?' I croaked.

'What are you not telling me?' he said, unmoved. 'You've been babbling this whole time about him, about the Baba coming for you. What does that even mean? How is he doing that?'

I opened my mouth to tell him about the bat and my suspicions about the policeman, and then I closed it. I wouldn't be able to handle it if he laughed at me; and if he believed me, that would be even harder to recover from.

'Let me out of here,' I ground out through my teeth, still mad that he'd let me fall and hit the floor.

He pulled the grille back and walked out with me, a hard hand on my elbow, steadying me when I swayed with the pain. 'I'll drop you home,' he said, his eyes flashing dangerously in the subdued evening light.

* * *

The house was quiet as a crypt when we pulled up the driveway. As if on cue, a miserable grey rain began to fall and thunder cracked its knuckles above us, booming in reverberation out over the sea. The stairs to the villa dimmed as the clouds swept away the last flicker of sunlight, and a dread grabbed hold of me. I stiffened.

Chris looked at me blankly when I didn't follow him out of the stolen car. 'What's the matter?' he asked.

'Something's different.'

He pulled my door open and looked at me curiously, made irritable by the drippy rain running down his nose. 'Come on, I'll settle you in. Unless you want to go somewhere else? Hurry now, you don't want me to catch my death with cold.'

I gave him a grim smile.

'Alia, what's going on? Should we go back to the hideout? Somewhere else? Tell me what you want me to do.'

I stepped out of the car; the skin on my face felt tight.

When everything fails us, we have only instinct; sometimes it's no more than the headlights of your car lighting up a few metres of road at a time. It may not seem like much, but even a few metres of light on the road ahead is worth having when all is darkness.

We walked past the threshold, and that's when I felt it descend on us like an otherworldly cobweb, the sweet decay, the inherent sickness of this house, its age-old secret slipping out like incense, wafting, spreading, permeating the walls, and sinking into the pores of our skin.

The chandelier above the staircase was lit up and I remembered the first time I had returned after boarding school. The way the floor had carried the incandescence to me as though I were walking through a cavern lit up by subterranean torches. There no reason for me to feel this gasp of apprehension, this choke in my throat, unless . . . I shut down the thought in an old Ctrl-Alt-Delete combination I had used when I was mortal.

'Come on, we need to shower before Mary sees us.' He dabbed away a tendril of red water that had crept down his arm. 'You look like Frankenstein's bride.'

I left him to it and walked to my father's bedroom without a word. If my feeling regarding my father was correct, this is where I'd find out.

It was a gloomy room, heavily curtained, the air so subdued that even my tread on the Turkish carpet felt deafening. The four-poster bed dominated it, framed by wrought-iron roses with a swollen heaviness; to stand in that room, to stand before that bed, was to be transported in time back to when I had first wandered in as a child, my doll Miami Sheila's golden curls floating out under the door as bait.

This is where I'd seen him first; this is where I'd found out who the otherworldly child that I sensed around the villa was. The child who used my red crayons to mark the walls around me, the child who lured me to the maze in order to wrap its deathly cold hands around my body, wrecking a violence on my seven-year-old self that I had been forced to repress for the better part of my life, just so that I would survive the memory of it.

My breathing had accelerated so fast I was dizzy. I forced myself back to the present, for the truth was that time had passed and I was not a helpless victim any more. The spirit child was no longer loose and wandering the villa as it had been towards the end of my father's command over him. We had locked it away, my father and I; it only emerged now to do my bidding, and I had not called on it, so it would not appear. I had to believe that.

'Dad?' I called out softly into the waiting gloom. I could feel my voice go through the room, touch every object, until it was swallowed up, dispersed like smoke into the cool air. I switched on the lights and screamed sharply before my throat closed up—a figure hovered before me, caked with blood, her paleness cadaverous in the spotlights, her clothes ripped to shreds, as she reached up grabbing her throat. I stepped away from my reflection in the gilt-edged mirror and dropped my hands, taking shallow breaths. Judging by how quickly the silence had settled, it was obvious that the only person in this room was my own hesitant self, quavering in the doorway.

I strode towards his dressing room and threw the door open. It was stacked full of clothes, dress shirts and pants, shorts and T-shirts, suits and pyjamas, all hung above an assortment of footwear. I combed through his things, looking for the exact things I knew my mother had got him. Gone!

I ran back outside, straight to the Van Gogh and yanked it off the bedroom wall, dropping it in my haste, the frame going *thunk*, the canvas bouncing off the floor with a soft thud. My shaking fingers released the catch in the wall and I punched his code into the safe. It swung open and I looked for the tiny photo frame which bore the only photograph he had with my mother from the time before the Change. Gone!

'Alia, what you are doing in Boss's room?' Mary bustled in, trying to look officious, but from the way her eyes widened, I knew there was more to the story. 'Why you are going to safe? You are wanting money?' she asked blandly.

I balked; of course, she would know about the safe. Mary knew everything about this house.

'Where are they?' I whispered.

'Boss is not telling me anything,' she said crossly. 'Not to worry, he will be coming soon.'

'So he's gone,' I said. 'They're gone.'

'Yes, that is to say, they haven't even taken their main clothes, or many nightclothes or party clothes or anything. They will be coming any time.' She dusted her hands on her wide, aproned hips to make her point stick. I had never seen her look this uncertain.

'Didn't they tell you where? Or why? Or—'

'If I met them then they would be telling me, isn't it?' Mary sniffed. 'But they have just packed few things on own and gone, so it cannot be for long time.' She sniffed to cover her irritation.

'Did he leave me a note?' I looked around the room.

Her eyes grew narrow. 'Why would he be doing that in twenty-first century? You can call him up and talk, no?'

I pointed at the switched-off Vertu I'd found in the open drawer.

'Not really, no,' I said, trying to rid myself of the choking sensation I felt every time I imagined life at the villa without my father to guide me. I gulped. It wouldn't do to panic, but it would help to get out of this room.

Mary's eyes narrowed as she examined me. 'Why is clothes like this torn and stained?'

'I was . . .' I shook my head, too ill to construct another lie that she wouldn't believe. I turned on my heel and concentrated on putting one foot before the other as I walked to my room, feeling the house ebb and flow around me. I shut my eyes for an instant and knew in that moment that the narrow corridor was the belly of a beast; it inhaled and exhaled, and was conscious of me moving through it, never at peace, never in one place too long. This villa had been home to me for a short while, for a brief, poignant interval that was already tunnelling away from me with all the speed of felt nostalgia. For something had changed the balance and it had reverted again to being a house of horrors with one chief attraction at the heart of it.

I let myself into my bathroom and peeled the clothes off my unbreakable body. Only fading scars and blotches remained, the pain had drained out of me. As I clicked on the latch to lock the door, my eyes ached with the burden of unshed tears. I wasn't Frankenstein's bride; I was Frankenstein's monster.

I stepped into the shower cubicle, pulling the lever all the way to the left, scalding my skin even as I scrubbed every inch of me clean. The glass partition around me began to mist up, the steam from the shower rising to film the surface. I watched my reflection disappear into the vapours, swallowed up as the nebula ate into my image. A minute later and I was gone, the air sweltering, until I finished and turned the shower off. I started drying myself, panting slightly from the exertion and the humidity. When I looked up again, the steam had begun to climb out of the enclosure and dissipate, sucked into the ventilation ducts of the ceiling.

I shuddered, for a sudden chill filled the bathroom, spreading quickly, robbing the air of its vapour, causing every tap and handle and shampoo-bottle surface to weep with condensation. The transparent glass began to defog and I glanced its way—and it was like ice water had filled my brain cavity, making me unable to look away from what was in front of me: the glass had been marked by fingers and they were not my own. This was no shadow cast by sunlight and cloud, it was no play of the imagination; there was no mistaking it, or what it augured.

I managed to kick the door open, too terrified to make more contact with the surface of the glass. I made my way out, the towel around my arms doing little to contain the burst of goose pimples that erupted on my skin. My breathing came in fast and shallow, and I was conscious of my heart thrumming in its cage as though I had run a marathon. For outlined in the steamy glass was the exact curvature of my own body. And I knew without a shadow of doubt now that my worst apprehensions had been true. Bobby was no longer locked away like he had been in the early days of the Change. Who else could have been with me in the shower to sketch out this reminder of the Running Man?

* * *

When Chris knocked and entered my room a few minutes later, I had changed into a pair of shorts and a white T-shirt; I continued to dry my hair with a fresh towel, unable to meet his eyes lest he saw the horror in mine.

'Huh,' he said, sitting down on the bed by my side. 'How weirdly domestic this is. I've never seen you do all this. I mean, somewhere I know that you must; that even Alia Khanna must have a home life, where she paints her nails and does her hair and, heck, I don't know, does other stuff.'

I was too numb to respond. Here he was, prattling about domesticity, while my world was coming to an end.

His phone vibrated in his pocket. 'It's Sid again,' he muttered, drawing it out and flinging it on the bed.

'Sid again? Have you told him what happened? That I was with you all this time?'

I picked up the phone. I stared at the display—seventeen missed calls. Fifteen of them from Sid and two from Somya. It was like the air was filled with poison from the moment I saw her name. Why would Somya be calling Chris? A dull ache began at the back of my eyes and intensified with every breath I took. Knowing that I had only to Want something to get it—or, make someone like Somya go away—didn't exactly help my self-control.

'Chris, why haven't you answered any of these?' I dialled Sid back and he picked it up on the first ring.

'Alia, thank God!' Sid's voice was tight with tension. 'I've been going crazy with worry! It's been three days since we spoke and you vanished without warning. Where are you? Are you okay?'

'I am okay. I am at the villa now,' I said.

'What happened to you?' he whispered. 'I came by the villa but you weren't there.'

'I know. I'll explain when we meet.' I felt an exhaustion that had nothing to do with tiredness. Where would I even begin to explain the terrible place I had found myself at?

'You've got to tell me now! I was so worried that something had . . . you know . . .'

'Why are you speaking in whispers?' A ribbon of jealousy spun out and began to wind its way around me. 'Are you with Somya?'

'As a matter of fact, yes. We were about to launch a proper search party with flyers,' he hissed. 'Your phone has been unreachable the whole time! I came to the villa, I went to college, I even checked the news. I had no way of knowing how you were doing.'

'So you decided to team up with your ex-girlfriend,' I said, feeling a stone settle on my chest. 'Sounds real lonesome.'

'Alia, don't be ridiculous! Whom else would I turn to?'

'How much have you told her?'

'Jesus, who are you? Of course, I've told her nothing important!' The anger in his voice crackled through the phone. 'You were gone three days without a trace. With no warning! And now I can barely recognize you.'

'That makes two of us,' I whispered back, thinking about his words earlier . . . whom else would he turn to? I was too overwhelmed with sadness to keep going.

I disconnected and threw the phone to Chris who caught it with a surprised expression. 'That didn't sound like a lovers' reunion? That didn't even sound like you on *this* end of the line.'

'It's none of your business,' I said, turning my anger outwards. 'Why didn't you tell Sid I was okay?'

'Because I hate his guts and I don't owe him!' He gave me a black look.

'Do you know what you've done?' I said.

'What are you talking about?'

'He was with Somya the whole time,' I spat out. 'Thanks to your little intervention.'

'Are you for real?' He took a step towards me and then stopped when he saw the steel in my gaze.

'Yes.' I was trembling with rage.

'What are you saying? You can't be serious!'

'Oh, believe me, I am.'

'Well, next time you're in an accident, don't wait for me to come and get you. Just call your precious Sid, will you?' His eyes blazed with anger.

I walked to the bedroom door and held it open.

He stood there for a minute, his mouth working like he was rehearsing what to say, and then his jaw hardened and he walked out of my room.

I bolted the door as soon as he was gone and lay on my bed waiting for the tremors to recede. The callous desire I had—to get rid of Somya—was so strong that it took all my willpower to resist it. I knew this wasn't really her fault, or even that much about her. Nevertheless, my father, the only guide I had, was gone, and now she was taking Sid away from me at a time when I could really use some comfort, some safe harbour to dock my feelings.

I didn't kid myself. Nothing about my situation had ever been easy, but there was little doubt that things had got beyond complicated. I was once more in the sway of forces beyond my control, and I knew why I had flown off the handle on the phone earlier. The thing that made me mad about Sid and Somya was not that they were together now; it was the hunch I had that they truly belonged together. So I lay there, my knuckles pressed against my teeth, and fought the Want down before I did something I would regret for the rest of my unnatural life.

EIGHT

The day that followed was dramatic and changeable, with gusts of wind calling the shots. Sunlight pierced through the clouds and razored away the last of the shadows that clung to the topiary bushes, and then, only moments later, the sun was watered out by drifting cloud cover, and an austere gloom rode over the lawn, flattening out all opposition and snuffing away the contrasts.

Too much drama for me; I drew the curtains, hit the LEDs and picked up my book again.

'Go away,' I shouted hoarsely, when Mary knocked on the door later. After my little performance last night, I was not to be trusted around people. I reached for my missing iPhone and then scowled. I used a lipstick to mark my long-memorized schedule on the desk calendar in big, sure circles. Turned out there were weeks to go before another scheduled Want.

Another set of knocks like little hailstones and I trained my ear to the door.

'. . . is waiting for you in roses.'

I bounded up and unbolted the door. 'What in roses?' I said to Mary.

'Ah, now you open! I was telling you he is returning soon.' She honked triumphantly and flapped her arms.

I ran past her and took the stairs two at a time. I darted around through the dining room and ran to the flower garden where, sure enough, just as Mary had predicted, stood my father amongst the dying roses in his Wellingtons. The rain pattered on my head, a steady drizzle that droned like mosquitoes, and the clouds gathered force, blotting out the morning light with military greys.

'He's out, isn't he?' His voice was taut with strain as he poked at the bent rose heads.

'Probably.' I came to a stop and looked down. A clump of mud fell away from the roots of the plant and a lone earthworm wriggled in the shallow spill, trying to burrow its way back into the upturned soil. I bit my lip and looked away.

An old power had been unleashed again, a power that would blot the lights out and fill every shadow up with dread. Somewhere beyond the trees lay the maze. The rainwater crackled through its bushes, accumulated in the clearing at the centre, and dripped down. And through the mud and the maggots and the decay it dripped, right to where the urn lay with its dreadful contents, gleaming, intact, biding its time as it always had, our mortal and immortal years already forfeit.

'Have you seen him yet?' he asked.

I shook my head. 'I—'

'She saw him two days ago,' he continued, adjusting his hat, his voice deliberately casual. 'He came into her room and it set her off screaming so hard I had to slap her to make her stop.'

'I'm sorry,' I said softly.

'It's not your fault,' he said, all his attention now on draining the mud around the roots of the roses.

'Then whose is it?' I watched with fascination as a long, dark centipede crawled the flat ground and made its way over my big toe, heaving its body up, one segment at a time. To my surprise it bit me, and I shook it off, sinking my foot into the mud.

'Alia, we did everything we could to lock Bobby away. You've been doing very well so far.' His voice had an urgency to it now; an urgent need, whether to convince himself or me, I couldn't say.

'No, I haven't,' I mumbled. 'I've broken the summoning bind somehow—that's the only way he could get out.'

'You've done far more than I ever could. When I was Changed, I was drunk, drugged, high—whatever you want to call it—on power. Not a day goes by that I don't admire your control.'

I blushed when I remembered the foxy bat. Now was not the time to dwell on failures; I needed his help first.

'It's because I've always had you.' I glanced at his strained face. 'I've been wondering, Dad, what if it was wrong to leave him, to leave Deesh like we did.'

He frowned. 'Why are you thinking about this again? Has something happened? Did you see him?'

'No, not exactly. How could I? I just . . .' I shook my head, trying to put some force into my words. 'I brought you and Mom back, and Chris from his coma, and maybe we should've brought Deesh back, too. Maybe it would be easier on my conscience if I did it.'

'Your conscience?' He gave me a thin smile but his voice was hard. 'Alia, we discussed it a year ago. You use too much of your power when you have such a Want; it will push you further into the darkness and we can't have that.'

'But he was innocent, Dad, he just wanted to free his twin and I . . . we let him be dead.'

He flung his tools down and the clang made me jump back. 'Let's get out of this miserable rain. Come on inside.' He wiped his hands on the sides of his jeans and we went into the dining room, tramping slush all over Mary's clean floor.

I watched him sip a cup of hot, sweet tea after he'd washed up and I wondered what it would feel like to have that sensation back. I ran my tongue under my teeth and willed it to remember hot or cold or sweet. I nipped the tip of it but it was no use.

He replaced his cup with a clink and it filled me with wonder that I had given him this moment by redeeming his soul in exchange for mine, even if I had given him a new world of grief to go with it.

He reached across and squeezed my shoulders.

'So tight,' he said. 'How do you carry such a weight around with you? The decision about Deesh was the right one and we made it together. You're not alone, Alia.'

'Sure feels like that,' I mumbled.

'I am failing you if that's how you feel. I thought you were okay for now, sweetheart, and that's why I concentrated on your mom. You give me this impression that you can handle anything, because you've already faced so much. But now I see how things lie. We could not keep your Familiar off you.'

I felt the muscles in my shoulders and neck loosen under the pressure of his hard fingers.

'Are you happy, Dad?' I shut my eyes all the better to hear the silence in his voice.

'I am glad I have you . . . that makes me happy.'

'What about Mom?'

His fingers paused.

'You must not expect that from her. It's not that she doesn't love you. It's just that everything is a trial for her.'

I nodded.

His voice trailed exhaustion. 'I just wonder sometimes what's beyond this life. What would have happened if we had all just died like we were supposed to? I like to think we would have been together—our souls, if not our bodies.'

'So we're disqualified from heaven now?' I looked at him. 'That's bullshit. You weren't meant to fall in love with Mom and you were not meant to die because of her father's honour code and we were not meant to be together in the afterlife after he killed all of us. Nothing was meant to be. We made it this way, our way. Even if we made a mess of it.'

'That's too cynical to come from you.'

'It's not cynical at all. Chris thinks we are an abomination. Yeah, that's his word; he says we are outside God's plan. But I refuse to believe that either.'

'Then what do you believe?' He lowered his head to look into my eyes. I felt a reflective tingle—coffee brown on coffee brown. I blinked.

'That you make your own plan. You do the best you can. And that's all anyone can do.'

'I admire your spirit, Alia.' He smiled ruefully. 'Even as I wonder where you get it from.'

'But you don't agree with my words.'

'It doesn't explain how cheating death has meant every form of punishment the world has to offer.' He withdrew his hands and put them in his lap.

I watched with horror as tears began to stream down his cheeks. 'Dad! Don't cry!'

'I promised her the world and instead I have given her suffering beyond words. I brought it down upon you, the daughter I never knew I had. And now you sit here, full of hope and expectation that I can help you, or that you can be helped. When I know what's waiting—'

'Don't say that, please don't say that.' I shivered.

'How long did all my thinking buy us?' he managed to spit out. 'We barely made it through six months before Bobby got loose. I wanted to give you a whole lifetime, Alia. I wanted to protect you so you would have lived well—would have lived even if it is this half-life that you have.'

I felt choked. 'This is not a half-life,' I said. 'It's a pretty good life in some ways.'

His voice was hollow. 'Without food and sleep and drink and humanity?'

'What?'

'Oh God!' He turned away with a groan.

'What did you just say?' I stood up.

He turned his face to me and I examined it properly for the first time. It was gaunt, his cheeks were sunken and dark circles ringed his eyes—the changing measures and sliding scales of mortality.

'You owe me the truth. We discussed this—food, and drink, and sleep, but what do you mean about humanity?'

'That goes as well,' he said in a hoarse voice. 'This conscience you speak of.'

'No,' I said, unwilling to believe this. 'It has not gone. Everything else went with the Change, but I have feelings; I have human feelings. I may not be a poster-girl human, but I have human feelings.'

'That's because we kept Bobby off you,' he said. 'Don't you remember me, Alia? How I was to you all your life? Do you think I had any compassion in me? I would have had you run over by a truck in the street if it hadn't been for Reshma. You were just a kid and I did not care what Bobby did to you because I saw you as a product of her forced marriage. I've had people taken care of for less. Nothing stood between me and what I Wanted. It was a compulsion of the blood.'

'Are you saying that that's what I will become?' The words broke off and crumbled in my mouth. A memory of my father when he was in the Change flared in the recesses of my mind—a grotesque, staggering figure, his body and intentions expanding, loose, malevolent.

'That is what you already are,' he said, his eyes on me. 'Keeping Bobby away kept the illusion going—'

'Normality,' I said bitterly. 'It was an illusion.'

'I did not mean to tell you like this. It's just . . . seeing your mother like that brought too many things back.'

'I know,' I said, recalling my Running Man in the shower. 'For both you and me.'

He drummed his fingers on the table. 'We can't go on like this, Alia,' he said, at last.

'No?' I said in a small voice.

'She needs to get away from Bobby,' he said.

'Oh. Of course.' The pain I felt was too familiar for me to not recognize it, like an old stitch on my skin that puckered on contact. The 'we' hadn't been him and me, or the three of us; it had been about Mom and him the whole time. It was like listening to an old song on the radio. So why did it still make me so sad?

I studied his face in profile, the long, broad nose, and the almost Grecian forehead; the only concession to age was a furrow in the middle where he frowned. Such perfect symmetry to his face—the teeth perfectly even when he placed them against each other, pearl-white and curiously tiny—and then he drew a breath through his teeth as he glanced behind him to check if Mary was around.

'My mother wants you to go away with her, doesn't she?' I cleared my throat and spoke up.

He hesitated for an infinitesimal second. 'It doesn't matter. I won't leave you alone.'

I looked out of the window and into the waterfall that poured down from the gutters on the roof.

'And you want it too,' I continued in a whisper, not trusting myself to say it in a normal voice, not trusting that I even had a normal voice. 'Because that's all you ever wanted—to be alone with her. Is that why you're here? To say goodbye?'

He couldn't meet my eyes.

I could hear Asif bhai lead some men carrying my parents' monogrammed suitcases down the stairs behind us.

'Just a few things . . .' my father assured me, 'a temporary arrangement until she's calm again.'

I felt my heart harden against the pain. Not in the spasmodic way it did when I was working up to a Want. This was an old, near-human feeling, or as close as I could get. My father wanted something from me. Absolution.

'I was wrong, wasn't I?' I said. 'When I tried to play the hero and bring you two back. You were done with it all.'

He shook his head. 'Alia . . .'

'It's okay, you know more than anyone else that I'm not a child any more and I don't need to be lied to.'

'What do you want me to do?' His voice was agonized. 'I should stay with you and be here in your darkest hour. But she is struggling,' he said. 'The thing is, how can I leave you here with Bobby on the loose?'

It was not a question. I felt the strings of my heart break, one by one; I would always and ever be an out-of-tune guitar when it came to family.

'If I go for just a little time and then come back . . . If I can make her see that we will get through this together.' He glanced at me but I had already composed my face. 'I will only go if you tell me it's okay, and that you're okay on your own for a little while. Because it's not worth it otherwise. I would not let you down again.'

'It's okay and I'm okay for a little while,' I said.

I said it for his sake. Perhaps I even believed it a little. I was still innocent about how low I could sink when the time came to rise. That is the nature of corruption; once it digs its fangs into you, the poison builds silently, lethally, and the blowout is unexpectedly sudden.

Mary shuffled in with carrot cake. 'For Alia baby,' she said, winking at my dad. 'It's her favourite, so no eating all cake up, Boss. When you returning from vacation with Madam, I'm making you apple crumble your style.'

I could not stand to look at his stricken face any longer. Of course, he'd had his exit all planned even before we spoke. I was the last to know. I carved a large hunk of a slice out, gave Mary a thumbs-up and went upstairs to flush it down the toilet.

My father left that evening.

I sat on the stairs of the villa and watched the Bentley gleam like a knight's black armour as it made its way in the moonlight, through arrows of rain, heading to the electronic gates and the world beyond the villa.

I had blocked out my father's words after a while; it was all I could do to nod numbly. He didn't want to know about the foxy bat or that I'd crashed the Maserati and lost my iPhone. He just needed me to send him on his way without feeling more wretched than he already did.

* * *

The music went on very loud all night. There was a high chance of blowing the speakers but I had to blast the silence away. My mother was away, my father was away, and Mary, deep in the kidneys of the villa, would have no objection. After all, she was already sleeping through a perfect storm. I got on the bed and danced the way you dance when nobody's watching—although I could no longer tell if that was true. A sick chill had fallen once more upon the villa, an old power had been unleashed. Nothing and no one was safe any more and despite what my father said, I knew I had myself to blame for it.

Outside, the rain fell in thunderous slaps against my windows and the black night raged. My breath came in pants and my chest heaved as I whirled around the room and when, at last, an orange dawn cracked with the slow seeping of egg yolk, I fell back on to my bed and shut my eyes. I kept them shut and slowed my breathing down, until it imitated the patterns I remembered from the nights of sleep. It saved me from doing stupid things that night. It kept an illusion going, which is not so very terrible to do when you want the real thing so bad that it makes your face hurt.

He was taking care of the one he loved and it was time I did the same. Well, at least I knew what I had to do next. When the rats start deserting the ship, you know it's going to sink.

NINE

St. Xavier's College was the same old, same old as I walked into it the next morning. For all its Gothic awesomeness, it had as much connect with the forces of darkness as a yellow rubber duck. Arched windows set in stone walls stared unblinking at the sunlit interior of the courtyard as I walked past. Motionless gargoyles remained perched atop sun-bleached turrets and did not plummet to claim me. I walked in through the dark, low corridor that connected the new wing with the old, and out into the 'woods' where a few carefully circumscribed trees maintained a decent living. As though to demonstrate wishful thinking, we called this square The Woods. The kids at Woodstock would've laughed to hear it.

Sid was waiting for me on the stairs to the chemistry lab. I sat on my hands to keep my white pants from getting footprints on them.

'How are you?' he asked softly.

'Now, isn't that the question of the day?' I said. A twist of breeze lifted a bunch of leaves, spiralling them into a bouquet and then collapsing them and teasing them across the courtyard.

He put his arm around my shoulders. 'I still can't believe he left,' he admitted.

'Not helpful,' I murmured.

'I know, I'm sorry,' he said. 'So what did you get?'

'A Jag,' I said, grinning.

'Really? You wanted to go for inconspicuous again, I see.' He shook his head while a smile played on his lips.

'I like that it's named after a predator,' I said, a minute later.

'Alia,' he squeezed my shoulders, 'tell me about the new car.'

'What can I say,' I shrugged. 'It gives a pulse-quickening performance, like they advertised. It's got a nice charcoal finish. Oh, and the handles retract on the inside, which is kind of cool.'

'Why do they do that? So you can lock me in?'

'Yes, and then subject you to an uninterrupted airflow. At least that's what the salesman says.'

'Never happening,' Sid said with a shake of his head. 'You already keep the air con way too cold for me.'

'That's because you're only human.'

'Guilty as charged,' he said, and then glanced at my face. 'Hey?' He held both my hands in his. 'I'm here, Alia. I'm right here. They may have left but I haven't. Look, I've been thinking about this ever since we spoke on the phone. Move in with me.'

'What?'

'Yeah, I mean it. Move in with me. Who says you have to live in the damn villa?'

'I do, Sid' I examined my hands in his. His hands were broad, the skin firm and soft and there was always this seeping warmth his palms transferred to mine. 'I don't expect you to understand.'

'Where is all this coming from?' He trained his molten browns on me. Except, the magic wasn't working. I knew now why his magic worked less and less. It was great magic; it was the compulsion someone who loves you deeply always has on you—a sort of ownership that draws you in—but it was a human magic, meant for a human soulmate. I was an Other.

He didn't know that this girl sitting by him would soon have as much humanity as the cool stonework we were sitting on. I had let him distract me but the truth was I hadn't called him here to talk about the new car or my precious little feelings; I had called him here to break up with him.

'What are you thinking? Why won't you let me in? I can help you. I love you!' His face was white. I gave him a thin smile. The oxygen had drained out of the atmosphere; we could only breathe in each other's longing.

'You can't even understand me,' I whispered. 'We can't go on like this.'

'That sounds like a crock of shit.' He was hoarse and his eyes twinkled, the lower lids raw with the effort of holding back tears. 'You're pushing me away because something is wrong, something is up and you don't want me to get in the middle of it.' He grabbed my shoulders and forced me to look into his eyes again. 'I signed up for this, Alia. No one made me. So go ahead and break up with me if it makes you feel better, less guilty, whatever. But we will never be separate.'

I hadn't wanted to go there, honest. The thing about having an Ace in your cards is that it's a mean card; it's vicious. To pull it out is to obliterate your opponent. And then what started out fair becomes moot, a fight that can only be dissolved in a win. But Sid was veering dangerously close to the truth and I didn't want him anywhere near it.

'I came to tell you I was with Chris,' I said at last. 'Those three days that I was incommunicado? Do you remember when you called and called and then I called you back from Chris's phone?'

'What?' It was like watching a light switch off in his eyes as he took in the implications of what I'd just said.

I almost couldn't do it, even though I was already coming colder to experience now that I knew that my humanity was corroding like a dirty pipe behind my ribs. So I thought about Somya and about how they'd been a little search party of two. And then jealousy dripped into the waters of my conscience, the pigment eddying out like smoke to colour everything. And I knew I'd been on the right course all along. I had to harness that pain and make him feel it too.

'I was with Chris those three days. And we had an experience together that I will never forget. It . . . it changed the way I feel about things.' I wrapped my arms around me. The best tip for liars is to infect your lies with a small tap of honesty. 'He gets me in a way that no one else can; he can sense me miles away.'

Sid's face changed. 'So nothing happened to you? You let me worry about you for ninety-two hours straight for no reason? Because Chris and you hooked up?'

I kept my face blank and nodded. 'Feeling separate now?'

Pain crossed his face like a bruise. I had put it there and I could take it away with the touch of my fingertips, with the kiss of truth.

Instead, I held on to my clenched fists so tightly that the nails ripped into the peach-soft palms of my hands. A warm liquid ran down my hands and I hid them quickly behind my back.

'Wow,' he said, his voice flattened out. He stood up abruptly and ran his hand through his hair, his jaw clenching. I stared at him, fascinated. He had only to run a hand through his hair and the beauty of disordered locks falling against his face disturbed the very air around the quadrangle.

'All I want from you,' he said at last, 'is your love. I can handle everything that comes with it. But you need to love me without ambiguity. Do you get it? You need to love me. You need to choose me. And when you bring ambiguity into your feelings for me, then yeah, it's time for us to think about what that means.'

'Maybe he and I, we belong in a way you and I cannot.' I forced the words out, forced myself to keep the tone even, the voice flat.

He shook his head.

'You have to admit Chris and I are made of the same thing,' I added, and like a viper I watched the venom I had injected work through his system.

'That isn't a get-out-of-jail card, Alia,' he said.

I merely shrugged.

He gave me a look and then he turned on his heel and strode away. In my imagination, I ran after him and threw my arms around him and told him everything, and the pain lifted from his face and we never parted again. In the real world, I just sat there and gripped my torn palms, trying to keep the blood from staining my pants.

* * *

The Jag sighed as I eased into the guarded entrance of the villa. I braked and watched the gates close behind me; a rosy, pink-cheeked dusk had settled in the garden, when on gossamer wings floated a gloom, thin as smoke, and I inhaled it and felt it curl into my lungs and thicken. Something flickered in my rear-view mirror; the bushes parted to reveal a shadowy figure and I hit the accelerator without thinking, skidding to a stop a few seconds later on the driveway, the pebbles ringing out like gunshots. Something had moved back there that didn't belong, and I had no idea what it was. I got out of the car, slammed the door shut and faced the approach, my heart pounding, and my back to the empty villa, every nerve ending firing on full.

Someone was calling my name in a high-pitched, sing-song voice. I froze, but I forced myself to stay loose, to keep breathing. Transitioning this early would render me incapable of dealing with whatever it was any other way but violently. Not transitioning, on the other hand, left me vulnerable, and I did not like the feeling one bit. I clenched my fists just as a head broke loose from the topiary bushes and a hooded figure floated up towards me, still calling my name. Then the voice splashed through me and I shook myself out of my dread.

'It's just me, you ninny,' the petite girl said light-heartedly, tossing the black hood off her head. She held her sides as she panted. 'Your face! Like you were expecting a ghost! How fast do you drive that thing? You should have a speed limit in here.' Her tousled curls caught the last of the sunlight bronzing in a flash as she stepped forward and grabbed my hand, and shook it vigorously.

'Aleifya,' I said wonderingly, 'what are you doing here?'

'I haven't seen you since, you know, the thing at the cafe.' She shuffled her feet in the dust.

I nodded. That still didn't explain her sudden reappearance.

'You know how it is, things didn't work out like I'd planned when I returned,' she said uncomfortably. 'I need a place to stay.'

'Why?'

'It's a bit of a long story.' She gestured at the building behind me. 'I think you can spare a room, no, if not a stable or two?'

'Aleifya, no,' I said, biting my lip. 'This is the last place you want to stay.'

'Fine.' She turned to go. 'Thanks a million.'

'No, wait!' I grabbed her by the shoulder. 'Don't take it like that, it's just . . . it's a bit of a long story. Can you accept that?'

'Sure.' She gave me a roving look. 'I can accept that. Are you okay here all alone?'

'There's no place like home,' I said with a wry shrug.

'Good, I'm staying the night. You can boot me out in the morning.' She crossed her arms over her chest.

'Why don't we both go stay at the JW Marriott?' I clapped my hands together in an attempt to sound excited. 'I have pretty deep pockets these days, what say? Fancy a swim in that infinity pool?'

She gave me the sweetest of screw-you smiles and marched up the steps to the villa.

The villa put on its pretty face for her. The shadows withdrew as the lights clicked on, and the freshly picked red roses on the countertops wafted welcome. Mary shuffled in and out of my room, feeding us as though we were an army.

'Not much protein in Ladakh, is there?' I said.

'Don't be a snob,' she said. 'I'm a growing child.'

'You're skin and bones, Ally; the life of a volunteer revolutionary is making you disappear.'

'And you aren't eating at all! Again.' She shot me a cross look. 'It's criminal to waste all this food!'

'I had so much to eat in college,' I murmured as the lie turned sour in my mouth.

'Oh, you went to college?' she said, blinking.

'Why wouldn't I?'

'Nothing! I had a bad feeling about you, that's all.'

'Okay,' I said. 'You show up after being incommunicado and it's because you had a bad feeling about me? Not at all odd?'

'What can I say? I'm soft-hearted like that. Now pass me the mushrooms.'

I passed her the bowl, thoughtful. Something was not right about this extempore visit.

'How did you even know how to find me? You've never been to the villa before.'

'Geez, it's not the best-kept secret that you are Khanna's daughter!' She rolled her eyes. 'Will you save the third degree for after I've had dessert?' She turned with reverence to the coffee-and-cream flan.

'How did you get through the gates?' I persisted.

'Oh please, what do you think I do in all the months I'm not at college, work at a telemarketer's?'

'Did Chris send you?' I asked softly. 'Is that how you knew I was alone here?'

'Oh, come on, boys are whatever, girlfriends are forever,' she said with a wink.

'Ally?' I whispered.

'Yeah?' She looked up attentively, her eyes sparkling.

'Forget all that. I'm really happy to see you.'

She smiled. 'I know, poppet, now relax those shoulders and eat something. Ally's here.'

* * *

We stayed up till 3 a.m. in my father's red-room auditorium and watched *Pulp Fiction*. By the time the credits rolled Ally was yawning her head off. She took a swig of her Breezer and threw some popcorn at me.

'Dude, come clean. What is going on with you? You don't eat? You don't drink? You don't get sleepy either?'

I faked a yawn and stretched. 'No, no, I just had—'

'Yeah, a lot to eat in college.' She leaned towards me. 'That explanation is getting old.'

'You're drunk,' I said after a heart-stopping five seconds. I pointed at the litter of bottles at her feet.

'That may well be true.' She hauled herself up. 'The girl gotta pee. Like a stallion.' She giggled.

I guided her to the bathroom and hung around while she sang to herself. Then I took her to the guest room and tucked her into bed. It was like handling a toddler; her already petite body had grown delicate from her time in Kashmir.

A small frown seated itself on the bridge of my nose and I couldn't shake it off as the temperature in the room began to drop slowly but surely. Distant thunder boomed and echoed around us—the howl of the departing monsoons. Why had I let my guard drop around her like that? I'd spent a year pretending to eat, to drink, to stretch, to yawn, to visit the restroom when around people. It was getting harder to care about fitting in.

I sat there and watched her chest rise and fall, and it made me want to scream all of a sudden—the way she could sink into a sea of sleep and wake up rebooted in the morning, having tasted oblivion. Her face was smooth in the night light, her curls fell over the pillow in disarray, and her white T-shirt had climbed up her thin waist to reveal the jagged careening scar she always kept hidden. Such abandon! The skin on her arms began to rise in goose pimples as the room grew steadily colder. Her breath came out in a fine mist now. I touched her icy cheek with one finger and she sighed but did not stir. There was something divine in the machinery of sleep. No wonder I had no access to it. I was a devil in the making, whether I liked it or not.

I sensed a movement behind me and spun around, and just like that, the French windows shattered and shards of glass hung in the air like an army of arrows aimed at us. There would be no time to duck once they were released, and they would slice through Ally and me with a lethal efficiency, and only one of us would ever recover.

The room drained of light and hope, and I raised a hand in greeting to a small figure that drifted at the periphery of my vision and cooled the atmosphere down further to echo a crypt.

'Outside,' I whispered, and in another heartbeat, the glass fell slowly to the Persian carpet, patterning the dark embroidery of the tree of life like a shower of snowflakes.

It was time.

TEN

I walked briskly through the woods at the back, heading towards the maze; I wanted to get as far away from the innocent sleeper in the room upstairs as possible. I could feel him tear through the trees along with me, his noiseless, icy approach no different in ferocity from a pack of panting hounds.

He was already there by the time I had breached the last of the passages and penetrated the centre of the maze, a corpse-like figure of a boy named Bobby. His skin caught the whiteness of moonlight like a fish on a hook and I watched with horror as his cadaverous paleness filled the air around him with an unholy halo. He was like a thing left too long in water, all colour bleached out of him until only an echo of his old form drifted through eternity. The shorn, pitifully oversized head on his little body made me catch my breath and had once filled me with pity, except I knew better now; he was a creature that traded only in fear. He had his chin bowed to his chest and hovered a few inches off the ground, the small, thin arms tight to his sides, the closed fists vibrating with wrath. I gasped as, slowly, ever so slowly, his eyes rose to meet mine, eyes I recognized from my deepest nightmares in the days when I knew sleep—dark-highway-headlight eyes, cat eyes, devil eyes, blood-red, eat-your-heart eyes.

'What do you want?' I shivered. He held his arms out, hands too big for his frail wrists, at the ends of limbs he had yet to grow into. Would *never* grow into, I realized with a start. 'No,' I pleaded. I backed away one step, and then another, circling him, and knew instantly that it had been a mistake. The weak curvature of his spine, jutting out bare in a loincloth, was a falsehood, a piece of trickery. His body responded with a quick coil forward, sensing my weakness.

I forced myself to stand my ground. 'How did you break loose from the summoning bond?'

He extended his arms and rose an inch off the earth, the fingers of each hand treading air as slippers dangled off his limp feet. The shallow lines of his ribcage exposed the vulnerability of the callow chest as he raised his head at last to follow my agitated movements with his eyes. His jaw jutted out and there was no time to see the rest of his features once his eyes locked into mine, and now the cold that emanated from him wrapped itself around me like a python, one revolution at a time, until my throat closed in.

'Go back!' I shouted, even as reality slammed into me with the force of a bullet train. I needed him, now that my Change had progressed further like an invisible cancer of the blood. I was slipping without him. But to admit that meant admitting I was no longer even a token mortal; I needed a Familiar to prop me up.

'Go back! Go back! Go back!' I repeated it like a mantra, like a prayer, like a curse, like a spell, like it was everything I had to keep myself sane. I backed away from him, stumbling. Then I turned and fled down the maze, my heart pounding in rhythm with my feet. I had to get out of there. I ran towards the boundary wall that separated the villa from the beach beyond and stopped before the rusted old gate. It swung open with a screech when I kicked it and I ran out on to the beach.

Clouds hung low, blotting out all but a few stars, smudging out the moon. The sea underneath was restless asphalt, broken bits surging to and away from each other in the incoming tide. The white-foamed breakers crashed into sand and cried out for relief but collapsed, hissing, and were absorbed back into the tug of dark water. I gasped and bit my knuckle to keep from screaming aloud.

My father was gone, my mother was gone, Chris was gone, Sid would soon move on, and the sleeping girl in the villa could be a friend, but was a mirage that came and went as she pleased. Perhaps it was best that I remained as I was, completely and utterly alone, while I became the monster the Change had activated in me.

I halted and looked back the way I had come. I had walked a long way down the beach without noticing it. When I glanced back, my breath caught in my chest. There were two sets of footprints trailing behind me in the sand. The first set was mine; I could see the indents made by the heels and toes. The second set was small and irregular, and occasionally dragged. I whirled around and around, yet I could not see Bobby. I knew then I was not alone, after all. Perhaps from this point on, I never would be.

Dawn was still an unrealized promise somewhere under the belly of the eastern horizon when I sensed a quickening in the air. I had walked a long way down the beach and the shapes of buildings along the shore began to thicken. Most of the clouds had drifted away after the cloudburst, and watery stars shed their light.

I was a mess; my dress was a second skin, my hair was plastered down to my skull and my limbs were breaded with sand.

'You shoudn't be out here like this.'

I startled and looked up. Three men had slunk real close to me without my realizing it. I could tell little more about them except that they reeked of alcohol and seemed to have spent the night on the street. Their aggression was tangible. Three men and a lone girl on a beach—that wasn't the opening line of a joke; it was the headline to a report in the *Mumbai Mirror*.

I stiffened. I did not want any trouble. Or did I? Their ferret-like glances and their ratty voices had teased out a pulsing point of pain in my chest and I knew that the way I was feeling tonight, only they could make it go away.

'I'm all right,' I said softly, crossing my arms on my chest.

'I can make you feel better than all right,' said the one who had first spoken, and moved closer to me. The moonlight glinted off his silver incisor. 'Let's give it a try.'

I made a wry face; I owed them a warning, but knowing that I was barely human to start with made me wonder what glory there was in pretending. My conscience had drained out of me like through a sinkhole. A mesmeric coldness entered my voice; the pitch of a predator that challenges even as it forewarns. 'Go back to where you crawled out from. You don't want to mess with me.'

'Oh, but you don't know what I want to do with you yet, my princess.' He was up against me now, the stench of unwashed limbs and a defiant swarthiness filled my nostrils. He had a roughly fashioned walking stick in his hand and he used it to draw a circle around me.

'Look what the sea washed up for me.' He leered. 'Where did you go in this pretty thing?' he then whispered, his breath hot on my neck as he came around to face me, tugging at the lace neck of my dress with his forefinger. 'Where's your boyfriend? Call out to him; I want to hear you shout.'

I swivelled to look at the other two who had fallen back a little. They seemed surprised that I did not panic but were obviously in on this deal. Their lips were parted, their hips relaxed, their arms loose, and their eyes shiny with expectation. I watched a bead of sweat rise and trickle down the forehead of the shorter one. They were ready for the show to begin.

I focused on the face in front of me and peered into his hooded eyes. I was a piece of meat to this man, a release to anger and frustration, nothing more. I would not be the last girl he did this to; I doubted I was the first. I had never felt less human than in his gaze, but I held back with one last stitch of willpower. I could still do the human thing: walk away and leave him breathing. Then he put his hand where he shouldn't have.

It was like a dam burst.

Rage ricocheted through me at his touch. Every other emotion that had ridden me this evening peeled off and was gone. All I had left was rage, a fury that was pure reflex.

'*Take him.*' Bobby was pressed very close to me now, his white coldness a welcome balm to the heat of my anger. His pale face occluded the men behind him, the small mouth drawn up tight with sullenness. His eyes burnt into me, the flames in them initiating a call I could not but respond to, sapping me of all resistance. '*Take him,*' Bobby whispered into my ear, and it was already too late for the three men on the beach. For the words became poison trickling through my system, trailing through me, igniting my lifeblood, loading me brimful with cruel intent as I was transformed into a predator. Evil had come to roost in the form of my Familiar, and I welcomed it home with every heartbeat. My pulse developed a new beat, the veins tightened and my organs grew taut and swollen with the surge of black blood. Pleasure embraced pain. I was in an ecstasy not of my making. I had initiated a Want.

Only later would I appreciate the irony of the situation. I was never going to be anybody's sweet release, but this man sure as hell would be mine. Their faces morphed, the lust evaporating into comic masks of terror as they witnessed me in the Change. It filled me with triumph that my Want would be the last thing they knew.

I would begin with hands-on man here. He crashed to the ground and flipped over. His arms and legs were spreadeagled and his skin strained over his ribcage, buttons popping as his shirt shredded apart. His eyes popped with terror but his mouth was already stitched close. I bent down and put my ear on his chest to listen to his rapidly beating heart, such sweet poetry in its bursting rhythm.

I sensed movement from the corner of my eye and I lifted the palm of my right hand in a gesture, freezing the other two in place. They were screaming something awful as they tore at themselves and each other, their pitiful feet scrabbling in the sand, kicking up a storm. I could turn them off but I liked the sound of their screams.

Bobby was my Familiar. Bobby was a long, cool drink I tossed back; Bobby was a scent I had inhaled, his powers were mine, and I would not deny him his play because we Wanted the same thing. Ever so slowly, the better to savour every pulsing second, I put my hands on to the man's hairy chest. It rose and fell, an inflating, sweaty drum, as he drew in breaths he could not expel, and an odour lifted up from it, fear loosening his bowels, and the stench of it was strong as the tang of salt in the air. I spread my fingers out on the taut skin, marvelling at its cadaverous moonlit whiteness and I revelled with a bliss bordering on delirium in the screams of his friends as I smiled and reached for his toy-like ticking heart.

* * *

'Alia? Alia!'

When I came to, I was on my back in my bed, the lights forming a halo over the dark head that bent over me. I turned to my side and groaned with pain. A breeze rippled through the garden, causing the leaves of the trees outside the window to dance, the supple leaf tips frosted with sunlight and flapping like tinsel against the windowpane.

I was disoriented; had I been dreaming of something terrible? No, that wasn't possible because I couldn't be sleeping. The throb that ran through my left arm took all my attention now and I winced as I looked around. Where had the night gone? The last thing I could remember was sitting on Ally's bed. It had got cold and I had reached out to touch her cheek.

In a perfect parallel, she knelt by my bed now and touched my cheek, her face a mask of worry. 'Are you okay? Talk to me! What happened! Oh, she's up! Thank God she's up!'

'Doctor, you are performing miracle!' Mary broke into prayers of thanks to baby Lord Jesus for protecting her girl.

Full consciousness returned, the pain in my arm so intense it was all I could do not to scream.

'You were unresponsive on account of hypoglycaemia,' the young man said, whipping out his pad. 'Your friend said you hadn't eaten for a day before you lost consciousness.'

'What did you do?' I whispered.

'Gave you a shot of reconstituted glucagon. Your vitals were abnormally low,' he frowned. 'I'm instructing her on what you need to do next because you need some tests done ASAP. It was lucky I could get here this quickly.' He turned to Mary.

I gritted my teeth as the pain throbbed its way up from the needlepoint where he had injected my body. A shock ran through me and then another followed close on its heels. I grabbed hold of Ally's hand and squeezed it so hard that her eyes widened. She brought her head close to mine. 'Alia, what is it?' she whispered.

'This injection he gave me is poison. Get them out of here now.' I whispered into her ear. 'Or something really bad is going to happen.'

Her face paled and then she sat back, stunned. A moment passed, then another, as her features quivered.

'She needs some privacy, please, female emergency,' she mouthed to the doctor over Mary's head as she shepherded them out and shut the door behind them.

'Lock it,' I grunted, raising my arm for the first time.

She gave a tiny scream of surprise, falling back against the door when she saw it.

'You have to cut it out of me,' I said.

'What? No! You're ill, you're horribly ill; you're having an allergic reaction to the medicine.'

'Does this look like an allergic reaction? You were right about me all along. No, listen to me! It's true—I don't eat, I don't drink, and I don't sleep.'

Her knees were knocking against each other. 'What are you?'

The veins were bunched up around a purple, snake-like bulge that extended halfway up my arm now. The opening where the medicine had gone in at the wrist had begun to ooze black pus. It hurt even to talk. 'You have to get it out. Trust me.'

She began to pace. 'I can't do it, Alia. I can't do it!'

I gasped. 'Give me Fiona.'

Her hand fumbled in her pocket and that's how I knew she had it; that absurdly beloved pocketknife she had carried around ever since her uncle had jumped her when she was in the third grade. She had told me about it over a cup of coffee and tears, in another life.

'Why won't you let me call the doctor,' she sobbed.

'Because I'm as likely to kill him as I am to let him cut me open,' I said with all the calmness I could muster.

I struggled to stay reasonable and not initiate a Want. There was no way I was going to risk Bobby when I was this weak.

Her eyes flashed and she tied her damp hair into a knot. She whipped out the pocketknife and held it with shaking hands. 'Calm. Be calm.'

'I am . . . bloody calm,' I spat the words out.

'Not you, me. I need to be calm.' She half pushed, half carried me into the bathroom, propping me up against the bathtub. When I looked up, she had towels ready and was soaping her blade in the basin.

'Oh God, oh God, oh God.' She looked blankly at her face in the mirror for a few seconds and then slipped the belt off her jeans, winding it around my upper arm. She pulled hard and buckled it in.

My teeth were ripping my lips to bits as I tried to control the tremors; I could transition any moment.

She was white-faced but steady as she knelt by me. 'Look away, love,' she whispered, and drove the pointed end of the knife into my arm.

The pain that ran through my flesh seared my brain. A little later, I found that I had been staring in an unfocused way at a bunch of folded towels. They were white and fluffy, like little clouds, but perfectly folded, of course, rectangular and taut with a spray of lilies pleated into the tuck.

Her sobs were what finally pulled me out of my trance.

I put my good arm around her awkwardly; my other arm was wrapped in her sweatshirt now. I held her until she quietened and the hiccups died down, and then I leaned back and tried to unwrap my arm. It barely hurt when I moved it. She shrieked and pushed my hand away.

'No! I can't see that thing just yet!' She clasped a hand over her mouth. 'I didn't mean it like that, I am sorry! I am so sorry! What am I doing? You are not a freak! You are my friend. You're maybe my only friend.'

'It's okay,' I said. 'You're allowed a meltdown.'

'Please! Leave the towel bandage on for now,' she said. The look in her eyes was wild.

'You're a man of steel, Aleifya Malik. Thank you.'

'And you really are something else altogether, Alia Khanna,' she said soberly. I followed her eyes to the tub. She had scrubbed it clean.

'What brought you here?' I asked.

'I was sent,' she said, getting off the bathroom floor.

'Yes, of course. Chris.'

A nervous chuckle squeaked out of her. 'Yes! Chris! How weird that I couldn't bring myself to say that before.'

'His effects tend to wear off in twenty-four hours,' I said, 'give or take.'

'His effects?' She frowned.

I shook my head. 'Never mind; he can be persuasive, that's all I'm saying, but you'd have come around.'

'What's going on, Alia?'

'What do you mean?' My voice sounded odd even to me.

'I woke up and you were gone,' she whispered.

I hugged my knees to my chest as I tried to retrace what had happened last night after I sat by her bed, but it was a blank beyond the knowledge that Bobby had appeared and threatened her. All I could remember after that was waking up in my own bed with this ache in my left arm. Each time I tried to remember what had happened in between, my mind skipped from her bed to my bed, night to daylight. I knew something lurked in my memory but I couldn't see it.

'Why won't your body accept an injection?' Aleifya interrupted my thoughts. 'You're not . . . fully human, are you?'

The gentleness with which she'd asked the last question took my breath away.

It struck me then that we never really know the people we love outside of the moments we've had with them. So much within them remains secret, unexplored, tantalizingly within reach, but never appreciated until a moment of crisis. If I could have told anyone the reality of my life, it was her. She had stuck by me when Chris had fallen into his coma; she had pulled me out of my all-too-human despair when I needed to be saved before.

Was it really a coincidence she had found me now when she had?

'Listen, chiquita,' Aleifya lifted my chin up with her hand until our eyes met, 'I don't know where your parents are or why Sid isn't sitting by you right now. I don't know why Chris had to pseudo hypnotize me instead of coming himself. But I see you, and you're in deep shit. Start talking.'

I reached for her hands and clasped them in mine. A vein ticked in my forehead as I thought about her words and thought about what it would do to her to lose every certainty, every belief, every bit of hope that made her who she was. The darkness of this world I inhabited would melt into her like butter off a hot knife, waft through her like smoke, and transform her even as she remained a mortal, because it would fill her with the immortal's truth. The world would never be the same for her after this, and her place in it would not be certain. Was I willing to surrender all responsibility to her and do this?

I did not know her reserves; I had never tested them like I would now. But I knew my own were tapped dry.

I unwrapped my arm, unlooping her sweatshirt, and pulled off the bath towel she had fashioned into a bandage for me. I held my arm out for her to inspect.

The wound was still livid, the skin puckered around the underside of my arm.

She ran a hesitant finger over the scar. 'You heal yourself.'

I nodded.

'But you feel pain?' she said. 'You felt this.'

'I can feel some kinds of pain,' I said. 'And not others. I cannot feel, for example, what you will feel when I tell you this.' I gave her a small smile. 'You sort of caught me at a bad time. I'm told my humanity isn't what it used to be.'

'What the hell does that mean?' She sat up straighter and her face lost colour. 'You're scaring me!'

'Second thoughts?' I asked.

Her eyes bulged a little. 'Are you a vampire? Are you going to eat me?'

I laughed. 'I'm not a vampire; those are just myths and fables people construct every few hundred years to explain things they don't understand.' I leaned in closer and lowered my voice. 'Phenomena such as I are all too real, however, so you're not too far off.'

'Stop this!' she commanded. 'Tell me what's going on.'

A desperate pounding sounded on the door. 'Alia? Alia? Alia!' It was Mary, and the agitation in her voice was unmistakable.

'What is it?' I called out. Had she and Asif bhai got into another fight over who ruled the kitchen? Was she here to administer a banana on the doctor's orders?

'Please be letting me in,' she said in a shaky voice, 'it is very, extremely urgently necessary.'

Aleifya frowned at me, marched to the door and opened it.

I chuckled and came abreast of her, peeping out to see Mary's latest theatrics.

Except Mary wasn't alone and these weren't theatrics.

ELEVEN

Mary had perspired all over the heaving front of her dress and a heavy scent came off her, a compound odour of sweat and lavender powder and fear. Her arms were by her side, solid as tree trunks, rigid, the palms gummed against the outside of her thighs. Only the quivering jelly of her throat and chin suggested her ability to move at all.

Except, why wouldn't she back away from the crudely fashioned stick that was held pressed up against her neck, slowly cutting off her air supply?

'Mary,' Aleifya screamed. 'What is it? What has happened?'

Only her convulsive gasps suggested that she would rather breathe than speak. She was on her tiptoes, the rod inching higher. It was like watching a hanging, but in reverse.

The dark figures that herded her between them were shades without substance. I could make out three, and the malevolence that rolled off them was more powerful than the stick they prodded her windpipe with.

Ally leapt forward to grab the stick, and it was obvious she couldn't see the source of its animation at all, because she went about it comically wrong. The figure to the left of Mary raised the stick for an instant and then brought it smashing down on Ally's head. A sick cracking sound accompanied the thud and she staggered, eyes fixed and staring, the blood swelling like a river and then gushing down, channelling around her ears and face and nose, and then her body slumped to the ground. A burgundy pool formed around her face, weighing down the fleece of her hair.

The stick returned to Mary, who had heaved in great breaths but was choking again, so systematically that the act suggested great patience, or a study in the art of torture.

The figures turned to me now, no longer spectres, the features forming the very real-looking faces of snarling men.

'Who are you?' I asked. 'What do you want from me?'

Mary's eyes gaped and she began to convulse; she could no longer stand unsupported, her limbs jerked out spasmodically around her.

'Let go of her,' I commanded.

The trio did nothing of the sort. Their eyes began to glow instead, a primitive lava-deep maroon that brightened into a lust-for-blood redness, and that colour, that is what lit the gut-wrenching fear in my heart. Despair flooded my being, coursed through my veins and turned my vision dark. He was coming to get me. What else were these demons, if not the Baba's messengers!

I spun around and raced towards the window. I flung it outwards and had grabbed on to the sides of the sill when a pair of hands held my wrists. The mere touch of the shadowy stranger filled me with a kind of numbing dread, leached my bones of power and paralysed my thoughts.

I was yanked back, my arms nearly cleaved clean off my sockets, and I was dragged backwards, the heels of my feet burning furrows in the carpet, before he flung me on to the bed.

My arms were held down, dark fingers sank into my flesh, scorched into my skin like acid, and I had no means to resist. The buttons on my dress began to pop, and the material ripped, as another pair of hands began to tear through my slacks until I was exposed like meat on a butcher's table. I looked sideways; Mary stopped struggling and fell to the floor as the third figure let go of her and drifted up to me, and mounted my legs, his mouth parting into a leer.

There was no suspense left as to what would happen next.

I tried to move something—my limbs, my lips, my mind, yet I could not transition. Every panicked breath I dragged in drew in bitterness and surrender, and I experienced the true breadth of Despair in my inability to save myself. My face rocked to the left under the impact of a punch, and then it was back and forth, my head slamming this way and that, my body jerking under the violence of those hands, my lips pulping out.

My ears were ringing and my eyelids had swollen shut when at last a thought crept its way into my head. I would heal. Whatever they were doing, I would heal, and so this could only be a form of punishment and not the End.

And then I heard it, the cry, as Ally threw herself one last time on me; she couldn't see it, couldn't see the forces that pummelled me any more than she could hurt them. And as her blood dripped off her wound and fell on to my face, as they lifted her up between them, the sacrifice of her, the innocence of her white-as-a-snowy-lamb fingers dangling limply in theirs, was enough to snap me out of my torpor.

The Want built so quickly that I barely had time to transition before they were obliterated by Bobby. And his coldness was a balm on my tortured skin, and his icy crypt-like breath was what soothed my heated thoughts. My Familiar turned to me and I nodded.

'Fix them,' I commanded, turning sideways, spitting out the gore and broken teeth from my mouth. 'Make them forget this happened.' And I watched as Aleifya the valiant slipped into a deep, healing sleep and Mary's shallow breathing from before became deeper, her brain mending with the supernatural magic even as she slept, her memory cleaned out like a trash can, the events of this evening flushed out and forgotten for good.

A few minutes later, I was able get off the bed and stumbled to my writing table. I yanked open the drawer, emptying out its contents. I slumped against the wall and powered it on the phone. The only sound in the room was the gentle snore emerging from Mary's now healed trachea and the quieter, cat-like breathing of Ally, who had her pink mouth partly open, the tips of her teeth showing like pearls in an oyster shell. I tapped out a number.

I had promised my father I wouldn't call him if there were any chances of Bobby being around. I didn't care any more for that promise.

The phone rang, and with every ring I could feel my throat constrict as I rehearsed my plea to him.

I mouthed it even before he picked up. 'Come home, please come home. You said to call if I was desperate and I'm desperate.'

I said it over and over and over in my head as the phone rang, and I kept hitting redial all through the hours, until one of our phones went dead; whether it was his or mine, I no longer remember. Time had no meaning for me. Time was the mechanical play of a pendulum ticking one way and then the next, taking mortals with it, and shuffling them along an assembly line from the cradle to the grave.

I put my head on my knees and kept it there, the sound of running water lulling me into a trance. Eventually the sound changed, and I looked up at last to find the water sliding out from under the bathroom door to run into the room. It licked at the carpet, lapping hungrily through its fibres, causing it to darken and grow heavier. It filled around the sleeping forms of Mary and Aleifya and had reached me by now, an innocent trickle that tickled my toes and then gathered force and swept forward. I pulled myself off the floor, walking on the water to the bathroom. I swung open the door to confront the overflowing bathtub.

No good ever came of oblivion. I turned the taps off and watched the surface of the tub settle and flatten out. No good ever came of oblivion, and yet I was going to take this invitation anyway, because the prospect of spending one more second alone was too painful to consider.

I lowered myself into the tub with the inevitability of surrender and stretched out, the water pushing me upwards as it received my body. Then it pulled me in and I was falling, I was sinking into it and it closed above me, drawing me into its world, an embryonic world that thickened around me, trapping me as surely as a fly in amber, preserving me as time stopped for real.

I would not be granted oblivion after all; a memory spooled out, unbidden.

It was a memory of Deesh.

We were in the maze together. Salty sea fumes hung heavy in the night air. I had helped Deesh sneak into the villa and I could see us in the light of the full moon. I was, as I was then, not just six months younger and mortal but innocent of any wrongdoing.

I had believed in my power to end this evil reign my father had begun. That in reuniting Deesh with the spirit child, I gave him a chance to lay Bobby to rest. How could I have imagined the terrible consequences of my deed? How could I, in my human innocence, have known the corruption that came with being the Baba's changeling?

Deesh had dug out the urn that contained his twin's ashes and I saw the look on his face, the look of relief, as he wept into his sleeve and clutched the urn. We could all go home now, his expression suggested; it was all over and we were done with the nightmare. When, in fact, it was only the first in a series of actions that would destroy us both. For Bobby was not cold ash in a vase; he was a demonic spirit who hovered a foot behind Deesh, and he bent over him, his eyes signal-red, his form poised like an oncoming locomotive, and Deesh, for all his love of a lost brother, could no more sense him than he could sense his own impending death.

The moon was a broken bulb by the time it was all over, its luminescence spilling into the darkness with as much effect as my tears had when it came to washing clean the events of that night.

My eyes fluttered open and I stared upwards at the ceiling lights in the bathroom. The water was a wall; it pinned me down to the bottom of the bathtub but as I came to and struggled, it exploded around me. I burst out of the memory, thrashing outwards until I had climbed out and was panting on the icy floor.

They were wrong, my father and Sid—they were wrong about me; they were wrong about everything. The Wants didn't only push me into darkness; they were what kept me going. They were what kept me sane.

The new Want building up within me right now was powerful enough to keep me going for a long time. Who knew what the Baba would throw at me next. Who knew what horrors lurked in the next room, the next hour, the next moment. If I was going to lose my conscience and humanity anyway, I was determined to lose it doing something that made me happy, doing something that righted the one mortal wrong I had inflicted on the world before my Change.

I closed my eyes and let the tremors race through me— fast, double fast—with a recklessness that was both new and curiously natural. The schedule could go to hell; my father's advice on moderation could go to hell with him. It was time to Want something I truly cared about.

It was time to bring Deesh back from the dead.

TWELVE

After it was all over, I pulled on a pair of jeans and a full-length blouse. I checked myself in the mirror; most of the bruising was hidden but there was little I could do about the state of my face. I brushed my hair to fall around my neck, and then in a move that made me laugh out loud, I ran a lip gloss lightly over my swollen lips.

When you're seeing a guy after having left him for dead, you want to make a good first impression.

I ran downstairs, ignoring the squeaking of my Skechers on the marble. I threw the front door open and stepped into the night.

The stars glittered dangerously in the void, sharp enough to cut my teeth on in the clear night. I sat on the topmost steps that led to the driveway. For a long while there was nothing; the moon rose higher and higher, dirty as a used coin, its craters like thumbprints from rough handling.

* * *

I heard him before I saw him, the familiar whistling as he walked down the long drive. By the time he rounded the bend and I could see his lean figure in the motorcycle jacket and black denims, I was already in some kind of disbelief. It took a lot of dark magic to end someone, but to make him begin again—to bring him back—that was a seriously magnificent Want. No wonder I was both enervated and triumphant at my success.

'You're here,' I said.

He came to a stop at the foot of the stairs.

'Here at Khanna Villa.' He spat the last two words out. 'Or here in the world of people?'

'Both.' I held my ground as he climbed up and drew closer to me.

The shine in his deep-set eyes, the smirk on his lips, the pits that shadowed his cheeks like the tracks of old tears, the sharp nose that revealed a dent when seen in profile—he was just as I had seen him last, except, of course, he was immortal.

'Took you long enough,' he said as he stretched his long limbs out beside me.

'Deesh,' I swallowed. 'I am going to make it up to you.'

His voice was dry. 'You seem to have your hands full surviving yourself. What happened?' He pointed to my bruised face.

I bit my lip and turned away.

'Well, you owe me a catch-up,' he said.

'I don't know where to begin, or how to make it up to you—'

He took my hand in his; his palms were cool to the touch, like Chris's.

'You begin from the beginning, Bambi. And one more thing; it's the grooviest thing, but I want nothing from you. Nothing at all,' he said. 'The last time you tried to help me out, you basically led me to my death. So I'm going to pass on your kind offer and just fuck off once you tell me what I need to know.'

I hung my head.

'Okay, chatterbox, Q & A time. Why did you bring me back? Why now?'

'I never intended for you to die.'

He glared at me. 'If I thought for one second that you wanted me to end up murdered in the fucking maze, like a dog, we would not be talking right now. But we are. So start talking.'

It took just a few minutes to sum up the catastrophes that had resulted in the end of that life and the beginning of a new one for both of us.

'You really are a bleeding heart,' he said at last. 'So no one is beneath your kindness, eh? You may have wanted to spare your parents but you've bought a one-way ticket to a bad place, missy. Speaking of which, where are those wonderful ancestors of yours? I have some special words I'd like to say to them.' He trained his dark eyes on the villa and despite everything, I was glad that they were as far away as they could get from the villa tonight. 'And where is he?' he said.

He was referring to his frozen-in-time twin. What would his feelings be now for Bobby?

'I have things under control.'

'Sure looks like that.' The smile did not even go halfway up his cheeks. 'I risked everything to help him, and the little rat killed me. Bobby's dead to me now.' He gave a bitter laugh. 'Khanna made sure of that. You understand, don't you? They're going to pay for this, your lovely parents, and there is nothing you will be able to do to keep them from their punishment this time.'

The moon cleared the clouds and I saw his eyes properly for the first time. It was as I thought—marble eyes with piercing pinpoints.

'What makes you think they aren't being punished already?' I said soberly. 'Nobody's happy, Deesh. Nobody's at peace.'

'Don't you see it?' He shifted impatiently on his hips. 'You're the only one in this mess who had the choice to walk away, and you didn't walk away. How's that working out for you now?'

'Not so great,' I whispered.

'Those two have scrammed as they always intended, leaving you holding the curse. What a surprise, right? But only to you.'

I let my gaze drift over the silent lawns. He was right. I'd never seen it coming.

He sighed. 'You can kid yourself all you want, but isn't that why I'm here? A part of you wants them to suffer the way you're suffering. You know that's my function in your little plan.'

'No,' I said. 'Of course not!'

'You're fighting it. It's a compulsion of the blood, though . . . you won't be able to fight it forever. The Change makes monsters of everyone it takes. What makes you so special, Alia? Why will you succeed in keeping your humanity when everyone else has failed?'

I shook my head dumbly. I had no answer to that.

He outlined the bruise on my cheek. 'Accept the devil within before it's too late, that's my advice. You may heal but you know you're just circling the drain. Try to deserve hell a little before you go there.'

'I didn't bring you back to harm them,' I said softly. 'I brought you back because you didn't deserve what happened to you.'

He sighed. 'And you thought you could use a friend with benefits; don't kid yourself with virtuous bullshit, Alia. We just wanted the same thing, briefly. All too briefly, in my case, and you would do well to remember that. Have you seriously brought me back to be your long-lost BFF? What makes you think our interests will align now?'

'They won't. But you're all I have, so you'll have to do, won't you?' I looked him in the eye.

He grinned and his face relaxed into something approaching amiable. 'There's that spark again; it's the one thing I liked about you, Alia. You may be in denial about everything that counts but you were always upfront with me.' He squeezed my hands. 'I can work with that. Now come on, let's go have a party loud enough to wake the dead.'

* * *

I turned sideways on my sparkly stilettos to get a good look at my ass in the silver dress that I had borrowed from my mother's walk-in closet. The back was so low it closed in pretty deep into the small of my back, but it fit like a dream. Deesh chose a charcoal jacket and designer jeans, and whistled as he tried on different pairs of shoes. We looked at ourselves in the full-length mirror for a minute—two un-shatterable immortals on a night out—and then I tossed him the keys to the Jaguar and we drove to Royalty.

The human infant learns to smile before it can even process what that means; some survival instincts come naturally. It turned out that Deesh could Haze people effortlessly, and he was just as careless with it as an infant is with smiles.

I went to the ladies' room and checked my face. The bruising was all gone, my lips had settled and the puffiness around my eyes had vanished. I reapplied a shimmery pink lip gloss and concentrated on having a good time on the dance floor; the giddiness that came with being irresponsible with Deesh would leave me soon enough, anyway.

By the time the club shut, I said goodbye to my two admirers with a pang, but I was in no mood to continue playing games with people. Deesh had no such scruples; he had a young woman on his arm now, and her husband stared into his Blackberry screen with panic in his eyes.

'He can't look away, can he?' I elbowed Deesh in the stomach when we were alone. 'What did you do to him? He looks like he needs to pee!'

He winked at me and grinned at the young woman who slipped her hand into his shirt and gazed up at him. The glitter on her red dress shimmered like mermaid scales as she moved.

'Where are you going?' I asked Deesh as he walked the woman to her car.

'Heck if I know.' His eyes shone recklessly as he tossed me my keys. 'You can go home and continue being a saint, Bambs, but I intend to sin tonight. I've earned a little downtime.'

'Wait, did you Haze this woman into coming with you?' I stepped in front of him with my arms crossed over my chest. 'Because that is no different from giving her a roofie or—'

'Did he what? Roofie me?' She gave me a supercilious up-and-down look. 'No, hon, I don't think your friend here needs to persuade his women like that. Go play with someone your own age.'

'Yeah! Go play with someone your own age, Bambi baby,' Deesh mouthed behind her.

I stepped out of their way and tottered towards the Jag; these stilettos were not meant for amateurs.

If she didn't want my help then it was her funeral. Frankly, I no longer gave a damn.

A wave of exhaustion swept over me, now that Deesh had gone. I tried to blink it away. I slipped my mother's sandals off and rested the soles of my feet squarely on the pedals. After the way I'd crashed the Maserati, I had no intention of driving rashly.

* * *

Aleifya was sitting up in her bed when I knocked on her door two hours later. I had showered and put on a pair of grey tights and a white button-down blouse. My face felt scrubbed clean, my hair swung in a well-combed ponytail and I felt as close to normal as I'd ever been. Except, she took one look at me and shrank back in her bed.

'What's the matter? What happened?' I asked.

'What am I doing in bed? Alia, how did I get here?'

'Um, the usual way, the door?'

Bobby had wiped her memory of the attack clean; now it remained to be seen how much of it was gone.

'No, no, what am I doing here?' She scrambled around and clutched at herself. 'Who put these clothes on me?' She grabbed at a ringlet and tugged it towards her nose. 'My hair smells expensive! How can that be possible?'

'Hey, Ally, it's me, calm down, okay?' I sat down on her bed and put an arm around her shoulders.

She threw my arm off. 'Don't touch me! I need to know what happened!'

'Okay, okay, what do you remember?' I put my hands up in a conciliatory gesture. 'What's the last thing you remember?'

'I remember the driveway, you flew in with the big car and then . . .' she shook her head, her eyes growing wide, 'and then a window shattered, a whole big window shattered. There was glass everywhere and now I'm here, in this bed?' she looked around.

'Okay, guilty as charged,' I said. 'Don't you remember watching *Pulp Fiction*? We got pissed and we had a whole Quentin Tarantino extravaganza. The window shatters in the movie, silly.'

We both turned to look at the windows in the bedroom. They were intact, of course. I'd seen to that when I'd carried her into the other room.

'Maybe you had a bad dream,' I said.

'You said something to me; you said something about not being fully human.' She blinked at me with a blank look on her face. 'Didn't you?'

'Duh, yeah!' I forced a laugh out, counting my stars that I hadn't confessed everything to her. It would have meant more dark magic being used to wipe her slate clean. 'We could barely walk down the corridor last night. Now come on, go take a shower and meet me downstairs for breakfast. It's time for college and I can drop you off wherever you want on the way. All right?'

'All right.' She still had a tremor in her voice. 'I'm sorry about that, Alia, I don't know what got into me.'

'Don't worry about it,' I said, unable to meet her eyes. 'We may have overdone it with the alcohol, that's all. I'll see you downstairs.'

* * *

It seemed like I'd get away with it. She spooned more scrambled eggs on to her plate and attacked it with the gusto of Orphan Annie. I heaped jam on my slice of bread and reached for the cheese spread before I dropped my hand. What was I doing?

'It's okay, it's calcium,' she said with a wink.

'Oh, I ate my weight in cheese before you got here,' I said, my tongue twisting on the lie.

'You really live in the lap of luxury,' she said, waving a hand around to indicate the doughnuts and muffins. 'How come you aren't a blimp yet?'

'Mary just brings out the good stuff to impress visitors,' I said idly, and then wished I hadn't, because Mary swept by and her ears pricked up.

'Oh, sorry, Alia,' she said, 'I didn't even notice you. We are so busy sweeping up in the small guest bedroom, the whole window had fallen in last night.'

'The window what?' The grape she was about to pop into her mouth fell to the table and Aleifya's mouth opened and shut.

'Glass everywhere on the floor, all over room. Cannot understand it how it happened. Thank goodness you slept in Alia baby's bed last night,' she muttered. 'Otherwise you would be becoming pincushion. Asif bhai is saying he has never seen anything like this. Must have been a storm, but nothing is coming in papers about it.'

'Ally,' I pleaded as soon as Mary had gone.

'Save it.' She pushed her chair back so violently it fell to the floor. Neither of us moved a muscle. Then she turned around and ran up the stairs. By the time I walked out of the dining room, she was heading downstairs with her backpack in her arms, her hoodie drawn low over her forehead.

'Ally, please, I can explain.' I blocked her exit.

'Yes, you can, but none of it will be true.' She looked me in the eye and I stepped back. 'I don't know what's going on, I don't know why I came here, or what happened here, or what I smoked up. But something is very wrong with this place and something is very wrong with you.'

I bit my lip. 'Ally, I'm sorry.'

'I'm not a pawn in whatever sick games you guys are playing here.'

I hung my head as she swept past me. I thought she'd left but when I turned around, she was standing in the doorway and had shouldered her backpack. Her voice lost some of its harshness as she called across to me. 'I've been in enough conflicts to know when something is off. If you have something honest to say, Alia, you come find me.'

And just like that she was gone.

Confusion seized me as I stared at the open doorway; the rectangle of light flickered on the floor of the dark hall as somewhere outside, the leaves rippled in the trees, and then there was a burst of rain and the door slammed shut, the noise resounding through the empty villa. I stood there for maybe twenty minutes, trying to gather my thoughts. Then I went upstairs, packed a sling bag and slipped out of the villa myself.

THIRTEEN

They say what does not kill you will make you stronger. People say careless things all the time, because so few of them have lived, really lived, through enough to know the twists and bends of any story. Yes, suffering is transformative where pleasure is protective, but these generalities are no more than a ripple in an ocean full of ripples. The truth is that certainty implodes into itself when you widen the canvas; it is pulled back and absorbed into the undulation and heave of the ever-mysterious deep.

The events of the last few days had left me hollow in a way I had yet to come to terms with. Driving to college without mowing through the slow-moving traffic took every ounce of control I had. I hit the brakes and put a hand to my forehead; I was immune from every kind of ailment and yet I felt as though I were gripped by a fever. I'd made it into the college gate when I heard a shy, polished voice say 'hello'.

It could only be Somya. She was walking alongside me now, her skin shiny with health.

'Hey,' I said.

'We haven't met properly in a long time. I meant to say hello at the party but I kept missing you, and then you left from the Kala Ghoda Cafe before I got a chance to talk to you.'

Every word pierced my brain like shrapnel. I imagined her hand on Sid's arm, her human, warm, pixie-perfect face smiling into his eyes.

'Hmmm,' was all I could manage.

'So, I was thinking, it would be great if the two of us could hang out sometime,' she said.

A vein in my forehead throbbed.

'So, anyway, um . . .' She fingered the lace hem of her blouse. 'We could go get a drink or something to eat after college, if you like? I finish at two,' she said. 'But we can go whenever . . .' She glanced at my face and trailed off. 'Even another day, there's no . . .'

The thought of having her alone and helpless in the Jaguar with the retracting door handles was more than I could take. I had to get away, and fast.

'I am late for class,' I said at last, and I left before the tremble in my body could give me away.

* * *

I made it upstairs with difficulty. The walls and corridor seemed to flicker and pulse, and I stumbled at the doorway. Sid jumped off his bench and steered me right back out before anyone could notice.

'What are you doing?' I said. 'I just got here.'

'Alia, lower your voice,' he mouthed. 'No, don't look around, just look at me. Look into my eyes and try to calm yourself. You're shaking all over. And you're as white as a . . .' He stopped himself in time.

'White as a? Go on, say it. And for the record, I *am* calm,' I bit out. 'Do you see me killing anybody?'

His eyes narrowed and whatever he read on my face made him lose colour. 'Okay, let's go,' he said.

'We broke up, remember? You don't need to do this.'

'I need to get you out of here.' He pursed his lips and began to hum nervously, his eyes leaving mine to dart down the corridor. 'That's all I need to do right now.'

'Somya wanted to go for a drink.' I laughed, the movement dislodging little pockets of pain in my chest. They coalesced again into a dark knot. 'What a joke,' I breathed.

He stopped humming, and his eyes narrowed. 'You don't want to be going anywhere with Somya,' he said a heartbeat later. 'Because Somya didn't break us up. You did.'

His words loosened a panic in my heart. He was right and I was wrong. What was the matter with me today? I leaned against the wall and shut my eyes for a minute; my body began to shake.

'What the hell! Alia is sick?' Binni, the best friend of maladies, was around, of course. 'It looks like seizures. Didn't she have them last year?'

'Oh my God, Alia! I'm calling the hospital,' Ronjy shouted.

'Alia! What's happening! Someone put something between her teeth!' It could only be Natasha.

'Don't touch her,' Sid shouted. 'Nobody touch her. Just stand back! Give her air. Ronjy, hang up!'

'She's having a seizure. Do you know what you're doing!' Ronjy shouted.

The bobbing heads gave way to a black Grateful Dead T-shirt.

'I do,' the owner said.

The black specks that danced before my eyes gathered around its black fabric and the pieces fit like a jigsaw, before everything went black.

'What do you think you're doing?' Sid asked.

'What you can't or won't,' Chris grunted as he gathered me up. 'Taking care of her.' He hauled me up and over his shoulder like a sack of potatoes, his bony shoulder digging into my stomach.

'What's the plan?' Sid asked as we went through the corridors.

'We let her get home and have a damn Want,' Chris bit out. 'It's when you try to control her that she gets like this.'

'You don't know what you're talking about,' Sid said.

'Really? And you do?' Chris's voice rumbled out to my ears from somewhere deep in his back. 'What do you and her dad want? For her to win Best Lifelike Human of the Year award? I have news for you. She isn't human and she cannot jump through hoops for you.'

'I don't do this for me,' Sid said. 'Fuck you for suggesting it!'

'Of course you do!' Chris laughed, and his body shook under mine. 'You think she wanted to meet her eighteenth birthday with a costume party where everyone dresses up like creepy monsters? Creepy monsters are already part of her life, Sid, or did you miss the memo?'

He turned a corner and ran down the stairs, making my head thump against his back. 'She doesn't get to be eighteen and you won't even let her grieve. You can't give her anything she needs.'

'So what *does* she need?' Sid asked. 'Since you know everything.'

'She needs to be allowed to feel like herself. Without being terrified that you or her precious daddy will judge her.'

'You think having out-of-control desires is what Alia is about? No, that's all you, buddy.'

Chris swung around to face Sid and his voice was like silk. 'I could hurt you right now and get away with it. But Alia would know. So, go back to your classroom and get through the rest of the day as usual. If someone asks you about Alia, say she was unwell and went home. That's all you will remember: Alia was unwell and she went home.'

I ground my teeth against the chattering. 'No!' I whispered but the sound would not come out.

'Turn around, friend. We never had this conversation,' Chris said pleasantly. 'Walk away from us.' And just like that, the Haze was done.

* * *

A comet travelled across the black night on a long burn into oblivion.

'Stare any longer at those and you'll have to pay the stars rent,' Chris said.

I shifted my sore shoulder blades and turned to my side to look at him instead. Chris lay beside me on the gravel; the steps to the villa reached up behind him, up to the towering stone edifice I had never called home.

'That's Orion's Bow,' he said, tracing out the bright constellation with his finger. 'You see that kite-like shape there and here? It's named after Orion, the mythological giant hunter. Legend has it that he wasn't the most popular man, not after he boasted about his ability to kill every animal on the planet. The goddess Gaia tried to kill him with a scorpion, but you know what got him in the end?' I shook my head. 'Love,' he said. 'Artemis, the goddess of hunting fell for him so hard that she was determined to have him. Her brother Apollo wanted to keep her from giving up her vow of chastity, so he dared her to hit a small target in the distance with her bow and arrow. It took a single shot for her to kill the love of her life. She didn't even know what she was shooting at, and all she could do in the end was place him among the stars.'

'That's a terrible story,' I said.

'Love can be a terrible thing,' Chris said in a voice so soft I wondered if I'd imagined it.

The silence stretched between us like a strip of gum.

We had only made it as far as the driveway of the villa before I'd collapsed. Chris had flung me down and we just lay there, and I talked and talked until there was nothing he didn't know about the last few days. What's more, there was no hiding any more from what I had to do.

'You're going to have to remember those things,' he said. 'Whatever it is that you did on the night that Ally arrived. You've done something bad and you've erased your memory; it's the only logical explanation for why you blanked out about it, and why you're being all crazy right now.'

'I don't want to remember something awful,' I whispered hoarsely.

'I know.' He turned towards me and stroked my cheekbone. 'But it's eating you up anyway. The Alia I saw today was a hot mess and a ticking bomb. You know it isn't a simple thing to take away a memory; it confuses everything.'

'I must have been pretty desperate to do that.' I bit my lip.

'I know you're scared but the only way forward is to face whatever you've been hiding from.' His voice was gruff. Then he raised himself on his arms and brought his face close to mine. His forehead rested against mine for a minute, and his breath caressed my cheek as he whispered, 'Be an underwater princess, Alia. Take a breath, go deep, swim through it, and come out the other end.'

I felt my eyes burn, the eyelashes twinning with the shimmering memory of shed tears.

'It's time you faced what's killing you or you really will wind up murdering someone.' He held my chin for a few minutes, his lips just an exhalation of air away from mine, and then he pecked me on the cheek and withdrew. 'This person who runs away from things isn't you, Alia; you have to find you.'

He hauled himself up and walked away, up the staircase and into the villa.

I shut my eyes. When I opened them, a form hovered a few feet above me, supine, its face staring into mine, its head blocking out the stars; the corpse-like coldness of Bobby radiated like a freezer's blast. I let him wait until I was ready.

His features flickered and he drifted slightly. His whiteness leaked into the night like vapour, sickening the fresh air that blew in from the beach.

Whatever spirit used this long-dead child and spoke through it was not childlike.

The garden held its breath. Every stem and leaf and insensate pebble prayed for sanctuary against evil, as he floated there above me.

'I Want to remember what happened the night that Ally arrived,' I said to the unholy creature, my breath condensing into cloud. 'Make me.'

FOURTEEN

Memory is not linear.

I guess I should explain how I came to be lying down in the middle of the road in Juhu, in the dead of night in a white dress, like an extra in an urban-legend slasher flick.

* * *

Apparently, violently annihilating three men on the beach and then doing unspeakable things to their remains had been a bit too dark even for me. I hadn't been able to bear the guilt. So I had asked Bobby to erase my memory of the event entirely. It had knocked me out, and Ally had found me like that, called the doctor and, well, the rest had followed.

Bringing the memory back and dealing with it hadn't been easy. It took me weeks to come to terms with it. I didn't doubt for a second that those men had been sent by the Baba to provoke me that night on the beach, or even that their actions were evil and they deserved punishment. It was the manner of punishment that I had meted out that filled me with Despair;

the merest contact with Bobby had been enough to spin me out of control. And now that the memory was restored, I recovered every sickening detail of what I had done to them, and that made me wonder if I had any humanity left at all.

Then there were the implications of the quickness with which my attackers had come back. The bat attack on the Maserati had been a walk in the park in comparison. I remembered the near-suicidal Despair I had felt, my inability to Want again and protect myself.

The cards were on the table—my bargain with the Baba of *Saat Rasta* was nearly out of time and there was no more hiding from his impatience.

* * *

Chris didn't leave my side over the weeks it took to recover my full strength.

When Deesh roared into the villa on a Harley-Davidson ten days ago, it had been like a Christmas gift for Chris who had heard all about it but now officially knew another member of the Undead. They bonded over bad jokes and worse films in the red room, while I read books or walked around the garden, poking at the plants and scratching out patterns in the dirt.

Chris confiscated my new phone because he said staring at the old schedule of red dots I had imported into its calendar was making me insane. He pronounced my nostalgia for simpler times as toxic.

What I didn't tell him was that I had also been secretly hoping against hope to hear from Sid. It made no sense;

Chris had Hazed away the memory of our last encounter and I knew I had told Sid he was to stay away. Then why did it hurt so much that he did?

A thin breeze plucked at my dress, cooling the sweat that marshalled at my forehead, lifting the strands of hair. I plucked a rose from the bush and turned it by the stem. A thorn caught in the delicate fish skin of my palm and I pulled it out and then watched the marvel of flesh closing up on itself; within seconds the skin was unbroken. I flung the rose to the ground in frustration and turned around.

Deesh was standing by in a biker jacket and distressed jeans.

'Is it the rose you are angry at or the thorn?' he said.

'Who cares,' I said in a moment of pique. 'It's just a stupid flower.'

'But he who dares not grasp the thorn/Should never crave the rose. That's Anne Brontë by the way. You quote surprisingly little poetry for a literature student.'

'Thorns can't hurt me,' I said. 'And Anne Brontë can't help me.'

'I know,' he said, and stepped forward to give me an unexpected hug. 'More's the pity, kid. Want some friendly advice? Feed your demons and you won't have to hear them howl at you all day.'

I shook him off. 'Why are you even still here? Go live your life, get your own villa and friends or whatever it is you want.'

'Uh-huh,' he said.

'You don't owe me a visit,' I said gruffly.

'That is true,' he said.

'You can leave anytime,' I said.

'That also is true.'

'What are you waiting for?'

'We are waiting for you,' Chris said as he walked up the path. 'I think you're all done with the brooding, Alia. It's time we had a little fun.'

'Speaking of brooding . . .' Deesh reached into the pocket of his jacket and pulled out a lighter. He wrenched it open and poured most of the fluid on to the rose bushes. Then he flicked on the flame and set fire to them. 'Who needs roses with thorns anyway?'

'These are my mother's rose bushes! What the hell are you doing?'

'Protests from the girl who tried to set the villa on fire last year?' he smiled. 'The Great Abandoners have pulled out their circus tent and departed, Bambi. It's time you did as well.'

'He's a bit heavy on the dramatics but he speaks for both of us. Now are you ready to have a good time or not? I have a little adventure planned.' Chris put his arm around my shoulders and led me away from the crackling bonfire.

* * *

Apparently, the only thing standing between a good time and me was the perfect dress.

'Show some cleavage, Alia,' Deesh said. 'Throw the dead guys a bone.'

'It has to be white,' Chris said. 'I don't care about the rest. A Sabrina neck with satin, maybe some sequins. Empire waist, you know what I'm talking about?'

'Do you spend all your nights reading fashion magazines?' I laughed out loud for the first time in what felt like a long time.

'Do you want her to look like Snow White?' Deesh said, frowning. 'I was really going for sexy here.'

'You guys have lost it.' I shook my head. 'You're acting like bridesmaids.'

'The way you're dressed now, whichever dude sees you on the road will probably run over you without noticing it. Come on, Alia, we said night out on the town and you went upstairs to put on black pants and a grey tee?' Deesh said. 'We are aiming to leave an impression, not road kill.'

'Did it occur to either of you that I might get hurt?' I asked.

Chris smiled at me, his teeth glistening whitely. 'Alia, nothing bad can actually happen to you when I'm around, you get that, right?'

I stared at him for a moment—something in his tone was off.

'You're excited about the possibility, though,' I said, watching with interest as his brow darkened at being caught out.

'If it happens, we will probably figure something out,' Deesh shrugged.

'We aren't really going for a smash-up,' Chris said in an unconvincing tone of voice.

'If? Probably? That's reassuring. Why can't we just go watch a movie or something?'

'No movie is going to give you the thrills like this is,' Chris huffed.

'And what I prescribe for you today, Bambi, as a recovering semi-suicidal Want addict, is life-affirming thrills. Serious thrills.' Deesh winked at me.

'But first, a dress, I prescribe a dress,' Chris said.

'There is no way I am changing into a dress to please you two.'

'Tell you what, I'll toss you for it. Heads you let us pick the dress, tails you come out looking like road kill.' He reached into his pocket.

And, of course, it was heads.

'Best of three?' I said hopefully, and was ignored.

Deesh snapped his fingers. 'Ah! Bandra, Pali Hill,' he said. 'I know just the place. And we have twenty minutes to get there before it closes.'

The shop was designer all right. It was a moodily lit, sprawling black box and smelled like money. The mannequins were headless tailor's dummies, and complemented the anaemic-looking saleswoman who drifted over in a spray of perfume. She heard Chris out with the attentiveness of a vestal, her head bowed and hands crossed in front of her, and took us to the back of the store to where vanity bulbs outlined a standout outfit. Its beauty burnt incandescent under the spotlights. Chris had taken about three seconds to locate the perfect dress.

I went to the curtained-off area. They were right. I felt something fall away from me when I shrugged out of my clothes. I was done with greys and blacks and cotton. I slipped this outfit on and was transformed in the silky reflection in the mirror.

It was a pearl-white sheath, not exactly what Chris had ordered, but close enough, and asymmetrical at the bottom, with jagged shards of sequins that ran like teardrops down the sides. Rock star meets . . . virgin bride. I pulled at the side of the heavy grey curtain and the saleswoman swept it away for me. We were inches apart, face-to-face, and I blinked into her severe face. She gave me a professional smile and led me to the viewing area.

Deesh and Chris were sprawled on a red sofa, both sets of eyes glittering like stones in the moody lights. I stepped on to the pedestal and ignored their expressions. When I turned to the three-sided mirror, I had a moment of shock. I loosened my hair-tie and let the hair float around my neck.

'Beautiful,' the saleswoman whispered through her red lips. It was the first word I'd heard her speak. 'This dress was made for you.'

My reflection telescoped and then split into two. I could see what she saw and I could see what I saw. This was not rock star meets virgin bride; this was a fallen-angel dress. I looked more carefully at myself. The corruption that had crept into me was irreversible, if slow; more drip than gush. The light caught the rigidity of my cheekbones, the pallor of my skin. The black blood that beat through me was evident to my kind even though the saleswoman saw only the false foreverness of youth. I ran my hands over my collarbone, and it was all I could do not to claw at myself. How long did I have before the chips were down? How long before I was too monstrous to recognize myself for what I was?

'Alia,' Chris cleared his throat. He stepped on to the pedestal with me and took both my hands, even though I would not meet his eyes. 'It's okay. You are lovely. You are lovely to Morticia here and you are lovely to us and you are lovely in every way that counts.'

I looked at Deesh. 'What about you?' I indicated our reflection. 'Am I lovely to you too? We aren't really friends. You see it, right? The three amigos waiting to see who falls first? We are a joke.'

'Speak for yourself, Bambs,' Deesh said. 'Because I ain't laughing.' He turned to the saleswoman. 'We will take it, and you will give it to us.'

Her mouth fell open before the Haze kicked in so that it looked a bit comical, her surprise and obedience frozen like that.

'You have no memory of meeting us,' Deesh continued. 'Bag Alia's old rags and burn them because you cannot tolerate such an affront to fashion.'

'And quit smoking before you get any thinner,' Chris called out to her as we left. He winked at me. 'This is me using my powers for good. Happy?'

'Happy,' I whispered back, feeling hollow, and yet, I sort of was happy in the moment to know that at least I wouldn't be walking out of here alone.

* * *

Which should explain how I came to be lying down in the middle of the road in Juhu in the dead of night in the white dress with my hair flowing out all around me.

The silver Audi had lights like a football stadium as it swerved into the quiet lane, tyres spinning to bite the concrete, and music spilling out into the kerb.

I was directly in its path, on my back, counting stars through the inky fur of a gulmohar. I had barely made out lopsided Orion before the techno beats and light alerted me to the oncoming car. I could tell the instant they saw me because the brakes screeched like banshees through the music. My eyes squeezed shut to avoid the kick-up of dust, stones and burning rubber, and it took all my willpower to lie there in the trembling dirt and let the event play out.

A searing wall of heat ate at me and the car bumper thundered to a jolting stop a foot from my face. I exhaled slowly. It could have as easily hit me, and then what? How much of a hit could I really take? What if it had been a truck? A tanker? How much could I handle?

What the hell! Chris was right, this felt awesome! The adrenaline had smacked my system awake and whatever it was that got my heart thundering and my pulse jumping, I wanted more of that sweet sauce.

A door opened and someone stumbled out.

'Oh my God! Oh my God!' a high-pitched girlish voice keened into the night. 'Oh my God!' I could smell the alcohol on her before her knees hit the ground. She bent over me, thighs splayed like sticks under her short dress.

'Don't touch anything. Let's get out of here.' It was a slurred man's voice.

'Oh my God. Oh my God,' she said. 'Let's go! Let's get out of here! Are you dead?'

I opened my eyes. 'Booo!' I said.

She screamed fit to shatter glass. Her friend cupped her mouth with his hand and began to drag her off. They were both shaking so much they lost their balance and began to crawl back to the car. I walked alongside, making zombie-like noises, even though I was laughing too much to be credible. Chris and Deesh appeared by my side just as the couple made it to the car.

'Oh my God! Oh my God! Oh my God!' The girl was hysterical.

'You are boring,' Deesh snapped. 'Which is worse than being a drunk and a lousy driver. What else have you got besides "Oh my God"? Hurry up or I'm going to eat your pretty face.'

Her eyes rolled back in her head and she fainted. The man took one look at her and tried to flee.

'Spot jog,' Deesh said. 'You're a real charmer. Don't you want to take Drunk Chick with you?'

The man's cheeks wobbled as he sped up. He was too terrified to talk.

'Well, she did stop in time,' I said. 'Maybe we should ease up?'

Deesh and Chris burst out laughing.

'What?' I was annoyed.

'So what do you want to do with them?' Chris said when he was done laughing. A spasm crossed his face and he pulled his right shoulder in.

'Wow, this one sweats,' Deesh observed.

'He may have a heart attack,' I said. 'Look at him.'

The man was panting desperately now, his shirt darkened with perspiration.

Deesh looked him in the eye. 'Don't have a heart attack.'

I giggled. 'Come on! It's not like you can control a heart attack.'

'It's not the size of the Haze; it's how you use it,' he said with a wink.

Chris turned to the man. 'You will remember everything that happened and you will tell everyone you meet about it. You will Tweet it, Facebook it and post an Instagram of your ugly face. Except for how we looked—you will forget that part. Now run on home.'

The man's eyes were like saucers, and sweat dripped off his chin.

'Go!' Chris muttered. And the man shot off like a bullet.

'What about Sleeping Beauty?' I said.

Deesh was already going through her shiny wallet. 'Hmm,' he said, and produced a picture. 'Soft kitty, warm kitty, little ball of fur.'

He bent down and his eyes glittered in the street light. 'Wake,' he said and snapped his fingers. Her eyes fluttered open, blank with terror, her breathing growing more hysterical by the second. 'You were driving drunk and you killed a kitty just like Mishka.'

Her eyes clouded over and she burst into tears. Her sobs for her kitty would have been heart-wrenching had this not been the same person who had just been willing to walk away from my corpse.

The girl fumbled with her keys and got the car door open.

'Why are you burdening her with an awful memory,' I said. 'After all, she did—'

I heard the car get into gear and then reverse slowly.

'Um, Alia, she didn't stop in time,' Chris said. 'She was too high to hit the brakes.'

'But I felt nothing, I just felt—'

Deesh chuckled. 'Romeo here wedged himself between the car and you at the last minute. He took the hit for you.'

'Do you really think I'd let some car run you over?' Chris said.

'Oh,' I said. Somewhere at the back of my eyes, I could see stars, as though he had let the Audi crash into me.

* * *

The street lights went out as we drove back silently. It was past dawn and the city was beginning to stir by the time we entered the villa grounds.

'I have an insane urge to put on the TV and watch an entire season of *The Big Bang Theory*,' Deesh said when we got out of the car. 'Man, I miss alcohol.'

'Chris,' I said, 'I've been meaning to ask. Don't you have to get home? You've been here all this while.'

'I left home a long time ago.' He climbed the steps after me.

'What? How do I not know that?'

He shrugged. 'I didn't like to talk about it.'

'Did something happen?'

'Let's just say I find it hard to take orders these days.'

'I thought your mom had turned over a new leaf after you . . . revived.'

'Delicately put,' he said. 'Look, I don't want to talk about it.'

'But say something?'

Chris scowled darkly at me.

'It's a sign she cares. When a woman nags—I read that somewhere—it's when she's silent that she's plotting to kill you. Adios amigos!' Deesh winked at us and loped off down the corridor towards the guest room.

I scowled at his retreating back.

'He's right. You are nagging me, you know,' Chris sighed.

'Okay, sorry.' I shrugged elaborately. 'I would've thought that you'd have more sympathy with my need for closure and—'

He punched me lightly in the arm. 'Nice try, Alia, but you must have me mistaken for some other sap.'

'Damn!' I said, 'You used to be so easy to guilt. But Chris . . . your mom. I mean we have to talk about it.' It hung in the air, that terrible, terrible, unstated thing. His mom had driven him to jump off his terrace before; what might she drive him to now?

A vein ticked in his forehead. 'Okay, Alia, what do you want to know? We went through a whole thing together, my mom and I. She dragged me to three parish churches; I had to talk about my suicide attempt and what it taught me.'

'What it taught you?'

Yeah, don't you know committing suicide makes me the worst type of Christian? Believe it or not, but it was a huge disappointment to her that I tried to end my life.'

'No way,' I shook my head.

'The priests were surprisingly okay; most suggested counselling. Of course, then she found a hell-and-high-water type and I had to go to him and seek pardon.'

'Why did you never talk about this?'

'I was all talked out.' He arched his brows. 'Okay?'

'Your mother sounds crazy!'

'We can't sit in the same room together for five minutes before she's blaming me for something and I'm wanting to kill her. I mean, actually kill her. Or better yet, get her to kill herself. I even have these elaborate little fantasies of how I'd get her to do it. I keep editing it in my head when I can't sleep—which, as you know, is basically every night.'

'That's disturbing.'

'You think? That's why I left her house.' His eyes were hard. 'So don't bring that woman up again, okay, chiquita?' His voice softened with the endearment.

'You got it.' I shivered despite myself. There was always something more than met the eye with him, an undercurrent of darkness despite his easy-going exterior.

He ran a hand over the back of my head and slid it down to cup my chin. He turned it slowly towards him and his cold hand did nothing to reassure me even if his eyes blazed into mine. His other hand curled around the small of my back.

We stayed like that for a few minutes, our eyes locked into each other's. And it felt like the moment of truth. Nothing good had ever come from getting intimate with Chris; we could be close, but when we got too close, one of us would crash and burn, like he had last year. I tried to pull away but it didn't translate into movement because my mind hadn't unstuck itself yet from the strange fascination I felt for him in this moment.

'Alia,' he said with a groan at the back of his throat. 'We need to talk about this thing, this thing between us.'

'There is no thing between us,' I whispered. 'Because I'm going to hell and it's soon.'

'Then I'm already there,' he said hoarsely.

'No, you're not. You're going to go on forever in this world, Chris, them's the breaks.'

'We don't know that,' he said.

'But we hope. Both of us do.'

'Do we? I have belonged to you completely from the moment I met you. There is no going on for me once you're gone.'

'You've been listening to too much bad pop,' I whispered to break the spell, to break us apart, delay the inevitable.

Instead, his arm pulled me closer until I was pressed up against him, and his face lowered to meet mine. My lips parted easily enough at the closeness of him, and I felt myself sigh with longing as his lips left tiny kisses on the corners of my mouth. And then, before I could pull away, the kiss deepened and my quicksand heart gave way so that my lips were no longer listening to the voice in my head.

FIFTEEN

'Alia baby, what you are wearing?' Mary's horror at my muddied clothes eclipsed her feelings over catching me kissing Chris on the landing. Grooming over morality. The average celebrity housekeeper's protocol, I suppose.

'It's just a little dirty.' I had sprung back and wiped my lips with the back of my hand. What the hell had I been doing kissing Chris anyway? Embarrassment flooded my face, making me unable to meet her eyes.

'A little dirty? This is not a little dirty, this is ruined! Ruined I say!' Mary crossed her arms over her ample bosom and flared her nostrils.

Chris was frowning. 'Are we still talking about the dress?'

'You be quiet, Chris baba! I am not tolerating bad behaviour in house. It is so late, it is still early in the morning and the house is sleeping! You are welcome to be guest but behave like guest only. What if instead of me Gail was coming to settle beds?'

'I'm sure she's seen worse; she's been living with us, remember?' I muttered.

'Shut up, Alia baby! Be quiet!' Mary rounded on me. 'This is a respectable place and if your father and mother are not being here then it is on me to maintain discipline and good behaviour.'

'Like they ever gave a hoot,' I said soberly and turned on my heel, leaving Mary with her mouth flapping open and Chris with a fast-fading smirk.

* * *

'What's the matter?' he said, when he snuck into my room later. He had rapped on the door with his knuckles and let himself in without waiting for a response.

I lay on my stomach, reading *Paradise Regained.*

'Geez, your Mary was patrolling the corridors,' he continued. 'But we should be okay with a door between us. You notice how I'm not Hazing the locals? It shows real willpower.' He paused. 'Okay, seriously, what's going on with you?'

'I don't think Milton had his heart in it the second time around,' I said.

'Who didn't?' he frowned.

'Milton. The poet of *Paradise Lost.*'

'What are you talking about?' Chris sat down on the bed.

'Not what, who. Milton, John Milton.' I shook his hand off my back and scrambled up. 'I don't think his verse is too convincing in the sequel, you know?'

'Again, Alia, why are you talking about him? You've lost me.'

'In *Paradise Lost* he tells the story of Adam and Eve, how they are created, and how they fall from paradise, right? And about how Satan is turned into a serpent. Basically, the whole shebang.'

'So it's a poem based on the *Book of Genesis*?' he said.

'Yeah, a really, really long poem.' I pointed the book out to him. It lay on my bedside table with about a million highlights in pencil. 'It's about disobedience, the cost of eating forbidden fruit and then the loss of innocence. Sin and Death make their way to Earth at this point. You know, "Treble confusion, wrath and vengeance poured".'

'Oh-kay,' he said, 'let's hear it for treble confusion. Whoa! Where did you get this copy? It's really old.'

'Yeah, long story—put it down carefully. But the sequel,' I waved my copy of *Paradise Regained* at him, 'is written so much more plainly, and it's unconvincing; it's basically undoing the damage caused by the Original Sin.'

'Sounds like it's a problem-solver.'

'Except, Milton can't pull it off,' I said. I showed him the excerpt I had in mind.

'Um, do they have an English translation?' Chris said.

I threw a cushion at him. 'How is it fair that Adam and Eve had no choice but to fall for the serpent's words and learn their lesson?'

'Alia, my love,' he said, putting his hand on mine. I shook it off.

'What is this really about?' he sighed.

'It's about this one fatalistic interpretation of their sin.'

'No, it's not.' He put an arm around me, drawing me to him. 'Don't you dare!' he cautioned, as I made to shrug him off. He stared into my eyes. 'It's about you searching for an answer, or at least something to blame for where you are right now.'

It was my turn to stare at him. 'No, it's not. Everything is not about me, you know, not even to me.' I rolled my eyes.

'It kind of is, Alia baby,' he teased. 'And it's okay, because what you've done for your parents, what you have to bear today as the result of that, isn't just superhuman; the way you are, it's suprahuman.'

'What's suprahuman?' I grimaced.

'I'm not sure but it got your attention, didn't it?'

'Would you be serious for five seconds?' I snapped, pushing him away.

'Fine. Let me put it in serious words. Alia, a bad thing happened to you when you chose your parents' lives over yours, because they're scum.'

'No!' I said.

'Some people are just bad investments, Alia; your parents are among those. Heck, my mom is, too.'

'Stop it!'

'Who looked after you when you fell apart?' he challenged. 'I did. And Deesh did—this is your family now, the community of people who truly understand what you're going through. Not people who may think they love you but try to turn you into something you're not.'

'Not Sid, you mean,' I said softly.

'Especially not him. He doesn't know what you are going through or what you need. Nor does he take no for an answer. You've told him to stay away but he still tries to break his way into the villa.'

'What are you talking about? He hasn't come here since . . .'

Chris tried to freeze his face but it was too late; a shadow of self-doubt flickered across it.

'What did you do?' I said. 'Chris?'

'He came to the villa when you were . . . convalescing,' he shrugged. 'You were in a bad way, Alia; there was no chance I would let him see you like that and disturb you.'

'He came to the villa,' I repeated. 'But why?' I felt my heartbeat quicken at the thought of Sid coming looking for me.

'It's his general bossiness when it comes to you. He kept calling and texting. I finally had to tell him to stay away or you were going to officially call him a stalker. That did the trick.'

'You what? What do you mean I was going to call him a stalker? How could you speak for me?' I thought back to that dark period of time. I covered my face with my hands. 'Chris, tell me you didn't message him from my phone?'

'So what,' he scowled. 'I could do a lot worse.'

'You really think you get brownie points for that? For lying to my boyfriend?' I scrambled off the bed and shook off his attempts to hold on to me.

'Oh, you must be joking,' he said. 'Really, Alia? He's your boyfriend? Like, again? Why doesn't it surprise me?'

'He didn't just walk away, even after we broke up. He tried calling and he came to the villa; that means something!'

'All it means is you'd rather be in love with a myth than a man. Sid is just Mr Perfect to you, isn't he? He's a statue that's bloody unbreakable. God forbid you two stay in an actual relationship long enough for you to see his flaws.'

'It's not like that,' I said.

'Me, on the other hand . . . all you see are my flaws. Why won't you see how much I love you? How much I struggle over you?' His eyes glinted as he turned away.

'How can I trust you if you go through my phone, send messages pretending to be me?' I shook my head in disgust. 'I know you are on my side but you think that means you can act for me, speak for me and think for me. Don't you get it, Chris, I love you too, but—'

He jumped off the bed and fixed his angry eyes on me. 'It doesn't matter how you love me; what matters is what you are willing to do with that love. And you've done nothing with it but push me away again and again. We just kissed, damn it!'

I turned my face away.

'So you regret it? Already? Within the hour?' he bit out.

'I don't know. But what else are you keeping from me? Chris, we have a history of crashing and burning, and now is not . . . wait!'

He'd already walked to the door and his voice, when he spoke at last, chilled me to the bone. 'You want me gone? I can go and not be found again. But be careful what you wish for.'

I looked at him in the doorway, a cold fury building up within me at his threat.

'Go,' I said, the harshness in my voice a whip. 'Be gone.'

I stared at the closed door for a long time after that.

How long could I have kept up this charade of half friendship, half-love with Chris anyway?

* * *

A knock on the door a minute later, and I was flying to open it with an apology of sorts in my eyes. Except, it was Gail.

'Please to join the family for breakfast,' she said, her dark eyes radiating sympathy. 'Immediately.'

'What family?' I said, trying to cover up the break in my voice with a cough.

'Family is back,' she said. 'Waiting for you in dining room.'

I didn't know quite how to digest this.

'Gail?' I asked. 'Would you wait for me, please?' I didn't want to be alone.

A tumult of emotions accompanied me into the shower. When I returned, she had laid out a denim jumpsuit with a white tank top for me. I slipped into it and she fastened the straps over my shoulders without a word and brushed my hair, the rhythmic strokes doing me good. I grabbed a clip and ran downstairs, twisting my damp hair into a bun.

* * *

It was exactly as she said when I entered the dining room. Except it was impossible.

My mother was seated beside my father. The curtains were pulled over to one side and roped; wide French windows opened to the cheerful day outside; the oppressive wooden tones of the room were transformed by birdcalls and sunshine. Her auburn hair tumbled out over her shoulders, its animation, sparkle and bounce in the daylight, a distraction from the shuttered hazel eyes. Her skin shimmered with skilfully applied make-up as she leaned in towards the man seated across the table, put a manicured hand on his hand and laughed, her head thrown back to more advantageously reveal her swan neck.

The sound of her honeyed laughter had me enchanted, and then stupefied. So this is what the trophy wife of last year had been like, the Reshma I never got to see, who had dangled on the arm of a superstar and driven the paparazzi wild.

And then I saw the man who had made her laugh, and my pulse thundered so hard it felt like I would explode, as if the whole room would explode; like it was a hot, unstable sun—no, it was the dark nucleus within that sun, in churn, in fury, in a kind of negative energy that belonged to a black hole and not to this ordinary-looking day. For this was on me. I had invited him into the world of the living and into the villa and here he was, fulfilling his chilling vendetta.

'Come on in, Bambs,' Deesh called out to me. 'I was just regaling Mrs Khanna here—'

'Oh, Reshma to you, please!'

He bowed. '—with a story of how we first met at a party for—'

'Get out!' My gut twisted with pain. How could I have been stupid enough to let Deesh come into contact with my parents?

'Alia, what's the matter with you?' My mother's expression turned cold.

'Did something happen?' my father said.

'Why did you even come back? Do you know who he is?' I shouted at my father.

'Alia, my darling, slow down.' My father walked over to me, his face lined with concern. 'We would never have abandoned you even for this long had we known how hard it was on you. It's okay. Deesh is not a stranger to us.' He lowered his voice. 'He is an inspiration, an angel, even, at a time when we'd lost our way.' He dashed a tear away with his fist.

'No, he really isn't a bloody angel,' I said. 'Deesh, what is this? Is it another of your cons? Is that why you came back to the villa in the first place? To get to them?'

I turned to my father. 'He does that, you know, when he needs something. He pretends he's a leaf with a leaf, a shadow with a shadow—a chameleon. Listen to me, he's told me this himself—he's done this before. Last New Year's Eve, that's how we met—he was pretending to be a journalist.'

'But I really was a journalist, Bambi. Well, just not *only* a journalist when it came to my interest in you,' Deesh said mildly.

'You had an agenda, you always have an—'

My father shook his head and put his hands on my shoulders. 'I hear you—'

'No, listen to me!' I pulled away. 'You're not really listening! He has every reason to hate you, and you have every reason to fear him. Dad, he is—'

'Bobby's twin,' Deesh said softly, his low brows pulled into a frown, his eyes shadowed with the sunlight behind him. 'Uncool to give away my big reveals like that, Alia.'

'You know this?' I turned to my mom. 'You knew who he was all along? You are not safe with him; he hates you both and he is up to something.'

'This isn't our first meeting since . . . well, since you resuscitated him. We are only here because he convinced us you need us.' She gave a pointed shrug. 'Besides, do you need reminding who brought him back? It was you; you don't like sharing your friends with us, do you?'

'This has nothing to do with my precious feelings! You have to stay away from him!' I said.

Mary walked into the room with a steaming tray and, sensing something in the air, thumped it down on the table and backed out again.

'Simmer down, Bambi,' Deesh said with a sigh. 'You're scaring the help. Take a chair. Where's Chris?'

I was too weak-kneed to keep standing anyway. I let my father lead me to a chair. He sat by me and held my right hand.

'Alia, my child, I am sorry. We are so sorry,' he said.

'Sorry?' I said. 'You walked out on me; both of you did. You taught me to trust you, to turn to you, to need you to get through things, and then when things got scary—'

'We bolted,' he said, releasing a hand to dash his palm against his damp eyes. 'We left you and we bolted.'

'I was attacked,' I said, my voice breaking with the press of emotion that tightened my throat. 'I am stalked. Do you understand what that means?'

'Baby.' He grabbed me and folded me into a hug. I pushed him away.

'How could you do this to me?'

'We are not proud of it,' my mother said. 'Not our finest moment by far. But that is where Deesh comes in, don't you see?'

'No, I don't see,' I ground out.

'Well, if looks could kill,' Deesh purred, fanning himself.

'What the hell are you doing here?' I said.

'Saving you, B-baby.' He sat up straight. 'Chris thought we could keep you going but it was always part of my plan to find them. You needed your mom and dad.'

'This is bullshit. You called them the Great Abandoners that night.'

'The Great Abandoners,' my father repeated, squeezing my hands. 'And so we were. He didn't just find us, he made us see how blind we had been to your needs, how desperately stupid. I am going to make it up to you, Alia. I am going to do whatever it takes.'

'Why?' I looked at Deesh. 'You said you'd be my friend. Why are you doing this?'

'I am your friend. Consider it a thank you.'

'So now we are even?' My eyes burnt into his but he didn't flinch. 'I bring you back from the dead and you guilt my parents into returning? I know there's more to this than you're letting on.'

'Alia, that is no way to—' My mother stood up.

'You both lost the right to tell me how to act,' I snapped. 'This is your house and you're welcome to it but don't for a second think that you can walk back into my life again,' I said.

My father, who had been pacing, hesitated; a strip of shadow caused by the panelling fragmented him, and the light went out of his eyes. 'We will make it up to you,' he murmured, almost to himself.

'But where are you going?' my mother asked as I backed away from them, from whatever this little act was. 'Come back and talk to us this instant. You must explain what you mean by saying that I'm not safe!'

A laugh bubbled up in my throat at her tone. The thing was, I no longer knew if I had what it took to care. Not after they had chosen to believe Deesh over their own flesh and blood.

* * *

He drifted alongside on a wave of contaminated air as I exited the dining room, although I only saw his figure in my rear-view mirror and I floored the accelerator, working the automatic transmission. The Jag leapt forward with a soft purr and I had slammed on the brakes a few seconds later to wait for the electronic gate to open, when I saw him once more, just a few metres behind me.

My Familiar hovered some inches off the ground, his toes dangling above the dirt. With my heart drumming against my ribcage the whole time, I waited to see what he would do next. The fingers in his hands curled towards his sides and he glided, as though with a gust of breeze, but he made no other move. His face blurred, like it was coming at me through a mist. 'Objects in mirror are closer than they appear,' I mouthed.

Then, in a move that chilled me more than anything I had seen before, he raised one hand in a wave. I was dumbfounded, my brain refusing to read the gesture. Bobby was saying goodbye. Numbness slid through my veins as the spirit fire within him faded out. My Familiar was coming apart, thinning out and fading like an old bruise, until all that remained of the corpse-like child was a thickness in the air, a disturbance of dark matter, and then even that evened out, the sunlight illuminating the driveway, and not a flicker of agitation in the air.

My throat dried up as I remained there with my eyes glued to the rear-view mirror; however, the scene was unchanging. Feeling returned slowly to my limbs and I put the car in gear and swung out into the city. But there was more where that came from—feeling returned slowly to my heart again, and that inhuman aloofness that had guided me for so long to seek isolation as a kind of power and solace left me at last. There were enough signs that I was running out of time and I had resolved not to spend what remained of it alone. My parents no longer mattered to me, but I knew someone who always would.

SIXTEEN

I searched the faces of boys tramping through the first quadrangle in college, a basketball flashing fast and slippery between them. The banality of it made me smile. There ought to be wild beasts running amok in the corridors; the doors ought to have rattled and banged until they fell off their centenarian hinges and into eternal blackness, as the whole stone edifice of the building chipped and fell away.

How fragile were the foundations of this mortal realm? Veils encircled us all, waiting for the moment to slip their evil charms around us, to whisper to us of bad things, until we ran out of ignorant breath and inhaled the suffocation of corruption. I stepped into the corridor and leaned against the column, studying the faces of kids who streamed past me, carrying bags, purses, folders . . . And all of them had something going on, but not one of them carried the cares I did.

My breath caught in my throat. It had taken my father seventeen years to lose his hold on Bobby. And here I was, forced to face the signs of my imminent return to the Baba within six months of the Change.

Why had my parents returned? I may know little of how the other world operated, but I knew enough to be wary of things that looked like coincidences. Were they also part of this plan, part of the welcoming committee to hell? Because that is what it had felt like, seeing Deesh with them; everything about it had been wrong in every way.

Sid grabbed my elbow and held me close. Heat rolled off his clothes, his body glittery with sweat and anger.

'Alia, Jesus!' His voice was tight as he tucked the basketball under his arm. 'It's really you.'

I stared at him. 'Where did you come from?'

'Where did I come from? Don't even . . .' His eyes streaked past me towards the staircase. 'Oh crap. Those idiots!' he said.

Ronjy and Raoul were lip-locked in a marathon kiss that would easily get them suspended. As we watched, the political science lecturer, who also happened to be an ordained priest, walked down the corridor, headed right to them. His head was buried in a file but he could look up any moment.

'Ronjita!' I yelled. It was no use. Sid lifted the basketball and lobbed it at them. They fell apart just as the teacher arrived.

'What the hell?' Raoul's head had taken most of the impact. He rubbed it and scowled at Sid who merely winked and strolled away.

'Not cool, man!' A player ran to retrieve the ball. 'You settle your scores in your own time.'

The bell sounded shrilly just above our heads and we jumped apart, momentarily confused.

Sid turned to go.

I put a hand on his arm. 'I really have to talk to you.'

'As do I to you,' he said with a formal bow. 'But first I have to submit my project for stats, without which I will lose my Honours mark. So do you intend to see me again after class or just disappear on me? I know being unpredictable is a big part of your kit these days, now that you're with Chris, but yeah, I think you owe me a conversation.'

'I am not with Chris,' I said angrily.

His brown eyes were flint.

'Well, then maybe you're with someone else or no one else. I was merely quoting your own words. Whatever it is, Alia, you owed me a proper debriefing.'

'Hey! I want to talk to you, Sid, stop being mad at me for one moment.' I grabbed his arm.

'Oh, you've made that kind of tough,' he said.

'I'll be in the canteen at two, okay?' I whispered.

'Will she? Won't she? Only time will tell,' he said as he backed away with an exaggerated shrug.

* * *

By the time I made it to psychology, it had become an 'incident'.

'Did you hear about how Sid attacked Raoul?' The skin on Binni's white nose was scrubbed raw by her morning cleanse routine. She lowered herself on to the bench and her chains tinkled around her neck. 'It was completely unprovoked. He hit him in the head and then ran. Raoul held back for Ronjy's sake, you know, he didn't want her to get involved in anything. I mean, Raoul used to, like, box, like, professionally, at school.'

'Professionally at school, huh?' I repeated.

'Did you see it yourself, Binny?' Khan asked. 'Doesn't sound like something Sid would do.'

'Half the college saw it,' Maya snapped. 'Which reminds me, Alia, you're on a blacklist. What are you even doing here back in class? And what's the deal with your boyfriend? Are you guys having problems? Why take it out on Ronjy?'

I groaned and put my head down on the desk. My life was ending and this was what I had to deal with as I went down.

Two o'clock couldn't come soon enough that day.

* * *

'But none of this makes sense.' Sid rocked back and forth on the bench. The canteen swallowed up the sound of his voice in the usual circus of clanking food trays, chairs being drawn, call-outs and conversations. I leaned in further towards him to whisper back and was conscious of just how close I'd got. I inhaled his aftershave and it took every ounce of willpower not to run a finger down his jawline, which looked sharp enough to give me a paper cut this morning. His eyes lowered to meet mine and then swept past them to hover on my lips. I closed my eyes for a microsecond, just to feel the ground steady around me again. When I opened them, he had leaned back.

'None of this makes sense,' he repeated. 'And yet I have just one question.'

'What is the question?' I asked, still dazzled.

'Why are you telling me all this now?' His eyes shifted colour with the sunlight—cat eyes, then pond-scum eyes. 'What changed?'

'I did,' I said. 'I've stopped trying to protect you from me.'

'Why now? All you've ever done is try to take care of people.' He held my chin between his thumb and forefinger and tilted my head towards him. I could smell his talc as well now, and the musky odour of sweat and perfume that was in overdrive, on account of the exertion he'd had on the basketball court. 'The thing I've never been able to figure is whether it's your greatest strength or your biggest weakness.'

'What do you mean?' I said.

'Taking on your father's curse didn't just Change you; it also made you who you are. You are someone who shoulders burdens, even if they are terrible deals and even when you could have walked away from them. I'm not saying it's smart and I'm not even saying it's crazy to do that. I'm just saying . . .' He ran his hand over his face and sighed.

'Tell me what you're saying?' I whispered.

'You wake up every morning and you go back to fighting the same fight you fought the previous night. I call that bravery. But, I wonder, when will you start caring for yourself?'

'Like, love myself a little?' I teased. 'That's what your advice comes down to?'

'Hell, yeah! Love yourself a lot, Alia.' He kissed my forehead. 'Take what you want.'

'That's what I came here to do.' I laced my fingers through his. 'Do you see?'

'I see,' he whispered.

We sat there like that for a while, our hands entwined, and our thoughts drifting, not together and not separate, but both those things in a new way.

'Seeing them in the dining room today,' I swallowed, 'it was unreal.'

'Deesh is a loose cannon, always was and always will be.'

'Literally, always, as it turns out,' I said, stressing the second word.

Sid gave a soft laugh, his boyish grin lifting up his cheeks just as I'd intended. The cleft flashed and was gone. 'Well, yeah. He's definitely up to something, and it isn't what he says he's doing,' he whistled. 'That's four people you brought back, Alia. You burnt a hell of a lot of good karma there.'

'Plus the three I murdered, not counting bat baby.' I chewed on a strand of my hair.

'That is a lot of Wants . . .' he said. Then he sat up straight and his voice was different, oddly stressed. 'How are the urges now?'

'You know, I haven't felt an urge in a while.' I smiled at him. 'Some good news, huh?'

'Are you sure? You aren't just burying them underneath something?'

I thought about it. 'No, I mean, yes, I'm sure. How is that possible? I'm actually getting the hang of this thing. Huh. It used to be insane before, like a kind of thirst that . . . what is it?' I said, alarmed.

Sid was pale and spoke very gently. 'Alia, you have to know that isn't good?'

'Why? I feel good. I'm more in control.'

'Alia,' he groaned, his face crumpling.

'I'm Wanting less, I'm . . .' I looked at him in horror, and then the reason behind his questions trickled down to me. 'Oh dear God, Sid! Sid, no!'

'You've run the gamut. It's happening. The prophecy is coming true. You have unlimited Wants, except once you can no longer Want—'

'That is when I fall prey to Despair and the bargain is complete. And he will come for me,' I said, my voice too soft for him to hear, but he didn't need to read my lips to know the finality of the awful statement I had made.

'I can't do it, Sid.' I clutched his arms so abruptly that he jumped. 'I can't go there with him again! I'm not ready!' My fingernails dug into his skin and his eyes widened, but I couldn't let go. 'I can't do it! I'm not ready. I'm not ready. It's too soon!'

'I know, my love, I know. We will fight it with everything we've got!' His voice was strong, rugged with something akin to faith, and the tears running down his cheeks were honest, and that is how I knew Chris was wrong; Sid was not perfect and he was not unbreakable, but he was perfect for me.

* * *

Fairy tales teach us that true love is all we need to overcome evil and ruin and death. That unadulterated, pure 100 per cent authentic love is everything, and that if you hit the bullseye, then love will save you from the most evil stepmom, and even from yourself. The kiss of the loving prince will rouse the sleeping beauty; the true love of an innocent girl will awaken the man within the beast. Of all the awful forces within the fabled universe, of all the vapours and mists that bubble and curl and swirl in the cauldron of fabulous make-believes, it is real love that is the most potent.

Well, I had it in that moment. When Sid brought his wet cheeks to mine, when my hungry mouth found his and I drew him in, it was as pure an expression of love as I'd ever known. Everything around us dimmed, the chatter of the college was forced out, as though from a vacuum, while we kissed, because the universe, in all its infinite vastness, could hold only that one precious happening.

We broke apart for breath and he grabbed my hand and pulled me up the wooden staircase to the first floor, then up another staircase, and then we were dashing past the library and up a twisting spiral staircase that led nowhere because it had been closed and forgotten about. We climbed and climbed the stone steps, and it was dizzying to do that with our hearts pounding and our feet stumbling. Our hands were in each other's hands and our hips and elbows and shoulders bumped against the crumbling iron railings, and yet we felt nothing but each other. We stopped where the top of the staircase had been cordoned off by a grille, and when we bumped our heads against the brick wall in the cramped space, we were giggling into each other's faces, breathing jaggedly as our hands rose to clasp each other in an embrace that had no memory of a time outside it.

Dust motes rose in eddies around us, a slanted sunlight streaking down on our faces and arms through the grille, and we were ribbed with zebra stripes of light and shadow.

Sweat bloomed on his skin and dripped on to mine and I realized with relief that we were alone here at last. A dry sob welled up inside of me and then I was still. His hands snaked downwards from where he held my face, our lips locked too tightly to part and he pulled me into him so that our hips were connected at the joints. It was as though we had made a circuit and the slow burn in my stomach plummeted lower and lower until I was on fire; there wasn't a part of me that wasn't burning up or sparking under his touch. I felt his fingers thread my spine, and I slipped my hands between us, pulling at his white cotton T-shirt, until they had slid into the intimate space between his T-shirt and his chest; the air there different, warmer, the planes of his torso moist to the touch.

I laid my palm against his heart for a few pulses and felt the beat vibrate up the length of my arm and into my own. The muscles on his chest were straining under my fingertips, his nipples growing hard as I felt their nubs.

Then he dropped his hands lower still, and he was cupping the roundness of my behind, then reaching up to find the hooks on the sides of the jumpsuit, impatient until he'd worked them off. The straps fell off, trailing down, hanging below our feet on the tiny staircase, the metal clasps clanking and echoing down the column. And I gasped at the shock of it, as his hand stroked my stomach under the thin cotton tube top I wore, his fingers making butterfly movements around my belly, tapping to see if there was any resistance, but there was none. I groaned against his tongue as I felt the hardness of him against me and it wasn't enough any more.

None of the reasons we'd gone over to keep us from making love made any sense. It just wasn't enough; the reasons to stay away weren't enough, the time I had left wasn't enough, and everything cascaded in a rush of emotion. I felt his still-damp cheeks rub against my collarbone as he slid lower, his lips blazing a trail of tiny kisses on my breast as he loosed it from its confines. And then I saw that the tears were still squeezing out of his eyes as he leaned into me, and I broke away for a second, just a second, to catch my breath, and to think about whether this was love or loss we were sharing, and whether it even mattered which was which any more.

I put a hand out against the wall, trying to cool down, trying to think, when I felt his hands push the jumpsuit off my hips, and it was down around my ankles now. I shivered despite the heat, standing there in my tube and cotton panties. His fingers curled into the lace that ringed my underwear and tugged at me. And it was all I could do to keep my knees from bending under the shock and the sharp, unexpected pain and the pleasure of it.

I gasped and turned my face away, and then I felt it, a weird hush that invaded the closed space, a sort of hum or hiss, a warning that bounced off the stone staircase and the brick walls. I tilted my head backwards and my eyes flickered up to where a shadow had come between the light and us. It grew steadily darker as I struggled in a daze to remain standing as Sid peeled my tube top off me and cupped my breasts in his hands.

I couldn't see Sid's face clearly any more; it was in shadow. I could just feel him as he coughed, and that was when I knew that something had indeed blocked the only source of light and air in this constricted space. It was hard to make anything out; I pushed Sid away, and then I pushed him away again when he returned to me.

I blinked and tried to distinguish the amorphous shape that was coalescing on the grille above. Was it someone from the college, a priest robed with a flowing hemline, who had stepped out on to the grille on the floor upstairs for some reason? Could he see us? We were so busted!

It shifted as I stared, and as beams of light streaked the borders, I could tell the shape—it appeared to be a white sari. Was it a woman then? A helper? Perhaps one of the office staff? Then it shifted again, moved in a way that allowed light to pierce down through the fabric, and I could tell it *was* a white sari. And yet the limbs, the stance, looked far too manly to be a lady.

Time slowed down and then stopped, and the only thing that was real was the way the object above us moved as it shuffled down on hands and knees, fingers twirling around the vent, white fingers with dark nails showing through the lattice. It was when it tilted its face downwards to meet mine that I saw the red eyes, dark-highway-headlight eyes, cat eyes, demon eyes, blood-red, eat-your-heart eyes that struck like matches through the dim, dusty column. Slowly, impossibly, even as the shifting planes of its face blurred and settled and blurred again, the shorn head began to mould itself against the grille, its substance advancing and retreating as it poured itself out into the space above us.

There was a moment of shock as my frozen brain restarted and I grabbed Sid and threw him before me, pushing forward, plunging down the steps. My outfit, still wrapped around my ankles, tripped me up at once and I fell, bouncing off the steps and hitting my head. I grabbed the railing strips with one arm and managed to stop, my spine striking the hard edge of a step in a blinding flash of pain. There was no time to cry out; I tore the garment off from between my feet and dragged Sid with me; round and round we went, down the spinning stairs, the claustrophobic brick column getting tighter in my imagination as I felt the dread apparition of the Baba descend on us, slinking slowly like dark mist.

The hum filled the air now, a hiss of many voices, but our feet were clattering and noisy, clumsy, caught in the gaps and yanked out, as we used our hands and legs to clamber down. I blocked the sound out, concentrating instead on pushing Sid ahead, keeping my body between the Baba and him. I could no longer see anything; it was like dust and darkness were coagulating to create a new substance, something that slowed us down, and something that would clot around us if we stopped, and never ever let us go. We had to get out of here, out of this cylindrical bottle, and then Sid would be in sunlight, Sid would be safe, even if I were ending. My whole story was ending now.

My blood responded, though—of course it would—to the call. I could feel the pull from within, the magnetic influence of the Baba calling me to him. My veins were thickening, the fluid inside growing viscous and dark, my heart pumping new blood, and this was not the transition of an urge or a Want; this was the preparation of a vessel called to duty. It became harder to keep going, harder to think about Sid. Sid, whose face was a field of confusion, who coughed and coughed and gasped for air, his hands and face bleeding from where we'd scraped and bumped and plummeted against the wall or rail on our way down; Sid, who had been shouting out words I could not hear, not over the rattle and hum of the many souls that followed the Baba down. I could see a bruise blooming rose-like on his forehead, and that is when I realized we were almost out; sunlight flooded in as we tumbled out on to the corridor and collapsed in a heap.

The noise cut off at once and there was silence—the ringing kind that hits your eardrums after a bomb blast. It deafened me, and I was curled in a ball around Sid, my eyes screwed tightly shut, my arms around him even as I knew I must let go. I needed to separate from him, so that when the End came to me, I would go alone. I felt him do it for me, separate so gently that it could only be him pulling my hands away, and my head was lifted and placed in his lap. I looked into his liquid eyes and it felt like he held my heart in his hand and it was safe there, far safer than it would ever be in my ribcage.

'You keep it for me,' I whispered. 'When I'm gone.'

He nodded, the tears flooding down his face again. His lower lip was bleeding, and even as I reached out to touch it, taking a dab of his blood on my finger, I realized we weren't alone; heads bent towards us like awkward buds on bent stalks. The silence was replaced by a medley of voices, until an authoritative voice boomed above it and the heads parted.

I raised myself to sit, learning only now that I was sprawled in the middle of the college building in nothing but a tube top and panties.

Sid pulled his T-shirt off and handed it to me. I put it on, my mind still struggling to understand what had just happened. A hand was proffered and I took it and scrambled to my feet.

Father Clarence cleared his throat. 'You both have some explaining to do at the principal's office, but right now I think some first aid is in order. Come with me.'

We followed him gratefully to the counselling room, aware of every stare and whisper that followed us down the corridors. I turned back once to try to peer into the mouth of the staircase we had climbed, but it had disappeared behind the students who milled around, trying to piece together what could have happened there.

'Ally cat,' Sid remarked as we entered, his arm still around my waist. A tiny figure was curled in an armchair, only the tumbling curls visible between cushions and rug. She sat up and glared at us. 'Let sleeping—Jesus! What happened to you two?'

She threw the rug off, yanked a skirt off her hips and threw it at me. 'Put that on, girl; I can make do with the tights.'

I stepped into it gratefully. It was still short, but a lot better than standing around in a T-shirt and Keds.

'I have nothing for you, handsome.' She looked speculatively at shirtless Sid and I fell into a time warp, remembering this time last year when Sid had joined college. There had been images of him everywhere in the city at the time, a shirtless Levi's model in a campaign he had never lived down.

'Disappear, my girl, I need to talk to these two,' Father Clarence said as he frowned at her, his forehead wrinkled and doughy with age and the cares of students over the years. He reached into a rickety cupboard and handed Sid a checked shirt.

'Good luck.' She gave my hand a squeeze, and was gone.

'Sit down. you two,' Father Clarence indicated to the chairs and bustled over his coffee pot.

Sid and I exchanged glances. In another life, I might have joked that the coffee here was dangerously bad.

'It's my fault,' Sid said. 'I took her up to see the secret staircase, and she and I, well . . .' He rubbed my arm. 'I'm sorry, Alia, I should never have taken you up there.'

I shook my head. I felt bad; I felt terrible about pulling the wool over an old friend's eyes, but what choice did I have? What on earth could I tell Father Clarence anyway but this bare-bones recital?

'We just—' I took a deep breath. 'We got carried away.' I couldn't meet the counsellor's eyes. He had turned around and handed us mugs of coffee. I placed mine on a side table, my hands still too shaky to hold it and pretend. Sid took slurping gulps, scalding his bleeding lips.

Father Clarence shook his head and pulled open a drawer, ruffling through it to slap Band-Aids, tiny bandages, surgical tape, Dettol and assorted items on the table.

'I will not judge you children, and I am not obliged to pass on information you give me to the principal's office, you realize that? I am here for you, to listen and to help.'

We nodded, sobered even further by the worry in his voice.

'But there are signs of violence here and I cannot ignore that.' He narrowed his eyes. 'And it seems evenly distributed; so either you went at each other, or something happened to you both.'

'It did happen to us both; we fell off the damn stairs,' Sid said, holding his hands out. 'Look, Father, I haven't done anything to her and she sure as hell hasn't given me this.' He pointed to the bruise on his elbow.

'Why did you fall off?' Father Clarence asked softly.

'You don't want to know,' I said.

He kept looking at me.

'Fine. My pants were around my ankles.'

'Alia,' he said with surprise. 'A sensible girl like you?'

I smiled despite myself. 'Father Clarence, even sensible girls kiss boys.'

'And you?' he turned to Sid. 'Did you think of the risk to yourself and to her? You do know you will both be rusticated at best and taken off the rolls at worst? It's mid year; where will you go now?'

'We didn't mean to end up like this,' Sid said.

'I can probably agree on that.' Father Clarence rubbed his chin. 'Let's hope you can put your point across to the principal, but I have to say, it's not looking good for you. You need to both get your heads checked after this—checked for concussion, I mean—in addition to being checked for good sense.' He tore the plastic off some cotton-wool bandages. 'Who wants to go first? Sid, I am going to ask you to take your coffee into the next room and wait for me there. Alia isn't drinking hers, so I'd like to start with her.'

'I'm really okay,' I protested.

'I will have to insist on this,' he said.

He held my hand in his after Sid had gone into the next room. He bent the wrist one way and then the other, and then tested my fingers.

'Don't bother, Father,' I said, indicating the bandages. 'I'm not really bleeding anywhere and nothing's broken. I just need a shower and clothes. Look.'

'Wait,' he said, blinking in confusion at the way the bruises already looked like they were on the road to recovery. I got up to call Sid.

'Wait,' he insisted, 'I need to ask you this, Alia: did anything happen that you were uncomfortable with? We can report it if necessary; we can keep you away from Sid or whoever it was that may have caused you these injuries. Was someone else up there with you both?'

'You don't believe we just slipped?'

'Occam's razor? The simplest explanation is generally true,' he admitted, 'but I also know you have a history of trouble, and I am very unhappy to see it has followed you into this new year as well. If you have been intimidated or pressured in any way—'

'Stop, please!' I said. 'I can't bear you even thinking about Sid like that.'

'I don't know this young man like I know you,' he said, 'but I meant what I said earlier. You are a sensible girl and it's not like you to do something this foolhardy in college. So I can only assume there were extenuating circumstances behind it. Will you share them?'

I shook my head. 'I'm sorry, Father.' I hung my head. The minutes ticked by on the big, friendly clock on the wall above his desk.

'Well, then there's nothing more to be said,' he sighed. 'Except that I will not forget it easily. The way he looked at you and the way you looked at him, it's obvious that you two are very much in love, but you are just overgrown children right now, and you are sharing a secret or some kind of sadness that you won't reveal. Do you understand love, Alia? Love is not foolish risk and love is not some form of daredevilry or seclusion or torture; it is a happy thing, a gift of God to be celebrated in the right way at the right time.'

I smiled. 'Tell me again, please.'

'Tell you what?' he asked.

'About what you saw when you saw us, how we looked.'

His face was worried, and then he grinned and ran a hand over my head, ruffling my hair. 'Child! It will be okay! You will face some consequences for today, but it will be all right in the long run. Yes, you looked like you love each other very much. Happy now?'

I grinned. 'Yeah.'

Rapid knocks on the door, and Ally burst in, holding my overalls.

'You can leave my skirt with Father C,' she said, and was gone.

'Thank you,' I mouthed as I went into the next room to call Sid.

* * *

I sat through the talk with the principal and stared out of the window beside us while Sid pleaded our case. Dr Mendonsa was more than fair, considering the circumstances; we were both suspended indefinitely, until he had spoken to our professors and made a decision. I nodded like it affected me.

'I am sorry,' I said to Sid as we walked out.

'Are you kidding me? Screw college! What would I even return here to? I can't live without you.' His voice broke at the end.

'You'll go on.' The bittersweet taste of Despair coated my tongue like after a fever.

'I don't want to live without you, you stupid, stupid, girl. You have to know that much if you know anything by now.'

'We do what we must,' I said. 'That's the way it works.'

'Let's get out of here,' he said, frowning. 'I can't take any more of these idiots staring at us.'

We drove to Nariman Point, parking opposite the NCPA. The sea shone like a tin sheet in the flatness of noon sunlight.

'What happened back there?' he asked at last, his voice raw. I glanced at his face, the bloody lip and the bruises, and then I looked at my own in the rear-view mirror, the skin already healed, unblemished. I was about as real as a Barbie. My thoughts flew to the imaginary friend of my childhood, Miami Sheila, the doll I'd had as a child. I had the pore-less perfection of her plastic skin. Was I any more real?

'One moment we were in each other's arms and the next, you were throwing me down the stairs and tearing after me as though we were being chased by a pack of dogs. I could only imagine the worst,' he said.

'I'd have preferred the hounds,' I said soberly.

'What was it? Bobby?' he shuddered.

I shook my head. 'Bobby is gone. I saw him leave the villa. I get it now. I have no more desires, Sid, no need of a

Familiar, because there's nothing to Want. The bargain is complete and that was the last link in the chain. Bobby is gone and the Baba came for me. I . . . I have no idea how I escaped that.'

He blinked a few times, his eyes streaked, and then they were overflowing. He put his face in his hands and his body shook so hard that I unlatched his seat belt, then mine, and held him in my arms.

He pulled away and looked at me with an expression that would have broken a mortal heart. 'We wasted all this time because I wanted you to be normal. I was too blind to tell you that you are extraordinary. You have always been extraordinary. I have to tell you something, Alia.' He dried his eyes and held me by my shoulders. 'You're my hero.'

'Hero?' A bitter laugh rose out of me. 'My life is ending. I feel like a fool.'

'You are the girl that stood for something and you . . . you made this world a better place by being in it.'

'How can you say that when you know I've done terrible things. I'm a monster, Sid; the prophecy came true.'

'You killed three rapists and a bat that attacked you. In my books, those guys got what was coming to them.'

'I could have done more with the time I had.' I bit my lip and looked away from him, ashamed. 'I was selfish and blinkered about everything. I had the power to really do things, and who have I helped?'

'Don't you realize what you're doing by beating yourself up?' he said urgently. 'You have to let go of this; this is the Despair that will get you.'

'It's real regret. You see, I didn't only have a weakness when it came to the Wants; I also had power, and I could have done something with it.'

'Like what?' he said. 'Save the world from itself?'

'I don't know. I don't know what. Maybe improve it a little?'

'The world is a big place to look after,' he said, 'but you have only shown mercy and generosity to the people you loved, Alia. That's where goodness begins. And you've always had it. How many people can honestly say they would do for their parents what you did? You lived a good life. You never had an easy one or a decent one, but you lived it with quiet grace and dignity, and I see it now.'

I buried my face in his shoulder, and I let him stroke my hair; yet all I could hear was the finality of his goodbye. He had given up and was already thinking of me in the past tense. I guess it was time for me to do the same.

'What will you do? When I'm gone,' I said.

'I don't know. It feels like the end of the world for both of us.'

The bleakness in my heart when he said that felt breathtaking; were there choric angels singing somewhere outside the Jag, their halos catching the slanting rays of the setting sun? It was almost beautiful to be resigned, to watch the sun go down over the Arabian Sea and be sort of accepting and noble. I felt like Joan of Arc, but post inquisition; no longer suffering the pain and throes of attachment. One last bonfire to go through and then at least this mortal torture would end.

Then he grabbed my chin and kissed me, crushing my lips against his, heating up my fading body with his warmth.

He pushed me away from him with a rough tenderness just as I began to kiss him back. His gaze pierced me as I touched his swollen lips.

'We have now, Alia; we are going to do something with it.'

'Okay,' I agreed, breathless.

Perhaps this was the bullseye of true love that the fairy tales promised. Evil and ruin, corruption and death, I did not doubt that they were coming, rising out of the vaporous mists that the other world was blowing my way, but what if they could be held back a little?

'I want you enough for both of us. Move in with me today. Leave that godforsaken villa and spend your time with me. Give me every second that you have left. And I will . . .' He took my hands in his and kissed each one, his lips moist against my palms. His voice broke. 'Promise me that you will do this. Promise me that you will be mine now, mine with all your heart, your soul, your everything.'

I nodded, overwhelmed. 'Of course,' I said, the sweet relief of return flooding through me. 'But, Sid, he will come back for me, you know that?'

'And he will have to pry you away from your last happiness and from my arms.'

I stared at him for a whole minute, trying to find the flaw in his plan. There was none. There were no other plans to make either. 'I am going to go pack my things!'

And on my honour, knowing nothing of the hell that would break loose once we parted that evening, I meant every word of it.

SEVENTEEN

Chris had once told me his basic problem with the notion of karma was that it made the universe sound like an old schoolmarm. This had been during the first week I'd spent in St. Xavier's college a year ago, and his argument had been straightforward.

'Let's say things are happening for a reason, and the reason is that you messed something up the last time. So everything swings around in a loop—day and night alternate, seasons change—everything is in a cycle that just brings you back to face that problem you messed up. So there it is, again, and you're supposed to get it right this time. Are you with me so far?'

'I guess,' I'd said. I'd been too distracted then by the activity in the canteen, and Maya and Ronjy at the next table, vying over who had more stories about the cute boy who'd just transferred here from St. Stephen's in Delhi.

'So my big question is "why"?'

'Why, what?' I returned my gaze to him.

'Why would the universe take all this trouble? How can it be doing that for billions of people every second? And, like, what if the lesson I have to learn is different from the lesson you have to learn? How does the universe choose which of us is going to have a "teaching" moment?'

'It's simple,' I said. 'It chooses me.'

He grinned. 'I can't really argue with that. I'd choose you over me.'

'Be careful, you,' I'd said, smiling into his dark eyes. 'This might be a teaching moment right now.'

'What might the universe be teaching me?' he said, taking my hands in his.

'The same thing fables do—not to trust strangers,' I said, laughing, shaking loose and giving him a theatrical wink as I gathered my books up. 'You never know when they might be trouble.'

* * *

I was the thirteenth fairy that turned up uninvited to the christening when I returned to the darkening villa to pack my bags. Posh cars lined up in the driveway and black-coated valets handed over tokens with silk-wrapped, long-stemmed roses to the guests who stepped out. Flute music played from concealed speakers in the bushes, and I screeched over to the side of the line, tossing my car keys to a young man as I ran up the porch steps. The hall was blazing with lights, the chandeliers at full strength, the dull-gold damask curtains drawn to keep out the night that streaked past the many small windows that ran along the room. Voices hummed, glasses clinked, and the occasional burst of laughter made it all seem unreal; the whole thing was like a stage set. A sudden flash made me blink as cameras went off, and I smoothed my crumpled overalls down, embarrassed.

'There you are,' my mother called out as she came down the hall towards me, her off-shoulder gown revealing perfectly formed collarbones with a heart-shaped diamond nestled in her clavicle. Her arms were held out towards me in a gesture of welcome, and she paused just a beat longer to let the paparazzi catch it.

'What's going on?' I said, my eyes drawn to the pool of light the diamond generated in the dip of her neck.

'Just a little party to liven up the house,' she said, still smiling with her teeth showing.

'Why?' I said.

'Because a certain birdie that we will not name told us that someone needs cheering up,' she said. Deesh broke off his conversation with a group of women as though sensing mention of his name. Something in the look that passed between my mother and him made the air in the room a little denser.

'And this is how? Seriously? Do you know your new friend burnt all your rose bushes?' I pointed to the centrepiece that dominated the white table. The scent of the roses hung nauseatingly heavy, like clotting milk, under the warmth of the lights.

'Oh, he brought me these by way of apology,' she said with a smirk.

'Oooh, let me guess, apology accepted?' I said.

'Don't be such a sulk, Alia,' she hissed. 'It's about time we livened up this place. Who knows what's coming for any of us. Your little warning made me realize I have to live in the moment!'

'You miss it, don't you?' I said. 'That life you had before, when you were a superstar's wife—the parties, photo spreads, the write-ups, the attention, the—'

'I miss being a part of the living, yes.' Her beautiful eyes narrowed into slits that brought her eyelashes, sharpened further by mascara, together like piranha teeth. She waved a photographer away.

'You should have thought about that before you shot yourself in the head!' I said. She had been so eager to push me into accepting the legacy that would save Khanna that she had thought nothing of raising the stakes by increasing the body count.

She grabbed my arm. 'I give up! I did what I did out of love. Why did you do it? Tell me, Saint Alia. Did you save your father and bring me back just so that you could roam around like a martyr all day and have us mourn you? Everything has to be about you, doesn't it? You queen over us with your sad little face even though you know you have everything and we are powerless.'

I only realized I'd done it when I felt the sting on the palm of my hand. I withdrew my hand from her cheek and stared at it in surprise. Her face reddened, a cut in her lip swelled outwards and a droplet of dark blood trailed down her jaw and stained her white dress.

Deesh was beside us in the instant it took for the cameras to start clicking.

'That's no way to treat your mother!' He brought a handkerchief to her cheek and dabbed gently at the tiny wound that had already begun to close.

'It's impossible to reason with her,' she said. 'Now do you see what I've been telling you about? I might seem a distant mother, but how does one talk to this girl? I only threw this party for her; so that she might come home to something special.'

'I know, Resh, I know, you've spent days planning it.' His voice was soothing as he kept his hand on her cheek, cupping her chin now, their dead eyes echoing each other's. 'You barely used the agency; you called every guest yourself, sent personalized invites.'

'Resh? You're calling her "Resh" now? You've got to be kidding me,' I said, recovering my voice.

'You've been struggling to make amends,' he continued, his eyes unwavering as they probed hers, as though I hadn't spoken at all. 'It hasn't been an easy journey on the spiritual level.'

She nodded and lowered her powdered eyelids that had all the artful symmetry of butterfly wings now.

'Are you for real!' I exclaimed, not caring who heard me any more. I turned to my mother. 'Are you buying this crap he's dishing out?'

He waved my protests away. 'You were right all along, Resh. We have to get you out of here; this is not helpful to your current state of mind,' he whispered into her ear, pushing back the thick, brown curl of hair that fell against his lips, and tucking it behind her ear with caressing hands. 'Let me handle this.'

He put his hand on her arm and guided her away from the
rippling crowd that opened up around them, heads swivelling
from her to me. I leaned against a pillar and watched them
walk away, their steps in perfect synchronicity, his arm
curved around her tiny waist with an ownership that you'd
have to be blind to miss. She leaned into him as they went
up the staircase. He returned a few minutes later, his face
wreathed in smiles that may have been appreciated by his
attentive guests but did not fool me for a minute.

'Where did you put her?' I asked.

'In her room, where she will brood and brood and wish
she were dead. Except, well, she already is, isn't she? So
that's not going to help at all.' He chuckled, glee turning up
the corners of his mouth. 'She's a real piece of work, your
mother; so used to being worshipped that she doesn't even
blink those starry eyes when I'm feeding her a crock of shit.'

'I don't get it. So this is your big revenge? Organizing
dinner parties? Aren't you tired of playing softball with their
emotions?' I said.

'Oh, some things are best kept mysteries.' The contempt
was obvious in the way he bared his teeth in the mockery of
a smile. 'You're right about my revenge, though. It is indeed
kind of slow, but don't you worry; it is coming.'

He steered me towards the staircase. 'Unfortunately,
you, my precious, will not be around to help them this time
around.'

'What makes you think I'd care any more?'

'Oh, your capacity to be a bleeding heart is not something
we are going to underestimate a second time,' he said.

'A second time? What do you mean?'

He gave me a piercing look. 'Never mind.'

'What do you mean by a "second time", Deesh? Who is "we"?'

'Keep your voice down, dammit!' He glanced around, and, for the first time, I saw real emotion flit across his face. 'Go upstairs to your room, Alia,' he hissed. 'If you don't want to be social at this party, then you should wait it out in your room.'

I kept my face blank even as I stared at him. I choked back the doubt that had risen in my mind. If I were to follow this doubt to its logical conclusion, then it would mean that I had been a pawn in a bigger game than I had realized all along. It would mean I had been played for a fool; that I was still being played for a fool, and that the worst was yet to come.

My mind snapped to alertness; I was going to have to be very careful with my next move. I needed to buy time, and everything depended on Deesh's complacency. He had to think I was the same clueless Alia I had been all along.

'Okay,' I said in a neutral voice, forcing my voice to stay calm. 'I guess I'll leave you to your party then.'

I took the steps two at a time, his gaze burning into my shoulders, until I got to my room and slammed the door so hard that the plaster surrounding it cracked to reveal a lightning bolt.

I threw a bunch of clothes into a holdall, trying to keep my hands from shaking. It was no use; I sat on the bed and thought about what I had just heard.

Who was the 'we' Deesh had been talking about? If that admission was true, then there was one obvious explanation.

I remembered Father Clarence's use of Occam's razor principle: the simplest explanation is usually the correct one. What if I had been played for a fool all along?

I had always believed that the blame for Deesh's death rested squarely on my shoulders. In fact, that terrible night when I led him into the maze to be murdered by Bobby was the first link in the chain of events that led to my taking on the Change. I needed to think about it now carefully. For it was no coincidence that my father had sacrificed one boy out of a pair of twins. What if Deesh's appearance in my life had been part of the Baba's plan all along? All along I had seen Deesh as an innocent victim but what if it wasn't just Bobby who had returned corrupted from the other side?

I shut my eyes and forced my memory to return to the vision of the unholy ritual conducted by the Baba at *Saat Rasta*. The events had been burnt into my memory and I replayed them now, allowing myself to remember the descent of mists and veils, as the vapours of the other world circulated freely around me, drawing me into the memory of *Saat Rasta* one more time.

I was in the Baba's hut where the initiates sat cross-legged around the sacrificial fire: my father, then a young man, and the seven-year-old twins, Bobby and Deesh.

The Baba stood over them with a mammoth bronze mask on that obscured his face and neck, its symbol a downward spiral, with wings like a flaming bird. Bobby's tiny chest was marked out with the same winged spiral. The Baba's Familiar, the raven, swooped in tight circles above the child who was shaven bald, and naked but for a loincloth.

The chants that followed were a series of assertions by the Baba; he was the in-between—the metamorphic, the transient, the liminal god—and he called upon the seeker to be transformed by the supplication. It was time for my father to make his sacrifice known. The ancient silver knife blazed as the Baba pulled it out of the fire and handed it over to my father.

My father plunged the blade into Bobby without hesitation and the child bled out, time swelling outwards and holding fast like a horrific bubble until he was drained out. His limbs snapped together like a puppet's when it was all over, and he walked into the blaze that had become an inferno, filling the tiny space with the fumes of his absorption.

The fire burnt for days, and when it had cooled at last and the little bones had been reduced to ash, then the Baba took a pinch of ash to draw the symbol of the winged downward spiral on the surviving twin's forehead. Deesh, paralysed through the entire ritual, was offered up as the anchor to dissolution. Thus had the covenant been balanced—one twin on the plane of the living, and one twin in the realm of the dead.

I had known all this when I allowed Deesh to unite with his twin. I had believed Deesh when he told me all he wanted was to set Bobby free; that in allowing him to do so I would right some part of the wrongs that my father had inflicted upon the innocent world. Then I had panicked at the thought of disturbing the remains of the long buried spirit in the maze. No wonder Deesh had resisted me and fought me when I tried to keep him away from the urn. I now realized my role had been anticipated all along. By uniting Deesh with his demonic twin, I had, in fact, dissolved the bond; the pact was no longer earthed in Deesh's mortal life.

My father may have stretched out his deal over seventeen years, finding ways to keep Wanting, to keep Despair at bay and keep going; however, my actions had terminated the bargain.

I had been given twenty-four hours to accept or renounce the bond that passed on to me by bloodline. It should've been open-and-shut, except, to Deesh's and the Baba's frustration, I had chosen to take on the legacy in order to save my father. Thus making the Baba wait even longer for the soul he had been promised in return, because I substituted my father. Why else would Deesh have said they were not going to underestimate my 'bleeding heart' a second time? They were in this together, they were both reapers of the soul and now they were coming for mine.

In my blindness and guilt I had depleted my remaining powers by using them to bring back my worst enemy.

EIGHTEEN

'Alia?' I couldn't place the voice. It called my name again, softly, melodiously even. It was coming from the bathroom. I looked irresolutely at the bathroom door. My name floated out again, and something about the sweetness in it compelled me to listen, to push the door and walk in, even though my mind screamed out that this could only be a trap.

The tiles were wet, cold water ghosted along the sides of my feet and I looked up to see her; she was leaning against the tub with the water running. She hummed a song from one of my father's old movies as she trailed her fingers in it absent-mindedly; her white-and-pink uniform was soaked at the bottom, revealing the outlines of her underwear.

'Gail! Gail, get up, for God's sake! What are you doing here?' I said. I turned the taps off.

I might have been talking to a mannequin.

I reached for her but she wriggled out of my grasp. Her fingers continued dragging through the water.

'Gail,' I said, carefully, as though addressing a tiger that might spring at me any moment. 'What's going on? Get away from there.'

'The water is good,' she said. 'Do it.'

I shook my head, my throat drying up even as my eyes wandered to the water; even as my eyes wandered to the water; I was lulled by the soothing lap of it against her fingers and the sides of the tub. Of course, this was it—the call to action. Would I ever make it out if I lowered myself into the tub?

'No,' I whispered.

'Do it,' she repeated, her mouth opening and closing like an automaton's, while her features remained blank.

I shook my head and backed away from her. Whatever this person was, it wasn't the quiet, mild-mannered Gail who cleaned my room every morning. She had been Hazed.

She got to her feet and dragged an armchair to the centre of the room. She climbed atop it and patted down her dripping skirt. Then she unhooked the satin belt from the midriff of her dress and began to ease it out of its waist straps.

The taps had turned on again; every tap in the bathroom began to run and the sound of the water filled my ears—the shower, the basin, the tub taps. The sound overwhelmed me, and my spine jarred painfully as I bumped up against the doorknob.

She fastened her belt in a loop. Then she slid her head into it and hooked the other end around the chandelier, tying it with difficulty, on tiptoes and using the ends of her fingertips. She checked to see if it was taut, and tightened the loop around her neck.

'For God's sake, what are you doing?' I took a step towards her and she lifted one foot off the chair in warning.

'Why are you doing this?' I sobbed.

'Do it,' she said.

'Okay, hey, okay, please just get down off the chair, okay?' I pleaded. I walked towards the tub and stepped into the water; it felt iciest where it cut off my knees. I sat down and felt the breath go out of me as I lowered myself into the water.

She slid her neck out of the loop, jumped lightly off the chair and walked out without a backward glance, leaving me there, the belt still swinging from the ceiling. My overalls sagged heavy with the pull of the water, and as the door swung shut behind her, the surface of the water closed in on me with a roar.

The nightmare world was very calm after it received me. So calm that I was in a memory of great quietude; it was the ICU of Lilavati Hospital from last December. A train of organza flashed by me and I took in a streaming sari, stiffly laundered and indicative of a woman on the go. A floral scent subdued the stink of disinfectant and medicines.

Her eyes were the same as her son's, a pitch black that reflected nothing.

It was the first day of the new year, and she knelt by Chris's bed, smoothing the sheets as if to rub away the question of how they might have got crumpled in the first place. She tucked in the ends of the pillow. Our eyes met over the impossibly neat bed.

'Coma patients rarely wake up.' She examined her bitten-down nails. 'The doctors called me in today. To discuss his situation and examine the options.'

The vision distorted, the face cracking up as the memory fast-forwarded to another time in the same place.

She took my hand in hers and stroked it with her hard fingertips. 'What do you know what it takes to raise a man? Chris was weak. And now we are stuck in this . . . situation,' she said.

I felt something move and I looked down. The body of the living boy lay between us, his mouth slack around the tube and his body wasted into a stringy thinness held together only by the machines. I felt his fresh burst of sadness now as I had felt it then, and a type of pain his mother had put there that only she could take away. Things had never been easy between them. But he would have, at the very least, wanted his mother to root for him to live. Here she was instead, talking about withdrawing life support while he still breathed and dreamed at our side.

The memory froze again, breaking up, and the next vision was so recent it was like I was living it in real time.

Chris and I stood in the corridor outside my bedroom and it was the morning after our road-kill episode with Deesh. The white dress I'd worn was a muddied mess.

'Your mother sounds crazy!' I said.

Chris's eyes were hard as stone. 'We can't sit in the same room together for five minutes before she's blaming me for something and I'm wanting to kill her. I mean, like, actually kill her. Or better yet, get her to kill herself. I even have these elaborate little fantasies of how I'd get her to do it. I keep editing it in my head when I can't sleep—which, as you know, is basically every night.'

'That's disturbing,' I said.

'You think? That's why I left her house.' His eyes were hard. 'So don't bring that woman up again, okay, chiquita?'

'You got it.' I saw myself shiver in response to the undercurrent of darkness that emanated from him.

The vision grew dark and I opened my mouth to gasp, only I let the water in and then there was no stopping it as it poured down my throat, my lungs collapsing under the water. I couldn't push myself up or even swing my arms and legs before another vision came to me, and for the first time, it was a vision of the future, a future I had yet to live.

I was in somebody's kitchen. I had my back to an old double-door refrigerator, and it burped and I saw myself spin around to notice the IIM Calcutta and Madras fridge magnets. A high-pitched shriek rent the air, cutting off abruptly, and an answering dull thud followed. I spun back around and all I could see was the granite counter where, nearly obscured by the biscuit tin, rested a cup of tea and a torn-open Glucose biscuit packet. The biscuits had spilled out of their packet, four collapsed like dominoes on the yellow daisy-print plate, two more on the table, and one had fallen to the floor to land on a spreading pool of blood.

I took a step backwards, or rather I wanted to, and the vision grew dark again as my open mouth and heaving lungs filled up with so much water that I had no choice but to fight my way up and out of the grip of the cold water.

I emerged spluttering, vomiting liquid, desperate for air. What I had told Aleifya all that time ago in the hospital by Chris's bedside had been true. There really was no telling what a person could or could not hear when they were in a coma, and what my gut had told me was that Chris had heard everything his mother had said about ending his life. No wonder he hated her. I held on to the sides of the tub and climbed out, my limbs energized with the enormity of the apprehension I had just had. That unfamiliar kitchen could only be Chris's mother's. Something terrible was about to go down, and I had to save his mom before he took his revenge in a way he would never recover from.

NINETEEN

Milton Apartments was an ocean-liner-sized dreary affair.

Cantilevered balconies with piped railings gaped out on the street like loose teeth. Colonial-style recessed windows smudged the brick facade, giving the building an air of heavy-lidded menace.

It was 3 a.m. on a weekday, in a cul-de-sac in Colaba. A stray cat picked its way between the parked cars, hunched over for the night in the compound. The security guard snored in his chair with a baton balanced in his lap as I saddled the chain-locked gate and jumped down by his side. I wondered how long it had taken him to get this comfortable after the boy fell out of the sky last year in the middle of a weekday night not unlike this one.

A flickering LED cast a ghastly pall over the foyer. I took the stairs. Eight floors of stepping over potted plants, sleeping manservants and overflowing trash bins, and I was outside the de Souza house.

Chris no longer lived here but I hoped to hell he had not turned on his radar. What on earth would I say to him if he came to learn that I stood outside his mother's front door? I remembered his face from the other night, the way his features had seemed to harden into a mask of anger when we talked about his mom, and I erased the image from my mind lest the elastic band we had between us tugged at him.

It struck me now that I had not worked out a plan. I rang the bell anyway.

I rang again, and then again. I could knock only so hard without waking the neighbours across the landing. And then, with an intuition that brushed against me like a whisper, I bent down and lifted up the welcome mat to find the key. She was a mom, after all; she wanted her boy to be able to come back home.

The key turned, and the heavy door unbolted, though I had to put my shoulder to push it open. It swung back and slammed shut behind me; this lady knew how to oil her hinges. I felt a cloud of malevolence at the thought of her crossing my back like a passing shadow, and I shivered. The hall and corridor ahead were in darkness, but a naked bulb blazed in a room at the end of a passageway.

I glanced around the hall, trying to imagine Chris growing up here, and I couldn't see it at all. The flat was in stealth mode and only grew creepier as my eyes adjusted to the dimness. China dolls leered at me through a locked wooden cabinet; the sofas looked dusted down with the fabric stretched impossibly tight; a flat-screen TV dominated one wall with a fitted synthetic cover; and artificial flowers sprung from a vase on the cane coffee table. Everything in the drawing room had an air of expectancy, as though arranged and waiting to come to life on the arrival of a special guest.

I went straight to the kitchen and switched on the lights. A quick glance confirmed that it was just like it had been in the vision I'd had before, except there was no pool of blood on the floor, no hint of violence in the air. I scanned it and was assured that nothing untoward had taken place here. I counted four other rooms down the corridor with their doors open, the darkness velvety around everyday furniture, and decided to investigate each one. First I walked through the passageway towards the room at the end with the light bulb on. A long, stale breath wafted down the corridor towards me, and I fought the insane apprehension that the house was somehow sentient and aware of me.

The room was a 10x10, probably a maid's room or a laundry room. My sandals crunched as I stepped on a lampshade that had once concealed the bulb in the ceiling. The curtains were roughly drawn in; other than the wrecked lampshades, there was nothing untoward. I hesitated a moment before pulling back the sheets on the low single bed—nothing. A flimsy-looking side table stood on a tiny rug with a copy of the Bible. A faded painting of the Last Supper hung slightly askew on one wall. I corrected it with one finger.

It was a cheerless room, but it made me breathe easier. That toothpick table would have collapsed at the first sign of disturbance in the air. Nothing had happened here besides the lampshade crashing down of its own accord. The aluminium sliding door across me was open a crack, a dark swirling vapour behind it, and I pushed it open all the way before I could change my mind. I slid my fingers across the wall until I hit the switches. Nothing. Just a cracked loo and a yellowing basin on old tiles.

I took a deep breath and clicked the lights off. Four more rooms and one kitchen to go; I could do that. The lights were always where I looked, and the rooms lit on and off as though magicked into existence. I swung every wardrobe door open, forced myself to look into every bathroom and sweep away every shower curtain. The plainness of his mother's room was startling—white sheets on a single bed, white walls, the monotony broken by an ornate wooden Pieta engraving. Only her wardrobe revealed any colour; organza, khadi and raw-silk saris rustled angrily as I parted them. The other rooms were tidy and revealed the expected debris of the de Souza brothers' childhoods—a forgotten cricket bat poking out from under a bed, an ancient boom box on a chest of drawers and Michael Jackson wall posters. That left only the kitchen, and while the vision I'd had was obviously a pack of lies, for there was no pool of blood or hint of violence, I decided to give it another once-over. The room was a model of Tupperware organization when I snapped the tubelights on.

I was about to switch off the lights and breathe a sigh of relief when the old double-door refrigerator burped and I spun around, and a chill ran through me as I realized what I'd missed before—the IIM magnets had somehow slipped to the floor. I walked around the kitchen table and bent to pick them up and there, at eye level, on the granite counter, nearly obscured by the biscuit tin, lay a cooled cup of tea and a torn Glucose biscuit packet. My heartbeat accelerated at the eeriness of the echo. The biscuits had spilled out, four collapsed like dominoes on the yellow daisy-print plate, two more on the table, and one on the floor. I went down on my knees and looked more carefully at the outline of the dried-up spill around the biscuits. This proved nothing. It could be anything, I told myself; it could be milk, or syrup, or even some tea. I watched the trail of ants as they made their way in and out through the kitchen window, and I sucked my breath in at the lulling domesticity of it.

I shut my eyes for a second and conjured her up—Chris's straight-backed mother in her clackety heels and linen sari, the unsmiling black eyes placed far apart in a thin face, and compulsive hands that smoothed out everything; not even ants would dare take up occupation for long in her house. There was no way she would have left the residence without cleaning up, unless . . .

A shudder passed through me and I walked quickly towards the front door that had banged so violently shut when I entered. It was only when I was upon her that I saw her, the malign shadow disentangling from the gloom to take on its own shape. She had been hanging on the inside of the main door all along. Her bloodless skin was stretched across the door hooks and her scrawny neck was a broken stem on which her head dangled forward, but I recognized her instantly; despite the bloated body, the severe bob of her hair was unruffled.

I felt terror bubble up inside me like bile, as the stink hit me at last and it made me hurtle through the air and run out of that house without even pausing to lower that poor woman to the ground. I ran downstairs and out of the compound, and I had to get into the Jag and go, and keep going, because to stop was to consider the reality of where we had got to—if Chris could do this to his own mother, it meant that all human feeling had deserted him, and the only one to really blame for this monstrous act was the one that had brought him back to life. Me.

Despair uncurled like a bud. Green stems of sickness furrowed into my mind, cracking into me, and I must have blacked out at some point, because I found myself pulled over at the side of the road outside Sid's building on Pali Hill, screaming into the airtight shell of the Jag. My phone vibrated in the next seat where I'd dropped it—thirty-two missed calls, all of them from Sid.

* * *

I was cross-legged outside his front door, nibbling at my fingernails, when he arrived with wild hair and muddy shoes.

'Oh fuck! Alia! Are you okay? I've looked everywhere. I was at your house, your bag was just . . .' He hefted it up to show me and then dropped it. 'I didn't know what to do; no one knew what to—' He staggered and leaned against the wall and put his face in his hands. His knees gave way and he slid down to squat by me on the floor. His voice shook even now. 'Where were you? Are you okay?'

'I need to get inside and take a shower. I need to get her smell off me.'

'Get what? I . . . what?'

I pulled him through the door, and his jaw dropped. I had pulled my T-shirt off in one fluid movement and thrown it to the floor as soon as we got into his room. I kicked my torn sandals off, threw off my jeans, and then dashed into the bathroom and turned the shower on.

The hot water ran down my face and through my hair and down on to the small of my back, and I picked up Sid's

Boots shampoo and emptied it over my head. I scoured every strand of my hair and every inch on my skin until all of me felt raw. I walked out in a towel and found him seated on the bed, his face a mask of pain.

'Wear this,' he said gruffly, throwing me a grey T-shirt and a pair of shorts. I did as he said, with neither enthusiasm nor embarrassment. He wasn't watching anyway. He led me to his bed and pulled back the sheets. 'Get in,' he said.

'I don't sleep any more, I don't—'

'Shut it,' he said. 'And get in.'

I got in and curled into a ball, with my back to him. He climbed in after me and held me. 'Now shhhhhh,' he said. 'You can tell me everything when you're ready, but there is no hurry, Alia; there is no hurry to get your clothes off, or to tell me, or to run out and do something.'

'How do you know?' A shudder ran through me. He held me tighter.

'All I know is that there is nothing more important than holding you right now. You know why?'

'Why?' I whispered.

'Because I thought you were gone. I thought you were coming back and then I thought you were gone, and that was it. And all I wanted was to hold you in my arms one time. Just one more time, and say goodbye properly. So that is what we are doing now. We are saying goodbye properly. So that whatever the universe does to us after this, we will always have had this.'

I shut my eyes and tried to forget until the tremors slowed down, and then I turned and held him, too, till both of us were soothed, cocooned by the warmth of dawn, the sunlight golden on his face, his irises expanding, his face turning away to take it on his cheek as it streamed through the window.

'Thank you,' I whispered, kissing him, feeling this pressure ease out of me, and feeling an unknown, mysterious ache I had carried inside me lift. He had taken away the most painful, the most unthinkable 'what if' I had ever felt. He had released me from the terror of not having had a chance to say 'goodbye' to him properly.

And then I told him everything. The geography of his face changed as the words left my mouth, and I knew I should go slow, or explain as I went along, except I could not slow it down. I led him straight to the dead woman hanging on a coat hanger, her skin stretched like leather, her odour violent, angry, and still alive. And then I left him to contemplate all that while I breathed in and out against his chest, nestled so close to his heart that his heart might have been my heart.

'Promise me one thing?' he whispered at last.

'Anything,' I said.

'Stay away from Chris. Do not—'

'Oh goodness!' The door was ajar and a woman stood frozen in the doorway, holding a bottle of water. 'Oh my!' she said at last. 'You have company.' She clutched her robe around her waist. Her eyes goggled at the clothes in disarray on the ground.

Sid sounded irritated. 'What do you want, Ma? Why won't you knock?'

'I thought you were out on your run,' she said with equal testiness. 'And really, it's too much that I'm the one that has to be offering excuses here.'

I nodded in agreement and then realized it was none of my business; it was between the two of them.

They locked gazes like wrestlers in a ring. I admired for the first time the way their colours and contours matched. They were a pair—mom and son—even in their hard moments.

'So the college called me in for a meeting, and now I see this.' Her lip quivered. 'I can only assume this is Alia. I want to see you both outside in a few minutes.' She withdrew, shutting the door behind her.

I pulled the sheets over my head. 'So this is how it all ends, after all.' Relief at the normalcy of this encounter had left me light-headed. 'I die of embarrassment.'

Sid groaned. 'What on earth does the woman need to see us for? Why does she need to workshop every damn thing! Why can't she just let it go for a change?'

I scrambled up and tousled his hair. 'Care to exchange moms, Sid?'

He pushed himself up on his elbows and pecked my lips. 'Oh, you're going to get a good dose of mine right about now.'

I stepped off the bed. 'Holy shit, I'm wearing your clothes; what is she going to think?'

'You were in my bed, Alia, and in my arms; what do you expect she's thinking?'

'She's thinking I deflowered her precious boy. Except, wait, that flower bloomed a while ago, am I right? I'm guessing mommy doesn't know that.'

'Oh, for Christ's sake,' he sulked as he led me out of his room. 'Let's just get this over with.'

* * *

I had only ever seen Sid's mom's face suffused with smiles in all his phone pictures, though she wasn't smiling now, as we went into the hall. She rotated a tiny earring in her left earlobe as she gestured to us to sit.

'What the two of you do when you're outside of this house is none of my business,' she said at last. 'You're both eighteen. But while you're under my roof, Sid, I am responsible. How much do Alia's parents know about this?'

'There is nothing to know, Ma. It's not what it looks like.'

'Then what is it?' She looked at me.

I cleared my throat and dropped my gaze.

She uncrossed her legs and sighed. 'Are you using contraceptives?'

Sid groaned. 'This is not happening.'

I shifted in my seat.

'Don't be blind to this, Alia; biology is not kind on the female when it comes to these things. And denial won't help if you get pregnant.'

Sid stood up. 'And that is my cue,' he said. 'Who wants an omelette?'

'Sid!' his mother exclaimed. He had already left the room.

I got up as well.

'Alia,' she called me back, gently.

'Yes?'

'You make him very happy, beta. I hope you will look after each other. Stay blessed.'

I nodded and looked away, not trusting myself to form the right words.

Then I wandered into the kitchen, my head spinning, and my eyes taking in everything, as though I were already a ghost here; so detached that a part of me was receding already, as though this were a diorama I beheld through a glass pane. So conscious was I of my separateness from the membrane of this reality that I blew on the pinned-up HDFC calendar to check if it would make the pages flutter.

My eyes took everything in as I said goodbye—Sid cracking an egg over the side of a canary-yellow bowl, the morning paper spread out on the round table, butter hissing in a pan, the noisy crows' nest outside the open window, an automated car alarm floating up the hill, calling out its dispatch as the city woke up to the promise of a new day.

TWENTY

'I read him Stephen King's *Revival*.' I put my iPhone down and frowned.

I had scoured the online news sites, but it had been three days since I'd discovered her and there was still no report about the homicide at Milton Apartments.

Sid looked up before scooping another plastic forkful of hazardously orange canteen-fried noodles into his mouth. 'So?' he said.

'*Revival*, the Stephen King novel. I read it to Chris when he was in a coma.' I waved a fly away from the table and it buzzed around the canteen, rising higher and higher, until it was gone. 'I was so stupid.'

'Why? Is it a stupid book? What? I don't get it. I'm not a horror fan,' he said.

'The book is all about "The Mother", this force that basically sucks the life out of everyone and cannot be put down, no matter what. It's evil incarnate, The Mother, it's a scourge, a—'

'And now you're wondering if you didn't just revive the dude, but if you also planted the idea of murdering his mom while he was still in a coma?' He shoved the plate away from him and shook his head, incredulous.

'Well, there is a body rotting in Colaba, and guess who made that possible?'

'Alia, he's unstable; he was always unstable. That's why he jumped off the terrace in the first place. Did you really think bringing him back would make an upright citizen out of Chris?' He put his arm around my shoulder and frowned. 'Okay, I see your point and I get that you're worried, but you've done what you could. There's nowhere else to look.'

'I will keep looking,' I said.

'If he wanted to be found, he'd be found,' he said. 'You know that.'

'I have to know what happened to him, Sid.'

'He doesn't deserve it.'

'Then it's just as well that I'm not doing it for him,' I whispered, an urgent sadness in the squeeze I gave his hand.

'Will I see you tonight?' He held on to my hand tightly, his voice breaking off on the last syllable.

'Sid,' I bowed my head. We had a deal. We'd said our goodbyes and now we were to take each day as it came.

'I know! I'm sorry.' He let go of me and stepped back. His voice softened. 'Is it ever too early in the day to say I love you?'

'I love you,' I whispered.

I walked away before he could react, and willed it to be enough to have said what I had.

* * *

Why was I spending the remaining hours of my life hunting for someone who had made it very clear he didn't want to be found? Because it is the things we don't say and do that can haunt us forever, and I was done with being haunted in this life or the next.

I exhausted every other possibility of finding Chris before I admitted that there was only one last stone to be unturned. Only it meant facing the worms that would crawl out from underneath it.

* * *

The electronic gates to the villa opened to let me in for what I swore would be the last time.

Deesh sat on the steps of the building, waiting for me, just as I had waited for him a few months ago. Although, unlike me, he looked quite at home, his features relaxed and his posture sharp, proprietorial.

'The prodigal returns,' he said, by way of salute.

I ignored the outstretched hand. 'So you haven't wrecked the place yet.' I looked around the villa grounds. 'Everything is blooming; I have to say the lawns have never looked better. I guess your kind of revenge really is on the slow side.'

'I have nothing against turn-of-the-century brickwork estates,' he smiled, displaying a set of perfect teeth. 'You, on the other hand, once set fire to all of this, didn't you? Ah, the nostalgia of past lives.'

'I need to find Chris. I don't have time for your games.'

'Oh, but I have all the time in the world to play games,' he said with a hollow laugh. 'You're the one with the tick-tock of the clock. Although I have to say, you look like hell, Bambs. Maybe it's just as well you're going before you . . . you know . . . go . . . like a piece of cheese that's been left out too long.' He curled his nose in distaste.

I blinked. 'That's low, even for you.'

'I'll take that as a compliment.'

'Where is Chris?'

He narrowed his eyes. 'So Chris is missing? How careless of you to lose someone who was so, how shall we put it delicately, cleaved unto you.'

He patted the step he was seated on and I sat down beside him, my hands tucked under my thighs, our knees leaning into each other. I looked out to where the topiary bushes tumbled in retreating perspective leading towards the massive gates. In all the years I had lived here, I had yet to see a gardener's team at work on the villa's enormous grounds.

'All of this will be yours one day,' I said. 'That's what you want, isn't it, to inherit this cursed place and be lord of the castle?'

'It's a funny little itch, isn't it, Alia, this fucking nightmare of a villa? You either want to burn it to the ground or possess it.'

'An itch isn't healthy, but then you were always obsessive.' I examined him, groomed to perfection, at ease at last among the wealth and the people he had always craved to conquer. 'You look good, Deesh. Death suits you.' I bit back the words that were on the tip of my tongue. The company he had been keeping had made sure he was looked after now. There was no need to let him in on my little discovery, though. The more he took me for a fool, the more he would slip up around me.

He tugged at the tip of my nose. 'I'll miss you, Bambi.'

'Really?'

'Does it surprise you?'

'Sure,' I said, 'in as much as you can still surprise me.'

'Touché.'

'Why do you want it, Deesh? This? Why don't you get in your car and drive to, I don't know, Cuffe Parade, or whatever the furthest tip of this island is, and just spook yourself a new place. Take the whole neighbourhood if you like. Live life king-size.'

'Is that concern I detect, or jealousy?'

'Either of those would assume I care about what happens to you or this place.'

'I see.' He smiled. 'Well, curiosity killed—'

'Yeah, well, I don't have nine lives. What can you tell me about Chris? I know you know something.'

'And how do you know that?' he purred.

'It's what comes with being an indifferent bastard. You watch all of us all the time, and you take mental notes, because this is a game to you. You've never cared for another person since you lost Bobby. You say whatever it takes to move the game along; it's your default setting to be deceptive. Oh, you can walk and talk and do a pretty good imitation of being a person but you can't feel.'

'So I'm an automaton?'

'You never had any humanity. That's why death suits you so well.'

He was rapt, and then a slow smile spread across his face. 'Hole-in-one on the observations! I've been trying my hand at golf these days . . . such a gentleman's game.'

I made an impatient sound.

He frowned. 'Your remarks are a teensy-weensy bit heartless, and that's new, because you never were low on heart. Way to go, Bambi! You are monstering up. We might have got along if you'd stuck around.'

I sighed. 'Come find me when you're willing to talk.'

I strode into the hall and headed down to the kitchen. I owed Mary a decent goodbye.

Asif bhai was hammering at a lamb shank when I poked my head in. He dropped the aluminium mallet on the counter and wiped his hands on his bloodstained apron.

'Baby!' he said. 'Are you eating dinner tonight? Want something special? Sir has ordered a four-course meal, but nothing is your favourite.'

'My father eats four-course meals now?' I smiled. 'You're making him fat!'

'No, no, Deesh Sir has ordered. He has friends coming for dinner.'

He registered the look on my face and spoke quickly, the words almost too fast to catch, 'I can make you Chinese and noodles and that manchurian you like with the mushrooms and baby corn and broccoli. I can call from market; there is enough time for me to serve by eight o'clock, latest eight-thirty or nine.'

I was awestruck. 'Asif bhai,' I said, and then shook my head, the immensity of my selfishness only now apparent to me. How easy it had been for me to imagine I could depart and not be missed.

'Don't be like that, baby,' he said, his neck twitching. 'This is your house only. We are all wanting you back.'

I sensed a movement and Gail slunk into the room, crossing through the doorway without touching me or unsettling the air currents. She stared at me with big eyes, as though seeing a ghost, while her pallor made me wonder how much she had retained outside of the compulsion the Baba had put her under. Was his contaminating touch enough to drag her into darkness forever? I hoped not.

'Gail,' I nodded at her. She gave me a sort of half-curtsey and I had to smile again despite myself. Where on earth had she learnt to do that?

'Baby is back,' Asif bhai announced. 'Gail, I am sending out for—'

'No, no, please wait,' I commandeered my shaky voice. 'Asif bhai, I . . .' I looked at my feet, trying to steady myself. I hadn't even thought of him and of saying goodbye to the man who had cooked me so many meals, both when I could eat them and when I couldn't.

'Come back, Miss.' Gail fingered the hem of her dress. 'The house is so empty without you.'

Asif bhai nodded and then turned around, overcome, and went back to pounding meat.

I stood there for a few minutes longer, trying to compose some words, some way of leave-taking. Finally, I went over to where he was and put my arms around his waist in the kind of childish hug I had never felt childlike enough to give to this man who had been here for all of my life, and probably most of his. He turned around, surprised, and patted my head before hastily taking his meat-drenched hands away.

'Thank you for everything,' I said. 'Asif bhai, your cooking has always been the best thing about this place. I am going to miss it very much when I go away.'

'You are going away?' Gail's mouth fell into an O.

I nodded.

'You are becoming student in foreign university.' Asif bhai's face was suffused with smiles. 'I knew it! We are very proud, Alia baby. We are very proud of your successes. You will become a doctor or a lawyer or something very famous. You are a very clever child, and always so well behaved!' He looked triumphantly at Gail. 'Didn't I tell you? Big future for baby.'

I forced a smile. 'Thank you for everything, Asif bhai. And I wish you all the best here.'

I turned to Gail who was sobbing into a kitchen napkin. 'Gail.' I licked my dry lips. I couldn't remember a single conversation we'd had that had meant something; more's the pity, and the fault was all mine. 'You should go work somewhere nice,' I said. 'You're too young to be stuck here. Go work in a mall or a hotel; how about Starbucks? Do you know Starbucks? Go somewhere cheerful. Do you need money to get started?'

She shook her head. 'I am marrying in December,' she said. 'Then it is Chennai.'

'Good!' I said. 'That is good. You know what—we are the same size—will you take whatever you want from my wardrobe?'

Her eyes popped. 'No, Miss, I can never do that.'

'Please,' I said, nodding emphatically. 'Seriously, you will be doing me a real favour.'

Asif bhai's shoulders shook. That poor lamb was being hammered to a pulp now. I had to get out before it liquefied.

'Could you tell me where Mary is?' I asked.

Asif bhai gave an angry snort.

'Mary is missing since last Wednesday,' Gail said.

'What?' It was my turn to have my jaw drop.

'Yeah,' she said with a shrug. 'Gone missing, no notes, no nothing.'

I rocked back and forth on the balls of my feet as I tried to take this in. 'Last Wednesday?' I repeated with difficulty. 'She's been missing since then?'

'Yes,' Gail whispered, her eyes darting from Asif bhai to me and then to the door, as though she was scared of being overheard. 'All Mary's things are still in the room. She even left her rosary here.'

I turned to Asif bhai. Last Wednesday made it the day that my parents had returned and Bobby had disappeared. Could it really be that much of a coincidence that Mary and Bobby should both vanish on the same day? I didn't like the odds.

* * *

Deesh was in the hall, making a phone call. He lay on the white sofa, head and booted feet propped up on cushions while he spoke into his headset. I grabbed the phone that lay on the coffee table and disconnected the call.

'Where is Mary?'

'What?'

'Did you Haze Mary?' I asked. 'If you ever Haze my staff or hurt them in any way—'

'Do you know whom I was talking to, you halfwit?'

'Oh, I'm sorry, was it someone very, very important?'

I held the phone up for him to see and then threw it across the room with all my force. It smashed into the wall and fell to the floor in pieces.

He sat up, his brows arched. 'Alia finally has a mood going.'

'Don't make me hurt you; I don't need the pleasure. Tell me where Mary is.'

'The fat housekeeping chick?' He looked around. 'Oh yeah, I haven't seen her around. I don't know, gone to her village or wherever these people go?'

'She's missing,' I said.

His eyes glittered. 'Again, Alia, what is it with you and losing people? Careless, careless girl. You'll have no fans left at this rate.'

I kept my eyes on him.

'Ooof, laser glare.' He pretended to shield himself. 'For your information, I don't screw around with the hired help who do what I want anyway because they're paid to. There's better places to employ my talents, wouldn't you agree?' He smirked and dropped his hands-free headset to the ground. 'How about Wanting up a new phone for me, love? Got time to spare before you go to everlasting hell?'

I kept looking at him.

'Why are you coming to me anyway?' he whined. 'Is there a sign hanging on me that says "Welcome Teen Derelicts"? When did I become your goddamn agony aunt?'

'I've told you this before,' I explained patiently. 'I don't like you. I don't trust you. But you're all I have.'

'Damn it, Bambi.' He walked over to me and grabbed my arm roughly, twisting me to look up at him. 'All this tough love is making you so attractive. What do you want? Why are you walking around looking for more trouble when you could be dry-humping lover boy or, I don't know, immersed in some happy drama for a change? Are you so badly in love with pain?'

'I need to find Chris before . . .'

'He did something, didn't he? What did he do? Kill someone?' His eyes glittered with excitement.

Something was off about the readiness with which he came to that conclusion, but I couldn't put my finger on it.

'It doesn't matter.' I turned away.

'Oh, but it does.' Deesh scowled and grabbed my arm. 'You can't have it both ways, Bambi; here I am, a noted admirer of your plain speaking, and then you turn the taps off and expect me to keep delivering the punchlines. Help me help you, Bambs, or fuck off!'

'He killed his mom,' I whispered. 'Happy now?'

'Did you actually see her strung out to dry with your own eyes?' He licked his lips, the slightest of movements, just the tip of his tongue darting out.

'She's dead all right.' I shuddered.

He exhaled slowly. 'So he offed the old lady, his own mom! What will you do with him?'

'Wait a minute, what do you mean strung out to dry?' I said, distracted. 'How do you know what she looked like when I found her?'

'Just an expression,' he said offhandedly. 'Why? How did you find her?'

'I . . . never mind.' It was my turn to look away. I didn't want to revisit the moment. 'I guess I need to get hold of Chris so I can say goodbye.'

'And then?'

'I need to make sure he doesn't hurt anybody after this,' I said, softly. 'If he does, it's on me.'

'There it is,' he whispered, clasping his hands to his chest in a parody of piety. 'Alia, the redeemer and the saviour of humanity.' His voice was vicious, anger radiating off him like heat from burning coals.

'Oh, shut up!'

'Bambs, are you really that stupid? I've been waiting for Grateful Dead Boy to snap, but wake up and smell the coffee, love! The only one he wants to hurt is you.'

'You're mad.'

'No, peach-puff, *you're* mad,' he said in a high-pitched, girly voice. 'Now quit fighting me, and listen when I speak. You want me to tell you what's what? You got it. You brought Chris back to life. Thus making him an Undead. Did you forget an essential little history lesson along the way?'

I scowled at him.

'Now, I haven't read the technical manual yet on the operations of the other life, but as one recently deceased and brought back, I can tell you some pretty strong feelings come with it.' He raised his eyebrows.

'Okay,' I said. 'So?'

'Okay, kitten, let's try this again. Why do you think your mommy dearest can't bear being in the same room as you?'

'Why are you bringing up—'

'No, don't fight it. You're almost there. Would you describe your relationship with mommy dearest as, let's say, a) comfortable, b) hostile, c) conflicted, d) like a Disney parade on cannabis. Tick one, and be honest.'

I gaped at him. 'Hostile, I guess. No, conflicted, yeah,' I fingered the pendant strung around my neck that Sid had given me on my birthday.

'Okay, so when you Undead a person, you release emotions too powerful and too complicated to even put in the same room. Everything from the old life—every obsession, every desire, every need—comes screeching back, only with a hunger like you've never known before. But there's more—you don't just have your old complexes, you have one pretty big new one.' He looked at me meaningfully. 'Ready?'

'As I'll ever be,' I said.

'Try to imagine a hatred for life that presses down on you so hard that your only desire is to release it. Except, there is no release because you are an immortal, and you have to go on and on and on, ad infinitum.'

'I'm Changed, I know how it feels,' I said.

'Oh, no you don't, buttercup,' he said, his face hard. 'You Changed because you chose to, and you are in a fight all right, but it's been a fight with yourself. But the Undead have only one fight. And it's with the person who made us what we are.'

'That can't be true,' I whispered.

'Remember all the Wants you've ever had and put them together. Now imagine if you had only one Want.'

'Which is?' My throat had dried up.

'Which is to see your maker extinguished in as painful a manner as you can devise.'

'So you're saying Chris hates me. You all do,' I whispered hoarsely. 'How can he not know that he hates me?' My voice was muted in the big hall.

'He doesn't. Well, not all the time. Keep up, will you? This is Chris we are talking about. In his last life, he defined himself by his feelings for you. And you know how it is with us fabulous Undead folk. We can get kind of obsessive about our past lives. To have such powerful feelings for you that are so opposite must be killing him—excuse the irony—and my guess is, he's fucked off to some place to keep himself from hurting you. Killing mommy dearest must have unleashed a real thirst for a spree, and he's doing the right thing by you by staying away from you.'

'But—'

'Why do you think he devised the road-kill game? Think about it. He wanted to see you hurt, badly hurt, and he couldn't resist dressing you up like a bride for it at the same time. Sound psychopathic enough for you?'

'Except I wasn't hurt!' I said. 'He couldn't go through with it; he took the hit from the car. Poor Chris,' I said.

'Poor Chris? Seriously? There's something about you two, isn't there? All I ever heard you talk about was Sid, Sid, Sid; and yet, when it comes to Chris, you don't even flinch when he knifes his own mother and wants to rip your throat out next.'

'You wouldn't understand,' I said.

'Do *you*?'

I stared at him for a full minute. Did I? 'Leave these mysteries alone,' I said at last. 'You're the Tin Man. You have no heart, remember?'

'With a mouth like that, no wonder everyone wants to kill you,' he said with a wolfish grin. 'The biscuit's crumbled, Bambi, the tea got cold, and you missed the party. Everything can't be neat and tied up with ribbons. You think guilt over his mom is what'll cause him to go on a rampage? Imagine the guilt he would experience if he tried to hurt you.'

'Why aren't you trying to kill me if this is true? You don't have feelings for me, too, do you?' I asked.

He chuckled. 'You mock my hard-heartedness but you see, darling, on lazy nights, when I have run out of supermodels and bored socialites, and other amusements that shall remain unnamed on account of your tender years, I sit around thinking fond thoughts of ways to end you.'

'So try it.' I squared my jaw.

'I'm a man of mature years, Alia. I appreciate the wholesome entertainment you provide, and I can handle delayed gratification. Basically, I cannot improve on what you're going to get once your time is up.'

'So why hasn't my mom tried anything?' I said.

'Why do you think it was so easy to get between those two cooing lovebirds? She's always had feelings of guilt over you, and now they're magnified and in direct conflict over the new feelings. She's a mess and much too terrified to talk about it with daddy darling who, I have to say, is proving to be rather mono emotionally. I'd have expected more depth from one who has lived like he has.'

'Enter Deesh,' I breathed.

'Bingo!' His eyes glittered. 'There's a villa full of broken glass for those two to walk over before I even get started with my plans for them.'

'You really are a creep,' I said.

'And you really are a loser,' he snapped.

'Excuse me?' I said.

'You lost. You lost the bargain, you failed the test, you ran out of time.' He made a crying face and then gave a fake yawn. 'It's all very pathetic but no one gives a damn.'

'Loser?' I repeated, intrigued. 'What was there to be won?'

His eyes widened involuntarily and he coughed to cover his sudden confusion. 'Hadn't you better say goodbye to dream boy than worry about semantics? Tick-tock, remember?' He walked away quickly, before I could ask him any more.

* * *

I stood in the middle of the hall, the conversation replaying in my head, until the sounds of his retreating footsteps died down.

The perfect silence swelled up and held. Not a leaf stirred outside, not a soul stirred within. It was like the villa had fallen into an enchantment outside of time, or perhaps I had. I had to act; the time to acknowledge the truth was now. I could feel my resolve speaking, and I wanted to hear what it had to say.

We are more than our stories. The mystical exists within all of us and it seeks to be claimed, it aches to be claimed. For far too long I had chosen to ignore it, to dismiss it, to fall into the heated distractions of my circumstances. Now I chose to listen, and in doing so, I allowed something greater than myself in, something greater than Alia Khanna, monster, murderer, and that thing too terrible to give a name to. I was no longer a juggler with a flaming torch, and I no longer feared the flames would burn me up.

Yes, the world had become a darker place for my Change, and yet it provided me opportunities to know better if I would only meet it halfway. The pieces of the puzzle had been drifting together before me all along, like a jigsaw taking shape, and Deesh's involuntary slip had given me the last one I needed. Now I had to allow myself to see the picture that had taken shape before me.

A new power was unleashed within me; it stretched out, viscous like a bead, and then it ballooned, an all-encompassing bubble that wasn't a mirage or a chimera to be popped. It was clear as glass, a separation of myself from the world around but not an occluding, or a hiding away. My thoughts took wing now, shimmering around me like snowflakes in a snow globe. I took it all in. I allowed them to swirl and dance and I allowed them to settle, and I knew what I had to do next was entirely outside of what had been written in my script. I was no longer an actor forced to react to the circumstances the Baba threw at me; I was no longer mouthing lines because I had no other things to say. I was more than my story, and when the time to confront the Baba arrived, he wasn't going to face the puppet he had dangled on a string for so long. He was going to have to face me.

First things first, I had unresolved business to take care of. My gaze hooked on to the dining-room door and the glass bubble around me shattered as I stepped back into my circumstances. There was only one place where people went missing in the villa. Mary had found me there twelve years ago, bruised and terrified, and she had gathered me into her arms.

Now it was time I rescued her.

TWENTY-ONE

The night I had wandered into the maze, eleven years ago, the maze was a living web, and I its prey. I hadn't known it then, of course, I was only seven and I darted in and out of dead ends, retracing my steps, my heart fluttering like a frightened little bird. I had hardly even realized it when the spider descended on its trap; a cold companion slipped his hand into mine and held it. He coasted with me as we burst into the clearing, and once the moonlight struck, I could see him through a fish-white haze that coated his limbs.

A bald boy with the burning eyes of a forest fire drifted before me, waiting to consume me with the force of his hatred. He was not much bigger than me but skinnier, and he was white, so white, because being in perpetual darkness had bleached everything out of him. All that had remained of Deesh's twin was this spirit child, who would one day become my Familiar, although I didn't know it then. His pin-sized mouth was puckered with loathing.

'Where are you going?' Bobby had asked, as I fell to my knees and attempted to crawl away out of that evil place.

'*What about me, Alia?*'

My legs had collapsed under me and I curled into a ball, sucking in chilled breaths. The prickly walls of the maze shivered, the dark night intent on swallowing us whole. His face bent towards mine, and his features blurred like moth wings as the stars blotted out one by one. The moon had gone grey and turned its back on me.

I did the only thing I knew how to do. I denied him. I denied he existed. Mary found me hours later, after having had the staff sweep the villa grounds. She clutched me to her breast and picked me up, her face thunderous with weeping and anxiety, her nose raw and eyes overflowing again at the sight of my bruised and battered body. I burrowed into her chest and knew then that my denial of this ghostly tormentor would not hold. The illusory world I lived in peeled back like an onion skin, and all that remained were tears and the realization that any notion of shelter, of care, love or comfort, was a deception. All was trickery. All was lost.

* * *

The mouth of the maze yawned open once again and I stepped in despite every impulse to run in the other direction from the horrors awaiting me. Bobby was gone at last, but the Baba's minion remained in the mortal world, and I knew that he would have shown Mary no mercy. I had been protected as a child by my usefulness to the Baba; what might they have done to Mary, who had no such protection?

I don't know what I expected to find as I tore through the maze and burst into the clearing at the heart of it, but it wasn't this. It wasn't Mary, queen of hearts, seated in the centre of the labyrinth, her curly hair flowing mermaid-like to the grassy ground, the maze gleaming around her, taut with all the promise of a well-kept secret. She had a crown of twigs in her hair, interwoven with roses; the petals haemorrhaged thickly down her shoulders and on to the ground. Her eyes were lustreless, like dead snakeskins.

I jolted to a stop, throwing myself down before her.

I reached out, but drew my hand back as her eyes flashed with sudden wrath.

'Who are you?' Her eyes raked over me with the indifference of hot coals.

'Mary, it's me, it's Alia,' my voice cracked.

To be forgotten by Mary was to be entirely unmade, to not exist, because I was her little girl, the child she raised in anonymity at the villa, the girl she welcomed home from boarding school like no one else had.

I hung my head and watched the petals drift around my knees; she had forgotten me in this instant as I had forgotten her in the year gone by since I was Changed; just as I had forgotten Asif bhai or stained-teeth Su or Father Clarence. So many people whose debts I would never repay; so many people who had carried me even when I had felt most alone.

'I am sorry,' I said to her and to them.

'What are you sorry for?' she hissed.

'Mary, what did he do to you? Will you be okay?'

'Can you be okay?' she muttered, her eyes evading mine as I searched for some glimpse of sanity.

'How can I be? Why are you asking me these questions?' I said.

She looked like Mary all right, and an updraught that whittled its way through the poky bushes sent the comforting lavender scent trapped in her dress my way. Yet something was different; something about her wasn't even her.

'Mary,' I whispered. 'Come away from here.'

'What are you coming for?' she hissed. 'Why here?'

I shook my head to clear it. I was here to save her; except a strange aura surrounded her and it suggested she wasn't the one who needed saving. Her chapped lips moved as she chanted in a low voice, her back ramrod straight. I strained my ears—these were no Christian hymns.

'Talk to me, Mary. No more questions!'

'What questions must you be asking?' She closed her eyes. The pupils were agitated under their covers, and her eyelids fluttered as though she were withdrawing within herself. 'When will you ask them?'

'Who are you?' I was seized by a terrible apprehension that the person before me was no more mortal than I was. Dark matter seethed under her skin and I knew then that what was on the outside was merely a plaster bust, her old form, good old reliable Mary's body merely a convenience that she might dash away with an impatient gesture when required.

'Who are you?' she echoed, the blast of her voice forcing my eyes shut, as the sound of her words went into a crescendo, causing my eardrums to cave in. I fell back on to the ground, the tunnels of my consciousness collapsing as the sound exploded out of the clearing, igniting the seven folds in the wrinkle of the maze, burning through the hedges, spouting out at last from the mouth of the labyrinth, and pouring on to the undisturbed grass outside a flame, a missile, a thirst, and a question that could not be quenched. *Who was I?*

When I opened my eyes, Mary had shut hers, her face blank. She had gone to another place in her consciousness and I could not follow; I did not exist there. I spun around slowly to confront the figure that had walked into the clearing and towards me, clapping.

'And Alia finds the prize!' The mockery in his voice did not disguise the undertow of surprise.

'There you are,' I said, softly. 'The Baba's secret helper.'

'And here you are, still meddling with what needs to be left alone,' Deesh said, his voice a snarl. All pretence of good humour gone, his face was a mask of hatred.

'I have only one question for you,' I said. 'Why?'

'I'll ask you one back,' he said. 'Why not?'

'You suffered at his hands, at their hands,' I said. 'I don't understand why you—'

'Even the devil was once an angel, Bambi baby,' he spat out. 'You should've renounced the curse and walked away when you had the chance. Instead you tried to play the hero, and look where we are now.'

'Where are we now?' I asked.

'We are coming to get you, Bambs,' his voice purred with malice. 'And we are hungry because you made us wait a long time.'

'What took you so long?'

'I don't have to answer your questions,' he said blackly, the sulk in his face a giveaway of his discomfort at the subject. 'I don't owe you a thing.'

'I just don't get it,' I said, lying as easily as if I had been born to do it. Deesh thought he was a smooth operator but two could play the game. Every piece of information he gave me was going to help me. 'So why did you hang out with Chris and me all this while and pretend to be our friend?'

His eyes gleamed at that and I knew I had struck gold. The pride he took in my fall was what would keep him from discretion.

He sniggered. 'Isn't it funny when the ones you would take a bullet for are the ones holding the trigger? I'd been cultivating Chris all along. Unfortunately, the sap couldn't handle his true feelings for you.'

I looked him in the eye. 'It was you who killed his mother, wasn't it? You deliberately sent me upstairs during my mother's dinner party. You Hazed Gail, knowing I would submerge myself in the bathtub and that I'd try to save her. You wanted me to be so full of Despair that I'd give up on my humanity once and for all.'

His complacent grin vanished. 'How did you figure it out?'

'How else would you know she was knifed and strung out to dry?'

He grinned viciously. 'Chris should thank me for it. She was an ugly old crone.'

'Sure,' I said, the bile rising in my throat as I remembered the old woman's broken body with pity. 'Real ugly.'

'Some people have nothing to trade that's of any worth.' He sounded bored. 'Some people are just better Ended.'

'Like Mary?' I said softly. It took all my willpower to disguise my simmering anger.

He glowered at me. 'It was a waste of time,' he said. 'A failed exercise.'

'How did she resist you? She's just . . . Mary. There must be something special about her.'

He gave an indifferent shrug; I couldn't tell whether he had detected my probing or was just hiding his own puzzlement. 'Talk to someone who cares.'

'So what happens next?'

'You meet your End in style. We have a soul to reap, remember? A promise is a promise is a promise.' A wolfish delight shone in his eyes.

'Bring it on.' I pronounced each word distinctly, enjoying the look of astonishment on his lying face as I laughed into it.

I didn't need to stick around for any further confirmation of what I had suspected; I had my answer.

* * *

They were waiting outside the exit and their eyes gave away their confusion.

'Alia, thank God.' My father wrapped me in a hug.

'We heard you were back,' my mother said, her body looking waif-like in a linen dress. Her bracelets tinkled as she wrung her hands.

'Let me guess, a little birdie told you?' I disentangled myself from my father and stepped back.

'Are you okay?' My father ran a hand over his face. 'We have been so distraught, so distraught over you.'

My mother ran the tip of her tongue over her painted lips and looked away.

'It's okay,' I said to her, 'I know.' I held on to the pendant and yanked hard. The delicate clasp snapped at the back of my neck and I dropped the streaming gold into the palm of her hand. 'It's yours,' I said.

'Why?' she said.

'A keepsake.'

'Oh,' she said, and her eyelashes fluttered as she tried to disguise the excitement she felt at the thought of my End. 'Alia,' she said, struggling visibly, 'I don't know what to say.'

'Then don't say anything,' I squeezed her closed fist, the broken ends of the chain dangled between her fingers and blazed fleetingly in the slanting sunlight before they grew dull.

'We don't have a lot of bargaining power but I have an idea I've been working on,' my father said, his voice baritone with emotion. 'We can still delay the inevitable by—'

'There is no "we" in this,' I said. 'We made our own destinies, you and I.'

'Can you forgive me?' My mother trembled by his side. 'And him? Can you? I don't want you to go to the other side wishing evil upon us! We were as helpless as you are now. Will you accept that? We took what we could get!'

'I'm Saint Alia, remember?' I smiled to take the sting out of the words.

'I would not choose this for you.' She pushed the words out as though to better believe them, her colour rising. 'That is, I . . .'

'It's okay,' I said.

'Alia! What can I do for you in this last hour, my daughter who I begot and lost in all my foolishness? The tears running down his cheek leached the colour from his face. 'I was not worthy of your generosity or the chance you gave me to prove myself to you.' He hesitated, as though wanting to say more, and drew a trembling breath in.

'I have only two words for you, Dad.'

He nodded, choked.

'It's okay.'

'That's all? That's how you're saying goodbye to me?' He sounded heartbroken.

'That's all I have to say to either of you,' I said. I turned to go. His insincerity was his puzzle to solve; I had the terrible equation of my own life to balance.

'Is she . . . wait!' My mother pointed to the maze with a shaking hand. 'Is that where Mary went?'

'Mary, full of grace,' I said. 'Yes, she's in there. Not in the way you expect, though.'

'Dear God! We have to help her!' my father said, stricken.

'You can't,' I said. 'She has her own journey, but if you listen with attention, you might learn something.'

'Alia, wait!' he sobbed. 'I am sorry.'

'It's okay,' I repeated blandly, perhaps even a little bored at the maudlin nature of this drama.

I had no other truth to offer and one last loose end to tie.

TWENTY-TWO

We are raised, at least those of us who have well-meaning parents and caregivers, on the promise that everything happens for a reason. That there is a pattern to our lives, no less intricate, and perhaps no less contained than the inscape of a leaf. Everywhere we look, there are approaches to sounding out the central mystery around life. Religion gives us answers before we conceive the questions. Philosophy rephrases certainties as inquiries. Science autopsies the world around but cannot catch up with the living.

And the business of living? The business of living offers only crossroads without conclusion.

How, then, will we connect the dots to make a shape we can understand? Or find a reason for a thing when no thing is single and no reason awaits at the end.

* * *

I had looked for Chris everywhere when he was, in fact, cleaved unto me, just as Deesh had said. It was true that I didn't understand this bond we shared or what it meant, but I could connect the dots and find him. I unlocked my heart and opened my eyes to Chris and I saw him with such sharp clarity that I called out his name. Except he wasn't here in the garden with me, he was somewhere desolate, where the wind whistled around him, ballooned out his T-shirt like a sail, and turned his straggly hair into seaweed even as he narrowed his eyes against the glare.

'Chris,' I whispered, reaching out with my hand, but he might as well have been a hologram. Desperation logged itself in my chest; I could see him but where was he? All I could see around him was a blue sky without even a hint of cloud. He could be anywhere; he could be in Timbuktu for all I knew. I tried harder, tried to feel him, feel my way around him; I let my longing for him wedge deeper and deeper into me until I felt some sort of resistance break as the margins and outlines that held us melted. My separateness from him flowed off me, evaporated, and we were one.

The burning ball of the sun dropped into the sea, brightness puckering over the horizon. Immersed in the glimmering as radiance slipped off the sky and into the Arabian Sea like a pulled tablecloth, I realized I was no longer looking for him, I was looking at what he was looking at.

We were one, after all; the rubber band between us had indeed snapped into itself, a stretch that no longer held, and I folded into him, carried into the union. And we watched the steadily darkening sky some more as we sat atop the roof of a tall building, and then we looked up at the iconic red-swan logo with its scorching wheel of fire, and I knew at once where we were, and we laughed with relief because were no longer lost; I knew where we were and I knew how to find Chris.

* * *

'It's not the tallest and it's not the widest but it's definitely the coolest rooftop in the city,' I said by way of hello to Chris an hour after I had come out of my communion with him. I had driven along Marine Drive and broken warily into the Air India building only to find it deserted.

'Did you know they switch off the lift service when the staff leaves for the night?' I crawled towards him on all fours; the smooth surface of the roof and the wind did nothing to make it easy. I gulped in a big gust of wind. 'Twenty-three storeys, Chris, that's a long way to climb. And to haul myself up here to the rooftop took some serious upper-body strength.' I glanced down at the steep drop and my stomach plummeted. 'Good thing I'm not afraid of heights.'

'Bugger off,' he said morosely. 'You can jump off, for all I care.'

'You'd rather be watching constellations than saying goodbye to your best friend?' I said.

'We are not friends,' he said. 'And I'm not into goodbyes, so bugger off.'

I sat beside him, my knees folded to my chest. The wind buffeted us against each other, and the company logo with its flying swan and wheel groaned ever so slightly against its pole.

'Most of those stars are probably already dead,' I said. 'Me, on the other hand, for a limited time only, I am still burning bright and I am here.'

'Cute. Now go to hell.'

'All in good time,' I said. 'Aren't you curious about how I found you?'

'If I act curious, can you tell me and then go?'

I grinned. 'I used the Batman signal, and then I put two and two together with the logo on the Air India building. You know if you'd tried brooding on the building across there,' I pointed to the Indian Express towers, 'chances are they'd still have a functioning lift service.'

'What do you want, Alia?' he turned to me at last. 'I give up. You can talk an immortal to death.'

I blew on my fingertips. 'I don't like to brag.'

He gave me a dark look.

The top floor of the Indian Express building blazed with lights all of a sudden.

'Um, Alia.' Chris looked anxiously at the building. 'Fuck!'

'I know,' I said softly. 'It can wait.'

'Are you serious?'

'Dead serious,' I said. 'It can wait. What I have to say cannot.'

The wind howled into us now, almost tearing us off the slanting roof. I felt the seat of my pants lift off the surface and he put an arm around my waist, anchoring me against him so that our hips bumped against each other.

'So do you hate me and love me so hard that you want to throw me off this roof and then run down and catch me before I hit the ground?' I said.

'What?' he said. 'Are you drunk?'

'It's okay, Deesh told me about it. The other feelings you have for me. And I felt them just now when we were, you know, bonded; I felt everything. I knew everything.' I searched his face, momentarily unable to express what a relief it had been to read his heart.

He nodded slowly. 'You're right, actually,' he said. 'I do want to push you off the roof, but I'm not sure I'll catch you in time.'

'Too slow?' I said hopefully.

He shrugged. 'You haven't made it easy for the guy that loves you to win over the guy that hates you.'

'Tell you what,' I said. 'I'll toss you for it.'

'Are you actually out of your mind?'

'Let's check. Have you still got the coin?'

He sighed and pulled it out of his pocket.

'Heads you catch me, tails you let me fall,' I said.

He shook his head. 'What is a stupid coin toss going to prove, Alia? Why are you doing this?'

'No, I want to show you something. Are we agreed? Heads you catch me, tails you let me fall.'

'Your last few minutes with me and you'd spend them playing this game? Why?' He frowned at the lights in the building across the street. 'It's in there, isn't it? I can't see anything but I can sense it coming.'

I stared across. A large shape moved in the window.

'Yes.' I caught my breath before it was whipped away by the wind. 'Chris, toss the coin!'

There was this moment of stillness as I watched the silhouette lean into the window and the Baba stood there, outlined in light, and a shadow broke off from his shoulder and flew through the glass like it was a waterfall and not glass at all. His Familiar squawked its way to us, the spirit raven streaking across the night sky, its call reaching us before it did.

Chris tossed the coin at the same moment. It flipped over twice and rolled over, facing heads.

Two minutes as the crow flies, I thought, *so that's what it means.* I had overestimated the time it would take for the Baba to claim me. I reached out and put my hand over the coin and drew it to me.

'Heads you catch me,' I whispered, my teeth chattering for real now. 'Did you see it? You would never let me fall.'

Chris exhaled slowly. 'What is it? What is happening now?' His voice was laced with panic. 'I feel like a blind man!'

'Eternity is a long time to spend in doubt,' I gasped out. 'I needed you to know this. I needed to know this. Everything we have become, Chris, it hasn't made us monsters. Remember that! Remember who we are!'

The bird was overhead now, circling us, its wings scissoring the air. The loops got tighter and tighter as it drew its profane spiral. No wonder it was coming now and coming fast. The Baba had feared me just as I feared him all along; he had only ever revealed himself when I tried to make a human connection, to reach out to someone, and it had worked; I had pushed people away as a result of that. I felt my heart twist. I had misjudged so many things in the little life I'd had.

'Your mother is dead in Milton,' I whispered.

The last thing I saw was the look on his face as he faded out of my reality.

'Alia!' Only the sound of his voice remained, a note of passion that hung in the air, the rest of his words cut out and lost forever. And then just like that, even the sound of my name was swept away as the fabric of this mortal world gave way and I fell into the mouth of the other one.

TWENTY-THREE

I was transitioning to the world of veils for the final time, and I felt no regret at meeting my maker. I was ready to surrender the Change.

The streets of the roundabout stretched before me, noisy and chaotic, even this late at night, and already there was a glimmer, a thickening in the air, and then a release as the trappings of the mortal world began to spasm and fall away like illusions. Shopfronts, hoardings, cars, the crush of foot traffic and the honking of buses, all the things that dressed and disguised the seven rays of the dark sun that was the *Saat Rasta* began to pixelate before my eyes and disappear as the dimensions shifted around me. The street lights were the last to go, taking with them the cornucopia of stars. I waited in a space darker than the blackest night while the veiled world took shape, misting into air until the mortal plane had been completely taken over, atom by atom, by the other side.

The *Saat Rasta* was a labyrinth—it held its victims in infinite loops, and as the mists that still trailed across the roundabout cleared, a cold wind funnelled in from the seven corridors to vein into the centre and swirl around me in a helix. My heart staggered under the onslaught, my limbs turning rigid, corpse-cold. When the stars switched on again, they were dimmer this time, the shadows dense over now-vanished objects. The whispers around me grew fiercer—harsh whispers, the cries of souls through time immemorial who had laid down their lives in the pointless quest of dark desires. Things began to stir, and my heart quickened as they coalesced into forms that grappled with me. Dark fingernails clawed sightlessly at my cold flesh, gouged at my skin to draw blood, and fell back on tasting it and finding that I was no alien to this place; I was a true daughter of darkness, returning home.

Across the street the Baba waited, barefoot and patient, his limbs draped in the white sari of renunciation, his head shaven in the imitation of the ascetic. I studied his face but features rippled through it, ghosting like breeze on water. It was his eyes that made the nightmare real at last. There was no escaping them. *Dark-highway-headlight eyes, cat eyes, demon eyes, blood-red, eat-your-heart eyes.*

They burnt into me even when he turned on his heel and strode away down the street. I followed him like a lamb to the sacrifice, until we were inside his den, and I blinked in consternation, coming out of the trance I had been in, because this was not what I had expected at all.

The room of ceremonies was unevenly lit and empty of all things, the mud floor swept clean, the walls bare; in place of the sacrificial fire, a naked bulb swung from the ceiling. Before I had time to consider what this meant, a sound charged through my spine like the beat of a tabla, half-human, half-divine, causing the very fluid in my veins to freeze. For it was the command, the call to the covenant that I'd heard. The raven rose like smoke at the sound to emerge over the Baba's shoulders. It materialized into a spin of black feathers and beak as it began to circle me.

When I looked back at him, the Baba had donned the huge mask of the fox god to signal that the ritual had commenced. He chanted the words of the unholy rite as he watched me through bronze eyeholes.

'The hour of reckoning is come upon you as you answer for the transgression of your progenitor. Know then that I am the trickster god, the conjectural god, the ecstatic god, the god of metaphysics and chance. The prophecy is completed when the heir of flesh surrenders equal collateral to the divinities of balance—your deed in exchange for your father's. Beyond harm and mortality have you harnessed the spirit of the sacrificial child to settle your Wants. Know that your divine restlessness alone brings you to your reckoning. Know this that when you no longer desired you Despaired. Thus have you returned to my fold and thus completed the bargain.'

'The bargain is not complete,' I whispered, half surprised to hear my voice in this evil plane.

He stared at me impassively.

'Because I ran out of Wants but I did not Despair.'

The Baba's eyes flickered behind his mask.

'To have lost a bargain is to accept its consequence,' he intoned.

'If there was something to lose, then there was always something to be won,' I repeated, more confident with every word I spoke.

The spirit was lighting up within me as slowly as kindling buried under a hurricane; the spark mutated and flickered, but never went out.

My spirit was a light that would never go out.

'And I won!' I said to him in triumph. 'Because the prophecy is not complete and the bargain is not fulfilled; how could it be? For I could no longer Want but I did not Despair.'

Light had filled me up and surged through me now. I was so bright that my body was a celestial in this dark place. The light of the bulb felt feeble before the illumination of my knowledge.

'You want to make monsters of us all but you did not win this time. I always had a choice; it was worked into the bargain, wasn't it? You are the trickster god but you still have to follow the rules of the divinities of balance. You tried to make me believe I was lost, to force me into being inhuman, to isolate me from others, but nothing could make me a monster, just as nothing could turn Chris into a monster. You failed because you are a false god! So it is not complete. Your bargain will never be complete and you will never have my soul!'

His face was impassive when he pulled down the fox mask in one move, indicating the abortion of the ceremony. He flung the mask to the floor and crushed it underfoot so that it crumpled into ash. His features no longer flickered and changed, and yet he was no more recognizable as man or woman than he had been before. He was the composite stranger when he held up the ancient silver knife and pointed it at me.

'Then it is time that the demands of the Fate line be met.'

Was he really surrendering his claim this easily? I knew I had kept my humanity despite all his machinations. However, I had expected more of a fight, or at least some trickery or threats. His submission left me dumbfounded.

I held my left hand out for him to conclude the ceremony. If I had truly won my freedom then my Fate line would show it. He slid the serrated blade across the palm of my hand, splitting the skin open. I took a deep breath in and waited. Would the divinities of destiny accept my argument? And yet, the mere contact with the ancient blade that had Changed me in the past filled me with foreboding.

My lifeblood spilled out, pooling at my feet. I lowered my head for him to pluck a single hair out from the crown. He let it fall and the blood froze on contact, and then cracked like a mirror. A spiderweb of black veins spread out from the single hair, the branches criss-crossing, merging, inking out my fortune as the prophecy came a full circle. The horoscope I had searched for in vain amongst the constellations was before me at last—my Head line, Heart line, Life line, Girdle of Venus, Sun line, Mercury line, and then the Fate line that the Baba had severed and tried to claim as his false victory.

Except nothing was as it should be.

'How is this possible?' I said. Where there should have been resolution and the mark of my triumphant victory, there was doubt; the Fate line was incomplete. I shook my head uncomprehendingly. I should have been free. Why was I not free?

'A soul was wagered to me, the keeper of the Saat Rasta,' he said. *'That, in the bargain, is unimpeachable. Your Fate line*

awaits a decision. If you will not fulfil your bond, who will take your place?'

'You think I would barter another soul to you?' I said. 'I will never do that. I may have been collateral but I will never bring another into your web.'

'How then will you exit the keep of souls without due payment?'

'Then I will stay,' I said. 'I will stay here and I will not surrender my soul. The Fate line shows me in limbo? Fine, I will stay in limbo. You still don't win because I will not play your trickery of pass-it-on.'

'It is not for you to say. Only he who inherits your debt by right may bequeath his soul.'

'What do you mean?' I shivered, only now realizing why this scenario felt so unfamiliar. There was no spirit fire because the Baba never meant for there to be a rite of transition for me. It was all a set-up! He had been going through the motions with me. He never expected surrender. All of this had simply been preparation for the ritual to come. 'There is no one to inherit my debt,' I whispered. 'I have no dependant, no offspring.'

As if on cue, the raven rose into the air and shrieked, the unholy sound causing me to clap my hands to my ears as it circled the entire room, its frenetic wings raising turbulence in the confined space. The loops became tighter and tighter until it was spinning in one place, and then the single bulb above us exploded with a pop and sparks rained down to the ground.

By the time I opened my eyes, the blaze from the fire that raged in the centre of the room had already roared across space to tear at my cheeks and skin and scratch my eyes. I shivered despite the lick of heat. Why had the sacrificial fire been lit now? It made no sense. I staggered back, except, of course, the walls were all around me, the doorway gone, and there was, in fact, nowhere to run to.

Something had gone wrong; something had gone terribly wrong with my plan for vindication.

And that is when I saw it in the fire—a vision so sad that it made everything I had experienced in my life before pale into insignificance. For there he was, my one true friend, shorn of his signature spiky hair, the black heavy-metal T-shirt and jeans gone, he sat cross-legged in a loincloth before the fire. The mark of the downward spiral was carved into his chest. I saw him an arm's length away, just across the fire, but the unmoving black pinpoints of his eyes left me in no doubt that I was invisible to him.

A figure loomed over Chris, his face in shadow. He held out the silver knife that still bore traces of my blood on its blade. Chris raised his left hand as he repeated the chant that was fed to him. The mantra was in the alien tongue of the Baba but I could understand every word as I heard it.

'No!' I screamed. 'Chris! No! Don't do it!' I broke out of my paralysis and ran around the fire to the other side, only to encounter the emptiness of the hut. I ran back around and I could see Chris through the blazing fire again. I tried throwing myself into the fire, only it was impossible; the raw flames flung me back. I watched helplessly as Chris held his left hand out and his palm was slit open, and I screamed again and again as his blood rained to the floor and collected at his feet.

Everything the Baba had said made chilling sense now. He'd been on to me all along; both of them had, and they'd always had a plan in reserve.

Terror rode my veins now as Chris's red blood welled out of the fire, flowing outwards until it merged with mine. I struggled to prevent this synthesis but I was transfixed as though in a dream or a hallucination that was too powerful to let me intervene.

Chris bent his head forward and Deesh stepped out of the shadows to pluck a single hair off his head. In the moment it took for him to let it drop and hit the surface of the pooled blood, I knew it was all over. The spiderweb of black veins branched out thickly, hungrily, from his Fate line and shot stems into mine. My destiny was merged with his, and the profane fire was our witness. My Fate line swelled and solidified and was complete.

I was no longer in limbo.

I raised my eyes in pleading and my voice in prayer, but Chris's eyes were opaque; he was wedded to the ritual and beyond my reach. How I wished I could dash my own eyes out now to keep from seeing this dreadful sight before me. How could I have been so blind? So wilfully, stupidly blind?

Deesh's words from before replayed in my head.

Isn't it funny when the ones you would take a bullet for are the ones holding the trigger? I have been cultivating him all along. Unfortunately, the sap couldn't handle his true feelings for you.

Well, my heart couldn't handle the pain I felt at this realization. Deesh hadn't been warning me away from Chris like I'd thought at all. Instead, he'd carefully fed my desire

to see him one last time. I turned Deesh's words inside out.
It wasn't Chris who held a trigger to my head; it was I who
had once again triggered his ruin.

Deesh's plan had never been obvious, after all. He had
cultivated Chris just as he'd said. I had no doubt that he was
the one who had persuaded him to go away into hiding in
the first place, and all the slip-ups I had so cleverly pieced
together hadn't been slip-ups at all. He'd wanted me to figure
out that he was the one to kill Chris's mother all along. He
wanted me to search for Chris until I had no choice but to
complete the bond between Chris and me.

The rubber-band force that connected us snapped both
ways when I used it to discover where Chris was hiding. My
actions had energized the bond that existed between us ever
since I'd brought him back to life. In effect, I had done the
last thing remaining to cement Chris's position as heir to my
legacy. In convincing Chris of his humanity, of his love for
me, on the terrace of the Air India building, I had driven him
closer than Deesh could ever have done towards making this
ultimate sacrifice for me.

I knew all of this and I still struggled. 'Let him go!' I
howled to the Baba who stood impervious, hands folded
over his chest, as he watched the show in the fire.

'*Thus is the boy rid of his burden towards his maker. Thus
are you cleansed of your debt.*'

'No, you cannot do that! I do not allow it!' I cried. 'Take
me! Take me instead!'

Not a trace of emotion crossed the Baba's face; my hands
clutched air as I tried to grab him. Already I was losing
corporeality in this world. The fire stuttered and went out,

leaving me in near darkness and devastated at the loss of Chris.

The Baba's final pronouncement echoed in the room.

'*The prophecy is completed when an heir of flesh surrenders equal collateral to the divinities of balance—his soul in exchange for yours. Thus have you brought a soul to my fold and thus completed the bargain.*'

'I reject it. I reject his sacrifice!' I flung myself at the fading figure of the Baba only to encounter thin air, and I never hit the ground. I was falling, falling back into the mortal world.

My words were uttered in vain.

The bond stood paid for. The *Saat Rasta* had no further use of me. The *Saat Rasta* around me shimmered and began to dissolve. Shadows drew away from me and the whispers of the damned souls died out as the dimensions shifted, and the mortal world wobbled back into place around me.

* * *

I came to under a blood moon, the sibilation of air through the bristling bushes around me working up to a high-pitched whine that broke the moment I opened my mouth and began to scream. I thrust my hands into the dirt, mud and tiny stones piercing my nail beds, wedging into my fingertips and the soft skin of my palms as I lashed out in grief and denial.

I blinked, and in the second it took to unblink, I saw them smoulder in the darkness before me—the red eyes, dark-highway-headlight eyes, cat eyes, demon eyes, blood-red, eat-your-heart eyes of the Baba of *Saat Rasta*. The unholy midwife had seen me back to the mortal world. When I looked up again, they were gone, but I no longer trusted the moon, shrouded as it was in brick-red earthshine.

I lifted myself off the ground. I was in the maze but I had nothing to fear. I was no longer yoked to the tyranny of Wants or the terror of time running out. My Fate line had been sealed. I had freed myself from the Baba's leash and I had also been granted another gift, a priceless gift by Chris. For in exchanging his soul for mine, he had blessed me with his immortality. The pain of his apartness, the sheer missingness of him lodged in my chest like a spear that I would never pull out, not until I was with him again.

I unclenched my hands and forced my mind to focus. I was going to pick myself up off the ground and then I was going to find my way to the other world, no matter what it took. The Baba would pay, and Deesh would pay for what they had taken from me. I had no doubt that I would make them pay for it. I raised myself up and walked out of the maze with an unhurried tread; I had all the time in the world to figure out how to bring Chris back.

The world was a dark place, and full of terrors, but I was done running from them. Henceforth, I would walk the narrow, walk the ledge, walk the tightrope; I would walk on air if I needed to, but I wouldn't lose heart. Because that's what you do when you decide to face your terrors, you just keep going, and you don't look down.

Read More

I See You
Karishma Attari

Nothing haunts you like guilt

Seventeen-year-old Alia is back in Mumbai from exile at an elite boarding school and wants to keep life simple. Her new friends and almost-boyfriend have no idea about her true identity and her troubled past. All that stands between her and happiness is Bobby, a malevolent child ghost who has put a sick chill on life at the family villa. When the all-too-familiar symptoms of a haunting return, Alia's double-life is in jeopardy, and simple is no longer an option. She must face up to the dark pact her Bollywood stepfather and brittle mother made. But is she merely collateral or can she square off their debt to redeem the people she loves?

Read More

Hedon
Priyanka

Let me tell you what love is at seventeen.

When Tara Mullick meets Jay Dhillon at a stifling society wedding, she forgets, for a moment, that she's an awkward, chubby seventeen-year-old, dying to get out of her sparkly lehenga and back into the comfortable invisibility of an oversized T-shirt.

At seventeen he is hopelessly, comically out of your league.

And all Tara can do is carry him with her, a talisman, over half a decade spent oscillating between India and the American heartland.

Do you know the thing about frequencies, though? There's no denying them. You can call it chance, you can call it prayer, you can call it what you want, but dream all your dreams because if you push hard enough, even the universe will move.

Laced with pop culture and a heady dose of decadence, this is the hedonistic experience of heedless millennials out in an ever-shrinking world and, within that world, the struggle to find a place or person to call home.

This was always going to happen.

Read More

Split
Meenakshi Reddy Madhavan

Who needs love? It only leads to trouble.

Noor is having the worst year of her life. First, her mother decides to leave her father. Then, her dad's mother, the Horrible Old Crone (HOC), moves in to look after Noor (who's sixteen and doesn't need looking after, thank you very much). She just knows the HOC is going to be mean about her mother because she never wanted her son to marry a Muslim. And now Noor has to attend some children-of-divorce thing after school—and her gang canNOT find out.

THEN she meets Ishaan. He's funny and nerdy, and likes all the same things she likes. Except love is stupid, as she's told everyone, and Ishaan isn't her type anyway. He wears glasses, participates enthusiastically in the lame children-of-divorce thing, and would rather read than play football in the break like all the other boys.

Can love happen with someone who is the complete opposite of everything you've ever stood for? Can forgiveness squirm its way in with love?

CPSIA information can be obtained
at www.ICGtesting.com
Printed in the USA
LVOW10s1941150518
577261LV00001B/101/P